Withdrawn from
Library Records

D0929439

The Sable Cloud:

A SOUTHERN TALE
WITH NORTHERN COMMENTS

The Sable Cloud:

A SOUTHERN TALE
WITH NORTHERN COMMENTS

By
Nehemiah Adams

The Black Heritage Library Collection

 BOOKS FOR LIBRARIES PRESS
FREEPORT, NEW YORK
1971

First Published 1861
Reprinted 1971

Reprinted from a copy in the
Fisk University Library Negro Collection

INTERNATIONAL STANDARD BOOK NUMBER:
0-8369-8721-7

LIBRARY OF CONGRESS CATALOG CARD NUMBER:
78-138329

PRINTED IN THE UNITED STATES OF AMERICA

THE SABLE CLOUD:

A SOUTHERN TALE,

WITH NORTHERN COMMENTS.

BY THE AUTHOR OF
" A SOUTH-SIDE VIEW OF SLAVERY."

" I did not err, there does a sable cloud
Turn forth her silver lining on the night."
MILTON'S COMUS.

BOSTON:
TICKNOR AND FIELDS.
M DCCC LXI.

RIVERSIDE, CAMBRIDGE:
STEREOTYPED AND PRINTED BY H. O. HOUGHTON.

F
Ado

CONTENTS.

—◆—

iv CONTENTS.

CHAPTER VIII.

CHAPTER IX.

CHAPTER X.

THE SABLE CLOUD.

CHAPTER I.

DEATH AND BURIAL OF A SLAVE'S INFANT.

"The small and great are there, and the servant is free from his master."

SOUTHERN gentleman, who was visiting in New York, sent me, with his reply to my inquiries for the welfare of his family at home, the following letter which he had just received from one of his married daughters in the South.

The reader will be so kind as to take the assurance which the writer hereby gives him, that the letter was received under the circumstances now stated, and that it is not a fiction. Certain names and the date only are, for obvious reasons, omitted.

THE LETTER.

MY DEAR FATHER, —

You have so recently heard from and about those of us left here, and that in a so much more satisfactory way than through letters, that it scarcely seems worth while to write just yet. But Mary left Kate's poor little baby

1

in such a pitiable state, that I think it will be a relief to all to hear that its sufferings are ended. It died about ten o'clock the night that she left us, very quietly and without a struggle, and at sunset on Friday we laid it in its last resting-place. My husband and I went out in the morning to select the spot for its burial, and finding the state of affairs in the cemetery, we chose a portion of ground and will have it inclosed with a railing. They have been very careless in the management of the ground, and have allowed persons to inclose and bury in any shape or way they chose, so that the whole is cut up in a way that makes it difficult to find a place where two or three graves could be put near each other. We did find one at last, however, about the size of the Hazel Wood lots ; and we will inclose it at once, so that when another, either from our own family or those of the other branches, wants a resting-place, there shall not be the same trouble. Poor old Timmy lies there; but it is in a part of the grounds where, the sexton tells us, the water rises within three feet of the surface ; so, of course, we did not go there for this little grave. His own family selected his burial-place, and probably did not think of this.

Kate takes her loss very patiently, though she says that she had no idea how much she would grieve after the child. It had been sick so long that she said she wanted to have it go ; but I knew when she said it that she did not know what the parting would be. It is not the parting alone, but it is the horror of the grave, — the tender child alone in the far off gloomy burial-ground, the heavy earth piled on the tender little breast, the helplessness that looked to you for protection which you could not give, and the emptiness of the home to which you return when the child is gone. He who made a mother's heart and they who have borne it, alone can tell the unutterable pain of all this. The little child is so carefully and tenderly watched over and cherished while it is with you, — and then to leave it alone in the dread grave where the winds and the rain beat upon it! I know they do not feel it, but since mine has been there, I have never felt sheltered from the storms when they come. The rain seems to fall on my bare heart. I have said more than I meant to have said on this subject, and have left myself little heart to write of anything else. Tell Mammy that it is a great disappointment to me that her name is not to have a place in my household. I was always so pleased with the idea that my Susan and little Cygnet should grow up together as the others had done ; but it seems best that it should not be so, or it would not have been denied. Tell Mary that Chloe staid that night with Kate, and has been kind to her. All are well at her house.

Of the persons named in this letter,

KATE is a slave-mother, belonging to the lady who writes the letter.

CYGNET was Kate's babe.

MAMMY is a common appellation for a slave-nurse. The Mammy to whom the message in the letter is sent was nursery-maid when the writer of the letter and several brothers and sisters were young; and, more than this, she was maid to their mother in early years. She is still in this gentleman's family. Her name is Cygnet ; Kate's babe was named for her.

MARY is the lady's married sister.

CHLOE is Mary's servant.

THE incidental character of this letter and the way in which it came to me, gave it a special charm. Some recent traveller, describing his sensations at Heidelberg Castle, speaks of a German song which he heard, at the moment, from a female at some distance and out of sight. This letter, like that song, derives much of its effect from the unconsciousness of the author that it would reach a stranger.

Having read this letter many times, always with the same emotions as at first, I resolved to try the effect of it upon my friend, A. Freeman North. He is an upright man, much sought after in the settlement of estates, especially where there are fiduciary trusts. Placing the letter in his hands, I asked him, when he should have read it, to put in writing his impressions and reflections. The result will be found in the next chapter. Mrs. North, also, will engage the reader's kind attention.

CHAPTER II.

NORTHERN COMMENTS ON SOUTHERN LIFE.

"As blind men use to bear their noses higher
Than those that have their eyes and sight entire."
HUDIBRAS.

"One woman reads another's character
Without the tedious trouble of decyphering."
BEN JONSON. *New Inn.*

SO then, this is a Southern heart which prompts these loving, tender strains. This lady is a slave-holder. It is a slave toward whom this fellow-feeling, this gentleness of pity, these acts of loving-kindness, these yearnings of compassion, these respectful words, and all this care and assiduity, flow forth.

Is she not some singular exception among the people of her country; some abnormal product, an accidental grace, a growth of luxuriant richness in a deadly soil, or, at least, is she not like Jenny Lind among singers? Surely we shall not look upon her like again. It would be difficult to find even here at the North, — the humane North, nay, even among those who have solemnly consecrated themselves as " the friends of the slave," and who " remember them that are in bonds as bound with them," — a heart more loving and good, affections more natural and pure. I am surprised. This was a slave-babe. Its mother was this lady's slave. I am confused. This contradicts my previous information; it sets at nought my ideas upon a subject which I believed I thoroughly understood.

A little negro slave-babe, it seems, is dead, and its owner and mistress is acting and speaking as Northerners do! Yes, as Northerners do even when their own daughters' babes lie dead!

The letter must be a forgery. No; here it is before me, in the handwriting of the lady, post-marked at the place of her residence. But is it not, after all, a fiction? I can believe almost anything sooner than that I am mistaken in the opinions and feelings which are contradicted by this letter. In the spirit of Hume's argument against the miracles of the Bible, I feel disposed, almost, to urge that it would be a greater miracle that the course of nature at the South in a slave-holder's heart should thus be set aside than that there should not be, in some way, deception about this letter. But still, here is the letter; and it is written to her father, whom she could not deceive, whom she had no motive, no wish, to delude. Had it been written to a Northerner, I could have surmised that she was attempting to make false impressions about slavery, and its influence on the slave-holder. Why should she tell her father this simple tale, unless real affection for the babe and its mother were impelling her? This tries my faith. It is like an undesigned coincidence in holy writ, which used so to stagger my unbelief. Possibly, however, — for I must maintain my previous convictions if I can, — possibly her father is such as our anti-slavery lecturers and writers declare a slave-holder naturally to be, and his daughter, herself a mother, is seeking to touch his heart and turn him from his cruelties as a slave-holder by showing him, in this indirect,

beautiful manner, that slave-mothers have the feelings of
human beings. Perhaps I may therefore compromise
this matter by allowing, on one hand, that the daughter
is all that she appears to be, and claiming, on the other,
that the father is all that a slave-holder ought to be to
verify our Northern theories. But she herself is a slave-
holder, and therefore by our theory she ought to be imbruted. I beg her pardon, and that of her father; but
they must consider how hard it is for us at the North to
conquer all our prejudices even under the influence of
such a demonstration as her letter. I ask one simple
question : Is not this slave-babe, (and her mother,) of
" the down-trodden," and is not this lady one of the down-
treading? And yet she weeps, — not because, as I
would have supposed, she had lost one hundred and fifty
dollars in the child, but as though she loved it like the
sick and dying child of a fellow-creature, of a mother like
herself. Now, who at the North ever hears of such a
thing in slavery? The old New York Tabernacle could
have said, It is not in me; — the modern Boston Music
Hall says, It is not in me. None of the antislavery
papers, political or religious, say, We have heard the
fame thereof with our ears. Our Northern instructors
on the subject of slavery, the orators, the Uncle Tom's
Cabins, "The Scholar an Agitator," have never taught us
to believe this. The South, we are instructed to think,
is a Golgotha, a valley of Hinnom ; compacts with it are
covenants with hell. But here is one holy angel with its
music; a ministering spirit ; but is she a Lot in Sodom ?
Abdiel in the revolted principality ? a desolate, mourning
Rizpah on that rock which overlooks four millions of
slaves and their tortures ?

In a less instructed state of mind on this subject, I

should once have said, on reading this letter, — This is slavery. Here is a view of life at the South. As a traveller accidentally catches a sight of a family around their table, and domestic life gleams upon him for a moment; as the opening door of a church suffers a few notes of the psalm to reach the ear of one at a distance, this letter, written evidently amidst household duties and cares, discloses, in a touching manner, the domestic relations of Southern families and their servants wherever Christianity prevails. It is one strain of the ordinary music of life in ten thousands of those households, falling accidentally upon our ears, and giving us truthful, artless impressions, such as labored statements and solemn depositions would not so well convey, and which theories, counter-statements, arguments, and invectives never can refute. Our senior pastor would say that the letter is like the Epistles of John, — not a doctrinal exposition, but a breathing forth of the spirit which the evangelical history had inspired. I have come to know more, however, than I did when I could have had such amiable but unenlightened feelings. I have read the " Key to Uncle Tom " and the " Barbarism of Slavery."

Still, I am sorely puzzled. " Kate," she says, " wanted to have it go, it had been sick so long ; but I knew, when she said it, she did not know what the parting would be."

"The parting!" Has she read our Northern abstracts and versions of the Dred Scott Decision, and are there, in her view, any rights in a negro which she is bound to respect? Has she not heard that the Supreme Court of the United States has absolved her from all her feelings of humanity? "The parting!" Where has she lived not to know how, according to our lecturers, families are parted at the auction-block in the Southern States with-

out the least compunction? We are constantly told, — has
she not heard it? — that the slave at the South is a mere
"chattel," and that a slave-child is bought and sold as
recklessly as a calf, and that a parting between a slave-
mother and her children, sold and separated for life, is an
occurrence as familiar as the separation of animals and
their young, and no more regarded by slave-holders than
divorcements in the barn-yard. This being so, it must
follow that when a slave-babe dies, the only sorrow in the
hearts of the white owners is such as they feel when a
colt is kicked to death or a heifer is choked. This must
be so, if all is true which is meant to be conveyed when
we are told so often at the North that the slave is a mere
"chattel." Therefore I am puzzled by this lady's tears
for the mother of this little black babe. She says of the
mother of that poor little negro infant slave, " I knew she
did not dream what the parting would be." I repeat it,
my theory of slavery, that which I hold in common with
all enlightened friends of freedom, requires that this lady
should have a debased, imbruted nature, for she owns
human beings, has made property of God's image in
man. And now I feel creeping over me a dreadful
temptation to think that one may hold fellow-creatures in
bondage and yet be really humane, gentle, and as good
as a Northerner! What fearful changes in politics would
come about should our people believe this! It cannot be
that our great party of Freedom can ever go to pieces
and disappoint the hopes of the world; yet this would be
the case, if the feelings stirred by this letter should gain a
general acceptance. I cannot gainsay the facts. Here
is the letter. May it never see the light; people are
much more influenced by such things than by mere logic,
and oh, what would befall the nation should our Northern

1*

excitement against slavery cease, and should we leave the whole subject to the South and to God! What if people should come to believe that the Southerners — fifteen or sixteen States of this Union — are as humane, Christian, and conscientious as the North!

Who will resolve my painful doubts? I do crave to know what possible motive this lady could have had in taking so much thought and care about the last resting-place of this poor little black "chattel." You and your husband, dear lady, seem to be as kind and painstaking as though you knew that a fellow-creature of yours was returning, "ashes to ashes, dust to dust."

One great Northern "friend of the slave" tells us that the slaves at the South are degraded so to the level of brutes, that baptizing them and admitting them to Christian ordinances is about the same as though he should say to his dogs, "I baptize thee, Bose, in," etc. This, he tells us, he repeated many times here, and in England.[1] Nothing but love of truth and just hatred of "the sum of all villanies" could, of course, have made him venture so near the verge of unpardonable blasphemy as to speak thus. Yet your feelings and behavior toward this babe are in direct conflict with his theory. Pray whom am I to believe?

Perhaps now I have hit upon a solution. Some people, Walter Scott is an instance, bury their favorite dogs with all the honors of a decorated sepulture. Rather than believe that your slaves are commonly regarded by you as your fellow-creatures, having rights which you love to consider, or, that you do not mercilessly dispose of them to promote your selfish interests, we, the North-

---

[1] See "Sigma's" communications to the *Boston Transcript*, August, 1857.

ern people, who have had the very best of teachers on the
subject of slavery, learnedly theoretical, reasoning from
the eternal principles of right, would incline to believe
that your interest in the burial of this little slave-babe
was merely that which your own child would feel on seeing her kitten carefully buried at the foot of the apple-
tree.

One thing, however, suggests a difficulty in feeling our
way to this conclusion. I mention it because of the perfect candor which guides the sentiments and feelings of
all Northern people in speaking of slavery and slave-
holders.

The difficulty is this: Who was "poor old Timmy"?
Some old slave in your father's family, I apprehend.
You seem sad at finding that his grave is not in the best
place. "The water rises within three feet of the surface;" — we infer, from the regret which you seem to feel
at this, that you have some care and pity for your old
slaves, which extends even to their graves. But we had
well nigh borrowed strength to our prejudices from this
place of old Timmy's grave, and were saying with ourselves, Thus the slave-holders bury their slaves where the
water may overflow them; but you seem to apologize to
your father for Timmy's having such a poor place for his
remains by saying, "His own" (Timmy's) "family selected his burying-place, and probably did not think of
this." Very kind in you, dear madam, to speak so. "The
friends of the slave" are greatly obliged to you for such
consideration. You say, "His own family selected his
burying-place." Do slaves have such a liberty? Can
they go and come in their burying-grounds and choose
places for the graves of their kindred? This is being
full as good to your servants, in this particular, as we are

at the North to our domestics. You thought poor old
Timmy's grave was not in a spot sufficiently choice for
this little babe's grave, and, it seems, you inclosed a spot,
and inaugurated it by the burial of this child, for the last
resting-place of other babes, the kindred of this child and
of your other servants. This looks as though there were
some domestic permanence in some parts of the South
among the servants of a household; and as though the birth
and death of a child have some other associations with you
than those which belong to the breeding and sale of poul-
try. We are truly glad to think of all this. It is exceedingly pleasant to have a good opinion of people, much
more so than to believe evil of them, and to accuse them
wrongfully.

In speaking thus to you, I make myself think — and I
hope I do not seem self-complacent in saying it, for you
must have learned from the tone of my remarks, if from
no other source, that self-complacency is not a Northern
characteristic, especially in our feelings toward the South
— but I make myself think, by this candid admission of
what seems good in you, of a venturesome remark by
Paul the Apostle to your brother slave-holder Philemon, in
that epistle in which he sends back the slave Onesimus, —
a very trying epistle to us at the North, though, on the
whole, many of us keep up our confidence in inspiration
notwithstanding this epistle, especially as it is explained
to us by some at the North who know most of Southern
slavery, our inbred hatred of which, it is insisted by some
of our best scholars, should control even our interpretation of the word of God. Paul speaks to this slave-holder,
Philemon, of "the acknowledging of every good thing
which is in you," — which we think was exceedingly charitable, considering that it was said to a holder of slaves; and

perhaps quite too much so; for the truth is not to be spoken at all times, and especially not of those who hold their fellow-men in bondage. I am often constrained to think that it was an inconsiderate, unwise thing in the Apostle to take this favorable view of that slave-holder; he may, however, have written by permission, not by commandment; that would save his inspiration from reproach; for had he been inspired in writing this epistle, I ask myself, Would he not have foreseen our great Northern conflict with the mightiest injustice upon which the sun ever shone? and would he not have foreseen how much aid and comfort that epistle would give the friends of oppression on this continent? One first truth in the minds of the most eminent "friends of freedom" is this: "Slavery is the sum of all villanies." Other truths follow in their natural order; among them the question of the inspiration of the Bible has a place; but slavery leads some of them to think lightly, and to speak disparagingly, of the Bible, because it comes in conflict with their theories regarding slave-holding, which is certainly not always referred to in Scripture in the tone which we prefer. There was the Apostle James, too, writing about "works" in the same unguarded manner as Paul when speaking of slaves and slave-holders. Pity that he could not have let "works" alone, seeing it was so important for the other Apostles to establish the one idea of justification by faith. He made great trouble for Luther and his companions in their contest with Popery. Luther had to reject his epistle; "*straminea epistola*" he called it, — an epistle of straw, — weak, worthless; and he denied its inspiration, because it conflicted with his doctrine of "faith alone." So much for trying to be candid and just, and for presenting the other side of a subject, or of a man, when the spirit of the age is averse to it, and candor is in danger of being looked upon as a time-serving thing. Neither Paul nor James, however, had felt the tonic, bracing effect of good anti-slavery principles, or they would not have written, the one such a letter to a slave-holder, and the other such a back-oar argument against "faith alone." However, I am disposed to think well of Paul and James, notwithstanding these the great errors of their lives. Indeed I can almost forgive them, when I am reading other things which they said and did. You will please acknowledge, therefore, my dear madam, that in giving you credit for kind feelings toward a poor slave and its mother, we are disposed to be just; yet I beg of you not to think that I abate one jot or tittle of my belief that, in theory, slavery is "the sum of all villanies," "an enormous wrong," "a stupendous injustice."

I have just been reading your letter once more, and the foolish tears pester me so that I can scarce see out of my eyes. I find, dear madam, that you have known a bitter sorrow which so many parents are carrying with them to the grave. Your words make me think so of little graves elsewhere, that I forget for the time that you are a slave-holder. Nor can I hardly believe that your touching words are suggested by the death of a slave's babe, when you speak of "the heavy earth piled on the tender little breast." O my dear lady! has a slave's babe "a tender little breast"? Then you really think so! And you a slave-holder! "Border Ruffianism," perhaps, has not yet reached your heart; and yet I suppose — forgive me if I do you wrong — that slave-holders' hearts generally need only to be removed to the "borders," to manifest all their native "ruffianism." Can you tell me whether there are any mothers in Missouri (near

Kansas) who feel toward their slaves who are mothers, as
you do ? There are so many people from the North in
Kansas (near Missouri) who have gone thither to prevent
you and your brethren and sisters from owning a fellow-
creature there, that I trust their influence will in time extend through all Missouri, and that white mothers in that
State will everywhere have such humane feelings toward
the blacks as we and you possess.

All that I ask of you now, is, that you give Kate her
liberty at once. Oh, do not say, as I fancy you will,
There is not a happier being than Kate in all the land of
freedom. " Fiat justitia," dear madam, " ruat cœlum."
I cannot conceive how being " owned " is anything but a
curse. Really, we forget the miseries of the Five Points,
and of the dens in New York, Boston, Buffalo, and other
places at the North, the hordes in the city and State
institutions in New York Harbor, Deer Island, Boston,
and all such things, in our extreme pity for poor slave-
mothers, like Kate, whose children, when they get to be
about nine or ten years old, are liable to be sold. Honest
Mrs. Striker came to work in our family, not long since,
leaving her young child at home in the care of a young
woman who watched it for ten cents a day. I said to
her, Dear Mrs. Striker, are you not glad that you live in
a free state, and not where, when you return like a bird
to its nest at night, you may find your little one carried
off, you know not where, by some man-stealer, you know
not whom ? — We honor your kind feelings, madam, but
you are not aware, probably, what overflowing love and
tender pity there is among us Northerners, toward your
slaves and their children. We are disinterested, too ; for
we nearly forget our own black people here at the North,
and more especially in Canada, to care for you and your

people. And though hundreds of innocent young people are decoyed into our Northern cities yearly from the country and are made the victims of unhallowed passions, yet the thought that some of your young people on those remote, solitary plantations, can be compelled by their masters to do wrong on pain of being sold, fills us with such unaffected distress that we think but little of voluntary or compulsory debauchery in our own cities; but we think of dissolving the Union to rid ourselves of seeming complicity with such wickedness as we see to be inherent in the relation of master and slave. We at the North should all be wicked if we had such opportunities; we know, therefore, that you must be. Because you will not let us reprove you for it, we cut off our correspondence with your Southern ecclesiastical bodies. But I began to speak of little graves. You will see by my involuntary wandering from them how full our hearts are of your colored people, and how self-forgetful we are in our desires and efforts to do them good. And yet some of your Southern people can find it in their hearts to set at nought these our most sacred Northern antipathies and commiserations!

But I constantly hear some of your words in your letter striking their gentle, sad chimes in my ears. "It is not the parting alone, but the helplessness that looked to you for protection which you could not give;" "the emptiness of the home to which you return when the child is gone."

Now, for such words, I solemnly declare that, in my opinion, you, dear madam, never had a helpless slave look to you for protection which you could give and which you refused; you, surely, never made a slave's home desolate by taking her child from her. No, such words as those which I have just quoted from your letter, are a perfect assurance that neither you nor your kindred, within your knowledge, are guilty of ruthless violations of domestic ties among your colored people. Otherwise, you could not write as you do about " desolate homes " and " the child gone." While I read your letter and think of you, I am reminded of those words : " Is not this he whom they seek to kill ? " Why, if the insurgents' pikes were aimed at you and your child, I would almost be willing to rush in and receive them in my own body. Yet I would not be known at the North to have spoken so strongly as this. O my dear madam, if there were only fifty righteous people (counting you) in the South, people who knew what " desolate homes " and " the child gone " mean, I should almost begin to hope that our Southern Gomorrah might be spared.

But I fear that I am trespassing too far away from my sworn fealty to Northern opinions and feelings. I begin to fear that I may be tempted to be recreant to my inborn, inbred notions of liberty, while holding converse with you, for there is something extremely seductive to a Northerner in slavery; it is like the apple and the serpent to the woman; so that whoever goes to the South, or has anything to do with slave-holders, is apt to lose his integrity ; there is a Circean influence there for Northern people ; thousands of once good, anti-slavery men now lie dead and buried as to their reputations here at the North, in consequence of having to do with the seductive slave-power; they would fill Bonaventura Cemetery, in Savannah ; the Spanish moss, swaying on the limbs of its trees, would be, in number, fit signals of their subjection to what you call right views on the subject of slavery.

Though I fear almost to hold converse with you, yet, conscious of my innate love of liberty, I venture to do so. Bunker Hill is within twenty miles of my home. When I go to that sacred memorial of liberty, I strive to fortify my soul afresh against the slave-power. After hearing favorable things said, in Boston, about the South, I can go to Faneuil Hall, and there, the doors being carefully shut, walk enthusiastically about the room, almost shouting, " Sam. Adams ! " " James Otis ! " " Seventy-Six ! " " Shade of Warren ! " " No chains on the Bay State ! " " Massachusetts in the van ! " " Give me liberty or give me death ! " I can enjoy the privilege of looking frequently on certain majestic figures in our American Apocalypse, under the present vial, — but I need not name them. I meet in our book-stores with " Lays of Freedom," never sung by such as you. I see in the shop-windows the inspiring faces, in medallion, of those masterpieces of human nature, " the champions of freedom," our chief abolitionists ; — and shall I, can I, ever succumb to the slave-power, even though it approach me through the holy, all-subduing charms of woman's influence ? No ! dear madam, ten thousand times, No ! " Slave-power ! " to borrow Milton's figure when speaking of Ithuriel and Satan, the word is as the touch of fire to powder, to our brave anti-slavery souls. You have, perhaps, seen a bull stopping in the street, pawing the ground, throwing the dust over him and covering himself with a cloud of it, his nose close to the earth, and a low, bellowing sound issuing from his nostrils. Your heart has died within you at the sight. You have been made to feel how slight a defence is fan, or sunshade, against such an antagonist, though you should make them to fly suddenly open in his face. No

enemy of his was in sight, so far as you could perceive;
you wondered what had excited his belligerent spirit;
but he saw at a very great distance that which you could
not see; he heard a voice you could not hear, giving occasion to this show of prowess. That fearful combatant
on the highway, dear madam, is the North, and you are
the distant foe. You may affect to smile, perhaps, at the
valorous attitudes, the show of mettle in the bull, but
you have no idea, as I had the honor to say before, how
sturdy is our hatred of the slave-power and how ready
we are to do battle with it. We paw in the valley, and
are not afraid.

Never think to delude us, my dear lady, with the
thought that slavery in our Territories means such ladies
as you owning Kates and their little babes, and having
such hearts toward them as you seem to have; for that
would take away a large part of the evil in slavery. Nor
must you expect us, in thinking of slavery as extending into our Territories, to picture to ourselves an accomplished
gentleman and lady searching a cemetery for a spot to be
the grave of a little slave-babe, and behaving themselves
as though they had feelings toward it and its mother irrespective of the market-price of slaves. "Border Ruf-
fians" are the archetypes of our ideas respecting all who
wish to extend slavery into our Territories. On the score
of humanity, madam, we have no objection to you and
your husband taking Kate and living in Kansas; how
perfectly harmless that might seem to many! for, no
doubt, you and Kate are perfectly happy as mistress and
servant; you would need domestics there, and how could
they and you be better pleased than if they and you were
just as Kate and you now are to each other? but, O dear
madam, that would be slavery, and we are under sworn

obligations here at the North to oppose the owning of a human being with indiscriminate hatred. Say not it seems hard that if you wish to live in Kansas, for example, you cannot have liberty to go there with Kate, who is as much attached to you, I make no doubt, as any Northern or English servant is to a household. Perhaps it does seem perfectly natural and harmless, and no doubt Kate's relation to you is as gentle and pleasant, almost, as that of an adopted member of a family, who is half attendant, and half companion; this we understand. You see nothing terrible in such a relation. O dear madam, you have the misfortune to have been born under the blinding, blighting influence of slavery, and cannot see things in the true, just light in which they appear to us, whose minds are unprejudiced and clear, and whose moral sentiments on this great subject are more correct and elevated. What is making all this trouble in our nation? I will answer you in the burning words of a Northern clergyman in his speech at a meeting called to sympathize with the family of John Brown, after his death by martyrdom : " The Slave-Power itself, standing up there in all its deformity in the sight of Northern consciences, — that is the cause, [applause] and there the responsibility belongs." [1] Yes, you are sinning against the Northern conscience ! It is settled forever that you are evil-doers in holding your present relation to the slave. We are bound to hem you in as by fire, till, like a scorpion so fenced about, you die by your own sting. We must proclaim liberty to your captives. Step but one foot with Kate on free soil, and our watchmen of liberty, set to break every yoke and help fugitives on their way from the house of bondage, will be around you in troops, and shout in her ear those

----

[1] *Boston Courier*, Nov. 26, 1859.

electrifying and beatifying words, "You are a free woman!" There her chains will drop; she will cease to be a slave, and become a human being.

Must I refer to your letter once more? I hope to destroy its spell over me. But I wish at times that I had never seen that letter. "Tell Mammy that it is a great disappointment to me that her name is not to have a place in my household." Your little slave-babe, Kate's child, you named Cygnet, because Mammy's name is Cygnet, and she and your mother grew up together, and she has been your kind, faithful servant and friend, as much friend as servant, during all your youth till you were married. And you seek to perpetuate her name in your own household, and to have a little Cygnet grow up with your own little Susan. "I was always pleased with the idea that my Susan and little Cygnet should grow up together; but it seems best that it should not be so, or it would not be denied." All this is very sweet and beautiful; but now let me tell you, honestly, what the spontaneous thought of a Northerner is, while meditating on such an apparently lovely picture. Here it is: Suppose that Susan and little Cygnet, when both are three years old, are playing in your front-yard some morning, and a cruel slave-trader should look over the fence, and say to your husband, "Fine little thing there, sir; take a hunderd and a ha'f for her?" I ask, Would not your husband (perhaps in need, just then, of money to pay a note) lay down his newspaper, invite the fellow in to drink, and go through the opening scene of "Uncle Tom's Cabin," coaxing up the fellow's price; and finally, would he not sell little Cygnet while her mother was out of sight, push poor little Susan into a room alone to cry her eyes out, and you and your husband pocket the money? Many of us at the North, dear madam, if you will take my unworthy self as a specimen, and I am a very moderate anti-slavery man and no fanatic, are quite as ready to believe such things of you as the contrary. We have read " Uncle Tom's Cabin."

Nothing could exceed the disgust and ridicule which your letter would meet with at the hands of some of our best anti-slavery men. I am thinking of it, just now, as in the hands of Rev. Mr. Blank. The other day I saw a cambric muslin handkerchief, richly embroidered, blow past me out of a child's carriage. As I turned to get it, a dog seized it, shook it, put both his paws on it, rent it, made rags of it, threw it down, snatched it up, and seemed vexed that there was no more of it to tear. So will our abolitionists serve your letter, should they ever see it. And, my dear madam, though I disapprove their temper and language, yet I must confess that I sympathize with them in their principles, the only difference between them and me being that of social position and manners. I must tell you that, after all, you are probably unaware of the deception which you are practising on yourself, in supposing that you are really as loving and gentle toward a slave-mother and her child as some might infer. Let but a good sale tempt you! I wait to know whether you would then write such a letter. We have a ready answer to all the kind and good things which are said about you, in this, which you will see and hear in all our speeches and essays, namely, " Slavery is the sum of all villanies." That is to all our thoughts and reasonings about slavery what the longitude of Greenwich is to navigation. All your clergy, all your physicians, all your judges and lawyers, all your fathers and mothers, your gentlemen and ladies, all your children, are heaped together by us in one name, to us an awful name, — " Slave-power." We think about you as we do of Egypt, with Israel in bondage.

And now that allusion furnishes me with an argument against your letter, which I must, in conclusion, and sorely against many of my feelings, let fall, like a stone, upon it, and crush it forever. Pharaoh's daughter was touched with the cry of the little slave-babe, Moses ; but what does that prove ? that Egyptian bondage was not " an enormous wrong," a " stupendous injustice," " the sum of all villanies " ? or that a Red Sea was not already waiting to swallow up the slave-holders, horse and foot ?

You may write a thousand such letters, all over the South ; but though they delude me for a while, it is only until the moisture which they raise to my eyes from my heart, by the pathos in them, dries up, and leaves my vision clear of all the blinding though beautiful mists of that error which has diffused itself over one half of this goodly land, and, I grieve to add, which has fallen upon many even here in New England, recreant sons of liberty, traitors to the memories of Faneuil Hall and Bunker Hill.

LETTER FROM MR. NORTH, INCLOSING THE FOREGOING.
INFLUENCE OF THE LETTER UPON HIS WIFE.

My dear Mr. A. Betterday Cumming : —

I have, as you see, complied with your request, and
herewith I send you my thoughts and feelings in view of
the good Southern lady's letter. I came near, once or
twice, abandoning some of my long-cherished principles,
under the influence of the letter and of the reflections to
which it gave rise. But I have been enabled to retain
my integrity. I am sorry to say that the letter has made
me some trouble through its effect on my wife, to whom,
incautiously, I read it. Very soon after I began to read,
I perceived that some natural drops were finding their
way down her tear-passage, leading her to a frequent use
of the handkerchief. By this means she interrupted me,
I should say, six or eight times, during the reading, and
as soon as I had finished she rose and left the room.

I remained, and wrote a large part of the accompany-
ing reflections, and, near midnight, on repairing to my
room, I found that Mrs. North was asleep. She waked
me in the morning by asking me if I was asleep. I told
her that I would gladly listen to what she had to say.
She said, " Will you not please, my dear, stop the ——,
and the ——," (naming two newspapers,) " and take
others ? "

" Why," said I, " what is the matter with them ? "

She began to weep again. In a few moments she said,
" I would give the world if I could have a conversation
with that Southern lady."

" I fear," said I, " that it would have a deleterious effect
on your attachment to the principles of liberty."

" Liberty ! " said she. " Oh, how foolish I have been!
I see now that there is another side to that question."

" I hope, my dear," said I, " that you will say and do
nothing to occasion any reproach. Certainly, there are
two sides to every question. If you manifest any surprise at finding that there is another side to the Liberty
question, I fear that some will quote to you the fable of
the mouse who was born in a meal-chest."

" I never heard of it," said she.

" Why," said I, " the mouse one day stole up to the
edge of the chest, when the cover had been left open,
and, looking round on the barn-chamber, she said, ' Dear
me, I had no idea that the world was half so large.' "

" The cover has been down and the meal has been in
my eyes long enough," said she. " I have been so much
accustomed for a long time to read in our papers about
' enormous wrong,' ' stupendous injustice,' ' the slave-
breeders,' ' sum of all villanies,' that, unconsciously, I
have come to think of the South, indiscriminately, as
though they were Robin Hood's men, or " ——

" O my dear," said I, " you must have known that
there are many good people at the South, notwithstanding slavery."

" How can there be one good man or woman there,"
said she, " if all that those newspapers say of slave-holding be true ? Husband, depend upon it we have been
believing a great lie. Just think of that letter. What a
tale many of those words reveal. When the infants of
our former servants die, do our ladies write such letters
about them ? I should judge that owning a fellow-creature softens and refines the heart, if this letter is any sign,
instead of making them all barbarians. All the newspapers and novels in the world cannot do away the impres-

2

sions which that letter has made on my mind. I tell you, husband, having slaves is not the unmitigated curse to owners nor to slaves that we have been taught to believe."

"Perhaps," said I, interrupting her, "you would like to live at the South, and own a few."

"I could not be hired by wealth," said she, "to have them for help, even here. I never did like them; and when I think that there are good men and women who do, and who are as kind to the poor creatures as this dear lady, I think that we should give thanks to God."

"Oh, the Southern people are not all like this good lady, by any means," said I.

"'Peradventure,'" said she, "'there be fifty righteous.' There must be tens of thousands. People like this lady are very apt to make good the saying of the blackberry pickers when they see a blackberry, 'Where there's one there's more.' The letter reads as though it were an every-day thing, a matter of course, for this lady to be kind and loving to the blacks; and for my part I bless any one who has anything to do for her or for those like her. Our papers never tell us such stories as this letter contains. No, they do not love to hear them, I fear; but if a slave is beaten or ill-treated, then the chimes begin, 'enormous wrong,' 'stupendous injustice,' 'sum of all villanies.'"

"Why, my dear," said I, "you are getting to be pro-slavery very fast."

"Never," said she, "if you mean by that, as I suppose you do, approving all that is involved in slavery and all that is committed under the system."

"But," said I, "your present feeling toward this Southern lady may insensibly lead you to believe that it is right to own a fellow-creature. Does not Cowper say, —

> " ' I would not have a slave to till my ground,
>   To carry me, to fan me while I sleep
>   And startle when I wake, for all the wealth
>   That sinews bought and sold have ever earned? ' "

" How Kate must ' startle ' and go into convulsions with terror every time this mistress wakes ! " she replied. " If Cowper had written in Alabama, instead of describing a state of slavery such as existed in the British possessions, and not, as in the South, mixed up with his every-day life ; if the first face with which he had become familiar as a babe had been a black face, the face of his mother's ' slave ' loving him, and nursing him, and he, in turn, had tended his old ' Mammy ' in her decrepitude, his imagination would have contained some other pictures than those in the lines which you quote. Had there been a Mrs. Cowper, I fancy she would have been like this lady ; and perhaps we should have seen Mr. Cowper acting the kind part of this lady's husband toward a slave-mother and her babe, his ' property,' so called. I lay awake here, last night, while you were writing, and thought it all over. What were you writing about so long ? I wished that I had a pencil and paper near me. Those English and French people who got rid of slavery as one gets rid of a bunion, know nothing about slavery mingled with our very life-blood. How self-righteous they are ! Our people, too, are perpetually quoting what Thomas Jefferson said about slavery in his day. Pray, has there been no progress ? Why are we not permitted to hear what Southern men, as good as Jefferson, now say about modern slavery ? "

" My dear," said I, " perhaps you are not fully qualified

as yet to judge of this great subject in all its relations. The greatest and wisest men are divided in opinion about it."

" Great subject ! " said she, " please let me interrupt you ; there is but one side to it, I should judge, from reading our papers. What do some of the 'greatest and wisest men,' on the other side, have to say for themselves ? Are they all 'friends of oppression,' 'enemies of freedom,' 'minions of the slave-power,' 'dough-faces'? Husband, I am thoroughly disgusted. I have been compelled to have uncharitable feelings toward thousands of people like this Southern lady ; I confess I have really hated them, as I hate men-stealers and pirates. This letter has convinced me of my sin. It is like the Gospel in its effect upon me."

" But, my dear," said I, " recollect that good people may be in great error, and we read, 'Thou shalt in any wise rebuke thy neighbor, and not suffer sin upon him.' Now, to hold a fellow-being in bondage, — how can it be otherwise than 'stupendous injustice'? "

" I wonder," said she, " if Kate feels that she is in 'bondage' to this lady. I wonder if she would not think it cruel, if her mistress should set her free."

" But it is wrong," said I, " to hold property in a human being, whether the bondman be in favor of it or not."

" 'Property ! ' " said she. " I should like to be such 'property,' if I were a black woman. If it were wrong in the abstract," said she, " it might not be in practice."

" Oh," said I, " what a pro-slavery idea that is ! where did you learn it ? "

" I learned it," said she, " at our corn-husking, when

the Squire read extracts from John Quincy Adams's speech about China, in which he said that if China would not open her trade to the world, it would be right to make war upon her. Now war is wrong, but circumstances sometimes make it right. So with holding certain men in slavery, under certain circumstances. I cannot believe that it is right to go and enslave whom we will; but the blacks being here, I can see that it may be the very best thing for all concerned that they should be owned. This may be God's way of having them governed and educated."

I found that I was getting deeper into the subject than I intended, and, besides, it was time to rise. As I left the room, she said, " You *will* change those papers, won't you? then we will have some more pleasant talks about this subject." She called to me from the door, " Please don't send back the lady's letter; I wish to copy it." This is my reason for not sending the letter with my reply to it. You will certainly give me credit for candor in telling you all that my wife said. However, it is so easily answered that I need not fear to intrust you with it.

Yours, for the slave,

A. FREEMAN NORTH.

P. S. After all, I concluded to retain this, and wait till my wife had made what use she desired of the letter, that I might be sure and return it to you safely. In the mean time, I have changed the papers. How irresistible a pleading woman is, especially a wife. Her very want of logic makes her more so, when we are good-natured. She came upon me with just such another supplication a few mornings since. As soon as she awoke, she said, " Husband, do please have our parlor window-sashes let

down from the top." " For ventilation?" said I. " Yes,"
said she, "partly;" but I saw that she smiled. " What
has made you think of it so suddenly?" said I. " Do
you not want to catch some more canaries?" said she.
" I suspect," said I, " that you would like to have ours escape." " Perhaps," said she, " that would be a relief
to you from your present embarrassment." Then I saw
that all this was banter. She wished to teaze me a little.
The truth is, I have two fine singing canaries and a
mocking-bird. Some of my pro-slavery friends delight to
pester me about them. They say that they mean to issue
a habeas corpus, and take them before Justice Bird, (who,
you know, queerly enough, happens to be United States
Commissioner,) and inquire if they be not restrained
of their freedom. I tell them that man has dominion
over all the fowls of the air. But they say, " Then
might makes right! Is it not a fine thing that such a
lover of liberty and friend of freedom and enemy of oppression should keep those little prisoners for his selfish
gratification. Come, be a practical emancipationist to the
extent of your ability; set the South an example; break
every yoke." " They are better off with me," said I ;
" the hawks or cats would catch them, or they would die
from exposure." " Expediency!" said one of them ; " do
justice, if the heavens fall." " Fye at *justitia!*" said
one, who pretended to take my part. " *Ruat cœlum*, Let
them rush to heaven," replied the other. " Parse *cœlum*,
please, sir," said my boy in the Academy. " Yes, past the
ceiling," said the lawyer, pretending to misunderstand
him; " that's right, my son ; " — and more wretched
punning of the same sort. Hence Mrs. North's pretended supplication about the window-sashes. She has been in
excellent spirits ever since I stopped the papers. She says

that she wonders at herself so calm and happy. I heard her yesterday calling at the stairs to a little lisping English waiting-maid, who cannot pronounce *s:* "Judith," said she, " did you not hear the parlor-bell ? " Judith walked up, and said, "Mitthith North, lately you've rung tho eathy, that motht of the time I thought it mutht be a acthident, and didn't come up at futht. I thpect the wireth ith got ruthty." Mrs. North said nothing, but afterward, in relating the affair to me, she said she truly believed that it was owing to my stopping the papers. For she could remember how often she went to the bell-rope saying to herself as she pulled it, " sum of all villanies ! " then " enormous wrong," with another pull, and then " stupendous injustice," with another. Several times she says Judith has rushed up to the parlor with " Ma'am, whath the matter ! the bell rung three timth right off." She thinks that her nervous system will last longer without the papers than with them. As she told me this, she was shutting down the lid of the piano for the night. As it fell into its place, the strings set up a beautiful murmur. " Oh, hear that ! " said she ; " how solemn it is ! " " I suppose," said I, " you would not have heard it, if those papers had been in the house." I shall not tell you, a bachelor, what she said and did. I trust that her views on the great subject of freedom will get adjusted by and by ; and I am debating with myself what papers to take, having been obliged, for my own edification, to become a subscriber to the reading-room. There, however, I meet with a good many pro-slavery prints, and I am tempted to look into them ; after which I frequently feel as though I should pull a bell-rope three times.   A. F. N.

CHAPTER III.

MORBID NORTHERN CONSCIENCE.

"Heaven pities ignorance:
She's still the first that has her pardon sign'd;
All sins else see their faults; she's, only, blind."

MIDDLETON: *No Help like a Woman's.*

[Accompanying note, from A. BETTERDAY CUMMING to A. FREEMAN NORTH.

MY DEAR MR. NORTH, —

With many thanks for your kindness and frankness, and with my warmest congratulations to Mrs. North for the pleasant effect which the Southern lady's letter has had upon her, I send you another document, hoping that she will read it to you. It will not be worth while for me to say anything about this production. It purports to be from a young man in one of our New England literary institutions, whose aunt, with her husband, was residing at the South for the health of a niece, a sister to this young man; — they being orphans. The letter is so entirely in the same key with your feelings that you cannot fail to be interested. Knowing that you love rare specimens in everything, I send you this as "the only one of its kind," or as we say, "*sui generis.*" — A. B. C.]

—— College, —— — ——.

MY DEAR AUNT, —

I have not heard from you but once since your arrival at the South. It is because sister is more unwell? or because you are very busy with your arrangements for the winter? or is it because, as I more than half suspect, you are so much overcome by your first observation and experience of slavery, that you have but little strength left to write to me from that "—— post of observation, darker every hour"? Perhaps you are mustering courrage to tell me of the sights which you have seen, the little while that you have been among the poor, enslaved children of the sun in our Southern house of bondage. "Afraid to ask, yet much concerned to know," I wait impatiently for a letter from you. I expect to make great use of its details among my fellow-students, many of whom, I mourn to say, have their hearts case-hardened against the story of oppression. They will show an interest in everybody and everything sooner than in the slave and his wrongs. They are not only callous on that subject, but they laugh at your zeal and call it hard names.

No one can tell what I suffer in the cause of freedom, through my well-meant endeavors to interest and instruct others on the subject which absorbs my thoughts. I know that I shall have your sympathy; and when I come to hear from you what your own eyes have seen, ere this, in slavery, I shall esteem all my sufferings in the cause of the slave as light as air.

I employ the intervals of study in walking among the beautiful scenery of the village and its environs, if haply I may meet with some to whom I may open my mind on this great theme. The last time that I went out for this purpose, I met with a sad sight. A horse was running away with a buggy, while between the body of the carriage and the wheel I saw depending a foot, which I at once inferred was that of a lady. The horse rushed by, and sure enough, a young lady had fallen on the floor of the

2 *

buggy, holding the reins, evidently entangled and embarrassed in her posture, uttering the most heart-rending cries and shrieks, with intermingled calls to the horse to stop.

I could not help looking at the horse, as he passed, with feelings of strong displeasure. To think that anything having an ear to hear and a sensibility to feel should be so heedless of the cries of distress, roused up my soul to indignation. As I reflected, however, it occurred to me that no doubt this horse had been subjected to unkind treatment from his youth up. I began to blame his owners. Had the law of kindness been observed in the early management of this horse, doubtless he would have regarded the first appeal of this young lady to him. May we not hope, dear Aunt, that a new era is dawning upon us with regard to the universal triumph of love and kindness over oppression of every kind, and that the brute creation will partake of its benign influences? The tone and manner in which horses are spoken to often sends a chill to my heart.

This reminds me, if you will excuse longer delay in my narrative, of some unfavorable impressions which I received lately on my way to Boston, with regard to the imperious manner in which a traveller is assailed by advertisements on the fences, as you pass through the environs of the city. Every few miles, as the cars passed along, I saw, printed on the rough boards of a fence: "Visit" so and so; "Use" so and so; "Try" so and so. I would not be willing to say how often my attention was caught by those mandatory advertisements. At last I became conscious of some feeling of resistance. Whether it was that I began to breathe the air of Bunker Hill, and the atmosphere which nourishes our most eminent friends of freedom, so many of whom, you know, live in Boston and vicinity, I cannot tell; but I found myself saying, with quite enough resentment and emphasis, "I will not 'use' so and so; I will not 'try' so and so; especially, I will not 'visit' so and so, — First, It will not be convenient. Secondly, I have no occasion to do so. Thirdly, I do not know the way; but, Finally, I do not like to be addressed in this manner, as an overseer of a Southern plantation addresses a slave. I am not a slave. I am a Massachusetts freeman." This way of speaking to people, dear Aunty, must be discountenanced. It will, by and by, beget an aptitude for servile obedience; the eye and ear becoming accustomed to the forms of domination, we shall have yokes and chains upon us before we are aware. Some one says, "Let me write the songs for a nation, and I care not who makes her laws." So say I, Let me write imperative advertisements on fences and buildings, and all resistance to Southern encroachments and usurpation will soon be in vain.

But to resume my narrative. I began to look round, as soon as my excitement about the runaway horse would allow, for some one to whom I could open my overburdened mind on the subject of freedom. I espied a man with an immense load of chairs, from a factory in our neighborhood, as I supposed, on his way to Boston. Four horses drew the load, which I saw was very heavy; not so heavy, I thought with myself, as that which four millions of my fellow-men are this moment laboring with, over the gloomy hills of darkness in our Southern States. I felt impelled to address the driver on this great theme. So, before he had reached the top of the hill, I called out, —

"Driver!"

Perhaps there was more suddenness and zeal in my

call than was judicious, but the driver immediately said
" Whoa ! " to his horses, and he ran hither and thither for
stones to block the wheels to keep his load from running
back, down hill.

I felt encouraged, by this, to think that he was of a
kind and pliable disposition ; and seeing the wheels forti-
fied, and the horses at rest, I felt more disposed to hold
conversation with the man. " Who knows," I said to
myself, " but that I may now make one new friend for
the slave ? "

" A warm day," said I.

" Yes, sir," said he, a little impatiently, I thought,
The sun was very hot, an August morning, no air stir-
ring, well suited to make one think of toil and woe under
our Southern skies.

" Have you ever been at the South ? " said I, wiping
my forehead.

" No, sir," said he, picking out a knot in the snapper
of his whip, evidently to hide his embarrassment while
waiting to know the drift of my question. The sight of
his whip kindled in my soul new zeal for the poor slaves,
knowing as I did how many of them were at that moment
skipping in their tortures and striving to flee from the
piercing lash.

" Your toil in the hot sun with your load, my dear sir,"
said I, " is well fitted to impress you with the thought of
the miseries under which four millions of your fellow-men
are every day groaning in our Southern country. I make
no doubt that you are grateful for the blessings of freedom which we enjoy here at the North. I wish to ask
whether you are doing anything against oppression ;
whether you belong to any Association whose object
is " ——

"What on airth did you stop me for," said he, quite impatiently, and yet with a lingering gleam of respect, and with some hesitancy at any further rudeness of speech.

"My dear sir," said I, "four millions of Southern slaves are this very hour groaning under sorrows which no tongue " ——

" You " —— (he hesitated a moment, and surveyed me from head to foot, and then broke out,) — "putty-headed, white-birch-looking, nateral — stoppin' a load right near the crown of a hill, no gully in the road, such a day as this, and — 'Ged ehp,'" — said he to his horses, as the stones under the wheels that moment began to give way; and then he drew his lash through one hand, with a most angry look. I really thought that I should have to feel that lash. The thought instantly nerved me : — I'll bear it! it's for the slave; let me remember them, I might have added, that are whipped as whipped with them; but at that moment the horses had reached the hill-top, and the driver was by their side.

He called back, as he passed round the rear of his load to the nigh side of his team. I caught only a few of his last words; — "take your backbone for a for'ard X." I snapped my thumb and finger at him, though not lifting my arm from my side. The human spinal column, with its vertebræ, for an axle-tree of a wagon! And yet, I immediately thought, the poor negro's back is truly "the for'ard X " of the great wagon of our American commerce. But I let him depart.

Salutary impressions, I cannot question, dear Aunty, were made upon his mind. He had heard some things which would occupy his thoughts in his solitary trudge on his way to Boston. That thought comforted me as I was writhing a little on my way home, under his opprobrious epithets; for you know that I was always sensitive when addressed with reproachful words.

I could not help recalling and analyzing his scalding words of contempt. I took a certain pleasure in doing so, because, as I saw and felt the power of each in succession, I remembered what awful abuses flow from the tongues of Southern masters and mistresses continually, as they goad on their slaves to their work, or reproach them for not bringing in the brick for which they had given them no straw. So it was comparatively a light affliction for me to remember that I had been called by such hard names. "Putty-headed!" said he. I infer, dear Aunty, that he must have worked in the painter's department, and had been familiar with putty; hence he drew the epithet, into whose signification I did not care to inquire. "White-birch-looking!" I suppose he referred to the impression of imbecility which we have in seeing a perfectly white tree in the woods among the deep green of the sturdier trees. He may have referred to the effect of sedentary habits on my complexion. However, I soon forgot the particulars of his insulting address, retaining only the impression that I had suffered, and that willingly, in the bleeding cause of freedom.

It was a great relief to me that, just at that moment, a very fine dog approached me and fawned upon me, then ran ahead, and seemed afraid that I should send him back. After a while I tried to drive him away, but he insisted on following me, and I have no doubt that I might have secured him, had I wished to do so. I was not a little inclined, at one time, to take him home with me, and to keep him as a companion in my walks. But he had a collar with his own name, Bruno, upon it, and the name of his owner. The question of right occurred to me. I debated it. Applying some of the self-evident truths established by our own Independence, I almost persuaded myself that I might rightfully take the dog. I reasoned thus: 1. All dogs are born free and equal. 2. They have an inalienable right to life, liberty, and the pursuit of happiness. 3. All governments derive their just powers from the consent of the governed. These principles, breathed in, from childhood, with the atmosphere of our glorious " Fourth," I did not hesitate to apply in the case of the dog. I do not know what practical conclusion I might have arrived at, but suddenly I lost sight of Bruno in consequence of a new adventure, in the process of which he disappeared.

A matronly looking lady came suddenly out of a gate, with a cup in one hand containing a teaspoon, and a brown earthen mug in the other hand. She pushed the gate open before her, easily; but I saw that she was embarrassed about shutting it. I stepped forward and assisted her.

" Some kind office for the sick, I dare say," said I.

" A woman in that plastered house is very sick," said she ; " I have just fixed some marsh-mallow for her, to see if it will ease her cough. Sorry to trouble you, sir, but my cup was so full that I could not use my hands."

" I suppose," said I, " madam, if you will allow me to detain you a moment,"——

" I am afraid my drink in the cup will get cold, sir, but "——

" Only a moment, madam," said I ; (for I did not feel at liberty to walk with her ;) " only a moment ; I am led to think, by your kindness to this poor woman, of the millions of bond-people in our Southern country who never feel the hand of love ministering to their sick and dying "——

"O you ignorant thing!" said she, pouring the contents of the cup into the mug, and then setting the cup on the mug, all without looking at me; "where were you born and bred? You must be an abolitionist. Southern ladies are the very best of nurses; and as to their slaves when they are sick, — why their hearts are overflowing — why!" said she, "I could tell you tales that would make you cry like a baby — the idea! millions of slaves sick and neglected! Do you belong to ———— College?"

"Yes, madam," said I.

"Sophomore?" said she.

"Yes, madam." But it was a cutting question. She had an arch look as she asked it.

"Well sir," said she, with a graceful air, in a half averted direction, "you have some things to learn about your fellow-countrymen which are not put down in your Moral Philosophies. Please do not betray your ignorance on subjects about which you are evidently in midnight darkness." She was some ways from me, but I heard her continue : "Was there ever anything like this Northern ignorance and prejudice about the Southern people!"

I had nothing to do but resume my lonely walk. My sense of desolateness no tongue can tell. I whistled for Bruno, but in vain. She called me "an ignorant thing," said I. Ignorant on the subject of slavery! How easy it is to misjudge! Have I studied free-soil papers all these years only to be called "an ignorant thing!" I could graduate to-day from this institution, though only in my second year, if the examination were confined to the subject of slavery. I have thoroughly understood the theory; I have learned by heart the codes of the

iniquitous system. I know it root and branch, from pith
to bark. All the lecturers on the subject have not labored
in vain, nor spent their strength for nought, with me.
And now to be called "ignorant!" Just as though I
could not reason, that is, draw inferences from premises,
make deductions from facts. There is the great fact of
slavery; it is "the sum of all villanies;" men holding
their fellow-men in bondage for the sake of gain; the
heart naturally covetous, oppressive, and cruel, where
power is unlimited. As though the law of kindness
could, in such circumstances, possibly prevail and mitigate the sorrows of the bondman! The direct influence
of slavery is to debase, to make barbarous, to petrify; I
know as well as though I saw it that the South must be
full of neglected, perishing objects, cast out to perish in
their sicknesses. You doubtless are acquainted, dear
Aunty, with the great change in the mode of reasoning
introduced by Lord Bacon. We reason now from facts to
conclusion; this is called the inductive method, to collect
facts, then draw inferences. The facts which I have collected on the subject of slavery, in my reading and hearing, lead me to a perfect theory on the subject, and my
confidence in that theory is all which it could be if, like
you, I were now seeing it verified with my own eyes.

I reason on this subject of slavery, just as our philos-
ophers reason about the moon. You have learned, dear
Aunt, ere this, that there is no water in the moon. Certain things are observed by our telescopes, in the moon,
from which we are sure that there is no water there.
Now there are certain given facts in slavery. Slavery is
Barbarism. It consists in holding men to compulsory
servitude. The human heart is avaricious; it gets all it
can, and keeps all it gets. Give it complete power over

a human being, and there are no limits to its cupidity and wrong-doing, but the finite nature of the thing itself. Hence, does it not follow that there can be no disinterest-edness, no tender mercies in slavery? Yes, dear Aunt, as we are perfectly sure that there can be no water in the moon, so are we sure, by the same unerring rule of reasoning according to the inductive philosophy, that there is not one drop of water in slavery for the parched lips of a dying slave. I stated this to a member of our Junior Class who is a wonderful metaphysician. He was kind enough to say that he could discover no flaw in the logic. Your letter, which, I trust, is now on its way to me, I know will fully confirm my theory and conclu-sion.

This lady had probably been reading some miserable cant about Southern humanity, for there are people everywhere who take the wrong side of every subject, from sheer obstinacy. What can disprove the laws of human nature? They require that things should be at the South as our theories lay them down.

In our Institution I mourn to say there is much oppo-sition to the principles of freedom. Not only so, but the students, many of them, mock at us who stand up against oppression.

You may not be aware, dear Aunty, that I have a habit, in walking, of keeping my hands firmly clenched, and my thumbs laid flat and pressed down over the knuckles of my forefingers. This, I am aware, gives the thumbs a flattened look. One of our principal pro-slavery students delights to laugh at me to my face. Perhaps I am wrong in connecting everything with this all-absorbing theme, but, truly, my thoughts all run in that direction. Mother and you were ac-

customed to send me on errands when I was little, and
you placed your money in my right hand and mother
hers in my left, because, on my return to our house, your
room was on the right hand of the entry.   So I used to
go along, holding your respective moneys in my palms,
with my thumbs stopping the apertures.   And now I am
persecuted for the fidelity which led me to acquire a
habit that cleaves to me to this day.   But little did I
dream, dear Aunty, when I padded along like a straight
footed animal in the water, instead of having the free use
of my open palms to aid me in walking, that I was ac-
quiring a habit to be to me an inlet of torture in behalf
of our manacled four millions, whose hands feel the gall-
ing bonds of slavery.   I take it joyfully, because it is all
for the slave.

The day that I came home from my two interviews
and efforts just related, a pro-slavery student, a Senior,
invited me into his room.   He is exceedingly kind and
generous, though, I am sorry to say it, a friend of oppression.   He gave me a splendid apple, the first which I
had seen for the season.   He dusted my coat with his
feather-duster, and he even dusted my boots.   He asked
me how far I had been walking.   I told him all which I
had said and done, thinking that it would profitably remind him of the great subject.   He roared with laughter.   " Three cheers for Gustavus ; "   " isn't that rich ; "
— waving, all the while, the feather-duster, and breaking
out with fresh peals, as I related one thing after another.
The noise which he made brought in several of the students from neighboring rooms, and he related my stories
to them as they stood with their thumbs and fingers holding open their text-books at the places where they were
studying.   They were a curious looking set, in their

dressing-gowns, slippers, and smoking-caps; and the most of them, unfortunately, happened to be pro-slavery, and advocates of oppression; by which I mean, not in favor of my mode of viewing and treating the subject of slavery. One of them was so amused and excited that he lost all self-control. He threw down his book, caught me with his two hands about the waist, and tickled me so that I fell upon the floor. Then they raised a shout. We have cool nights here, sometimes, in the warmest weather, and we keep, on the foot-boards of our beds, cotton comforters, called *delusions*, because they are so downy and light. Two of the students took the Senior's comforter and laid it on me; then four of them sat down, one on each corner, to keep me underneath. I have told you that it was a sultry August day. I thought that I should smother. I told them so, as well as my choked voice would allow; but one of them said, in a soft, meek tone, as I writhed in distress, " Hush, Gustavus, lie still; you are certainly laboring under a delusion." This was all the more painful from its being so cruelly true, in a literal sense, while I knew that they had reference to my views with regard to freedom, in the word " delusion." What sustained me in those moments, dear Aunty? It was not that I had myself stood by when this trick was played on Freshmen, and encouraged it by my actions; no, a higher and holier power than conscience of wrong-doing wrought upon me in those moments. Oh, I thought, the very cotton which fills this comforter was cultivated by the hand of a slave. And shall I complain at being nearly smothered by it, when I remember what an incubus slavery is to the poor creature who gathered this cotton, and what an incubus it is to our unhappy land?

I was delivered at last from my load, because my tormentors were tired of their sport. Would that there were some prospect that they who load cruel burdens on the slave were increasingly tired of their work!

They would not, however, let me rise. So, thought I, when we have taken the burden of slavery off from the poor negro, unholy prejudice against color keeps him from rising to a level with the rest of the community. I begged that I might get up. They told me that my morning exertions required longer rest. I told them that I must get my Greek. Whereupon one of them stood over me, with his arms raised in a deploring attitude, and said, —

> " Sternitur infelix! —
> — Et dulces moriens reminiscitur Argos."

This, dear Aunty, is the lamentation of a Latin poet over a Greek soldier lying prostrate on the battle-field, far from home ; — " and dying he remembers his sweet Greece." So they made game of me with the help of the Classics, giving poignancy to their jokes by polishing the tips with classical allusions. While I was under the " delusion," they sung snatches of Bruce's Address to his army ; and when they came to the words

> " Who so base as be a slave ? —
> Let him turn and flee,"

one of them ran a cane under the delusion and punched me with it, keeping stroke to the music. This was little short of profaneness. They asked me if the chair-maker's harnesses were probably made by free or slave labor, alluding, unfeelingly, to a mistake which I made in a recitation one day, when two of those very students had kept me talking about slavery up to the very moment when the recitation-bell rang, so that I had not looked at my lesson. There are men in my class, and these were some of them, who, I am told, are plotting to prevent my having the first appointment, to which they know that my marks at recitation entitle me. But may I never be so prejudiced against those who differ from me on the subject of slavery as to deny them credit for things which they have fairly earned. I leave this to the avowed enemies of human rights. For the cause of the slave, I must gain the first appointment.

I alluded, just now, to my feelings at witnessing tricks played on the Freshmen. Had the Sophomores asked my advice before they played those tricks, I should have dissuaded them; but when they played them, with such courage and enterprise, I stood before them with admiration. But while I was under that quilt, I found that I did not admire the Sophomores at all, any more than I did the Seniors who then had me in their power.

The enemies of freedom, in College, had a great triumph the other evening. One of them, in one of the Literary Societies, read an Original Poem, the title of which was, "The Fly-time of Freedom." He spoke of " our glorious summer of Liberty " being infested and pestered with noisy, provoking things, which he characterized under the names of dor-bugs, millers, and all those creatures which fly into the room when the lamp is lighted; the swarms of black gnats which are about your head in the woods; horse-flies which stick, and leave blood running; and devil's-darning-needles. One brave man here, a great " friend of freedom," who, they falsely say, loves to be persecuted, and longs for martyrdom, and interprets everything that way, he described as a miller, who seems to court death in the flame. I think he aimed at me in speaking of soft, harmless bugs which creep over your newspaper or book. Many faces were turned

to me as he repeated these lines. I am sorry to say the
piece was much applauded. It has put back the cause
of emancipation in College, I fear, a term.

The following introduction to another piece was written, and was read, at the same meeting, by a member of
my own class. I fear that there is a sly hit intended by
the writer, which I do not discern, at somebody, or something, related to freedom. This I suspected from the
applause it excited on the part of those who I know are
the most deadly foes we have to free institutions. I obtained a copy of this introduction. It will serve, at least,
to show you, dear Aunty, what a variety of topics we
have to excite our minds here in College. You can exercise your discretion about letting uncle read it, as it is
on a subject of some delicacy. The writer says, —

"I am collecting facts from our daily papers illustrating the Barbarism of Matrimony. My list of wives
poisoned, beaten, maimed for life by their husbands, and
of divorces, cruel desertions, the effects on wives of intemperance in husbands, is truly fearful. I make no
question that there are some happy marriages. But a
relation which affords such peculiar opportunities for
cruelty to women, must sooner or later disappear. No
doubt the time will come when marriage will be deemed
a relic of barbarism, and a bridal veil be exhibited as one
of the mock decorations of the unhappy victims. Human nature in man is not good enough to be trusted with
such a responsibility as the happiness of woman. Let
Bachelors of Arts, on our parchments, suggest to us our
duty to aid, through our example, as well as by words,
in breaking this dreadful yoke, bidding those innocent
young women who are now, perhaps, fearfully looking at
us as their future oppressors, to be forever free. In the

language of young Hamlet: 'I say, we will have no more marriages.' "

Just before dark one evening, I was sitting in my room, meditating on the great theme which absorbs my thoughts. My eye was caught by the bright bolt of my door-lock, the part of the bolt between the lock and the catch showing, beyond question, that the door was fastened. Some one on the outside had turned a key upon me.

I had the self-possession to be quiet, for my mind had been calmed by reflecting, in that twilight hour, that now one more day of toil for the poor slaves was over.

But as I looked at the bolt, my attention was diverted by something near the top of the door, moving with a strange motion. It was black; it opened and shut. I drew toward it. I found that it was the leg of a turkey, the largest that I ever saw. It was held or fastened in the ventilator over the door, while some one on the outside was evidently pulling the tendons of the claw, making it open and shut.

There it performed its tragi-comic gibes for several minutes.

I resumed my seat, unterrified, of course, and proceeded to turn the spectre to good account. I addressed it, in a moderate tone; though I think that I used some gesticulation. Said I: Personation of the Slave-power! predatory, grasping, black! thinkest thou a panting fugitive lies hid under my "delusion?" or wouldst thou seize a freeman? The Ægis of Massachusetts is over me. Gape! Yawn! Thou art powerless; but thy impudence is sublime. — Ten or fifteen voices then solemnly chanted these words: —

" Emblem of Slavery
  Clutching the Free!
  We've digested the turkey
  That gobbled on thee.
  Sure as THANKSGIVING hastened,
  Cock-turkey! thy hour,
  Thanksgivings shall blazon
  Thy downfall, Slave-power!

" The Slave-power has talons,
  Like Nebuchadnezzar;
  Slaves are the Lord's flagons
  Our modern Belshazzar
  From the Temple of Nature
  Has stolen away.
  ' Mean!' ' Mean!' be writ o'er him !
  Wrath! canst thou de " ——

Here screams of laughter, and a scampering in the entry, and the turkey's leg tumbling into my room, ended
the trick and their cantillation. I was wishing to hear, in
the next stanza, the idea that as the tendons of the claw
were worked by a foreign power, so slavery at the South
owes its activity to Northern influence. Perhaps it is
due to myself to say that the word scampering, a few
lines above, has no revengeful reference, in its first sylla-
ble, to the author of the trick. The cause of humanity,
I find, has a tendency to make one cautious and charitable in his use of words.

They have anti-slavery meetings in the village, now
and then, which I attend. All the talent of the place,
and the truly good, are there. One evening, when the
excitement rose high, a tall, awkward young man mount-
ed the stage, and said that he wanted to offer one resolution as a cap-sheaf. You will infer, dear Aunty, that he
was an agriculturist. He lifted his paper high up in
one hand, while his other hand was extended in the other
direction, and so was his foot under that hand. He

3

looked like Boötes, on the map of the heavens, which we used to take with us, you know, in studying the comet. " Read it ! " " Read it ! " said the meeting. " I will," said he, flinging himself almost round once, in his excitement, reminding me of a war-dance, and then taking his sublime attitude again ; when he read, —

" Resolved, Mr. Cheerman, fact is, that Abolition is everything, and nuthin' else is nuthin'."

Some of the younger portion of the audience wished to raise a laugh, but the reddening, angry faces of the prominent friends of the slave were turned upon them instantly, and overawed them.

All were silent for a moment, when the Chairman rose to speak. He was a short man, with reddish hair, and his teeth were almost constantly visible, his lips not seeming to be an adequate covering for them. He had, moreover, a habit of snuffing up with his nose, — in doing which his upper lip, what there was of it, played its part, and made him show his teeth by frequent spasms. Being a little bow-legged, he made an awkward effort in coming to the front of the stage ; but we all love him, because he is such a vigorous friend of freedom, looking as though he would willingly be executioner of all the oppressors in the land. He said that he " utterly concurred " with the mover in the spirit of his resolution ; it was not, to be sure, in the usual form of resolutions, but that could easily be fixed ; and he would suggest that it be referred to the Standing Committee of the Freedom League. " I agree to that," said the pro-slavery Senior who gave me that entertainment in his room, (but who, by the way, being a friend of oppression, had no right to speak in a meeting in behalf of freedom ;) " I agree to that," said he, " Mr. Chairman, and I move that the

School-master be added to the Committee." What a cruel laugh went through the meeting! while the most distinguished friends of the slave had hard work to control their faces.

I could not help going to the mover of the resolution after the meeting; and, laying two fingers of my right hand on his arm, I said, "Don't be put down; he tried to reproach you for not being college-bred; he had better get the slaves well educated before he laughs at a Massachusetts freeman for not being a scholar." — He tossed his black fur-skin cap half-way to his head, and he wheeled round as he caught it, saying, "Don't care, liberty's better 'n larnin', 'nuff sight." — "Both are good," said I, "my friend, and we must give them both to the slave." — "Give 'em the larnin' after y'u've sot 'em free!" said he; "I'll fight for 'em; don't want to hear nuthin' 'bout nuthin' else but liberty to them that's bound." He stooped and pulled a long whip and a tin pail from under the seat of the pew where he had been sitting, making considerable noise, so that the people, as they passed out, turned, and the sight of him and his accoutrements made great sport for some whose opinions and feelings were the least to be regarded. I saw in him, dear Aunty, a fair specimen of native, inbred love of liberty and hatred of oppression, unsophisticated, to be relied on in our great contest with the slave-power. I have been told, since the meeting, that his Christian name is Isaiah.

The meeting that evening appointed me a delegate to an Anti-slavery Convention which is to be held before long. I am expected to represent the College on the great arena of freedom. They have done me too much honor. Since my appointment, the students have sent me, anonymously, through the post-office, resolutions to be presented by me at the Convention. I have copied them into a book as they came in, and I will transcribe them for you and send them herewith. The spirit of liberty is, on the whole, certainly rising among the students. As the blood of the martyrs is the seed of the Church, I cannot but hope that my trials in the cause of freedom have wrought good in the Institution. Some who send in these resolutions privately, are, no doubt, secret friends, needing a little more courage to face the pro-slavery feeling and sentiment which are all about them. Some one who read these resolutions suggested the idea of their being a burlesque. I repudiated the idea at once. They will commend themselves to you, dear Aunty, I am sure, as honest and truthful.

The President called me to his room yesterday, and asked me about the treatment which I received from those Seniors. While I was telling him of it, I noticed that he kept his handkerchief close to his face almost all the time. I thought at first that his nose bled, or that he had a toothache; but I afterward believed that he was weeping at the story of my wrongs. A Southerner, in the Junior Class, said he had no doubt that the President was laughing heartily all the time. None but a minion of the slave-power could have suggested this idea. The President felt so much that he merely told me to return to my room.

But I perceive, by the students with letters and papers in their hands, that the mail is in. I will add a postscript, if I find a letter from you; and I will send on the resolutions at once. Write soon, dear Aunty, to your loving nephew, and to

Yours for the slave,

GUSTAVUS.

CHAPTER IV.

RESOLUTIONS FOR A CONVENTION.

> "Nay, and thou'lt mouth,
> I'll rant as well as thou." — HAMLET.

I.

RESOLVED, That the continued practice of wild geese to visit the South for the winter, flying over free soil — Concord, Lexington, Bunker Hill, Faneuil Hall, — on their way to the land of despotism, cannot be too loudly deplored by all the friends of freedom in the North ; and that the laws of nature are evidently imperfect in not yielding to the known anti-slavery sentiments of this great Northern people so far as to make the instincts of said geese conform to our most sacred antipathies and detestations.

II.

Resolved, That the abolitionists of Maine, and of the British Provinces, resident near the summer haunts of said geese, be requested to consider whether measures may not be adopted whereby anti-slavery tracts, and card-pictures illustrating the atrocious cruelties of slavery, and appeals to the consciences of the South, or at least instructions to the colored people as to their right and duty to assert their liberty, may not be fastened to these birds of passage, to make them apostles of liberty; so that while they continue to disregard the bleeding cause of humanity, their very cackle may be converted into lays of freedom.

III.

Whereas we read in the Revelation a description of the wall of heaven as having "on the South three gates," a number equal to that assigned to the North,

Resolved, That this description being in total disregard of the great modern anti-slavery movement, the book which contains it cannot have been divinely inspired; and that a true anti-slavery Bible would have represented those pro-slavery gates as shut, with the inscription over them: Enter from the North.

IV.

Resolved, That the great abolitionist who represents himself in his speeches as baptizing his dogs, in just ridicule of the baptism of chattel slaves, is worthy, with his dogs, of a place in the heavens among the constellations; and that anti-slavery astronomers be requested to make a Southern constellation for them somewhere near the head of The Serpent, as rivals to " *Canes Venatici*," which pro-slavery astronomers no doubt designed, in blasphemous profanation of the heavens, to represent their bloodhounds hunting fugitive slaves, placing it in disgusting proximity to our own Northern *Ursa Major*. And the friends of the slave are hereby invited to make that new constellation their cynosure, vowing by it, and anti-slavery lovers arranging their matrimonial engagements, if possible, so as to plight their troth only when it is in the ascendant.

V.

Resolved, That we shall hail it as a sign of progress and an omen for good, when anti-slavery women, with the sensibility which belongs to their sex, shall become so interpenetrated with the sentiments of freedom, that they can distinguish by the sense of taste the oyster grown in James River, Richmond, Virginia, and handled by the toil-worn slave, from that which grew on free soil.

VI.

Resolved, That our noble anti-slavery poets be requested to compose sonnets addressed to the whippoorwill, appealing to that sorrowful-tuned bird by our associations with his name, and by his own historic relationship to the victims of oppression, to desert the South and to frequent our woods and pastures in greater numbers, that the sensibilities of our people may be continually touched by his notes and his name, so suggestive of the monstrous lash which rules over one half of this great nation. And the anti-slavery members of the Legislature are hereby requested to seek legislative enactments whereby the whippoorwill may be further domiciliated at the North, and be provided with protection during the winter season.

VII.

Resolved, That bobolinks, blue jays, orioles, martins, and swallows, who visit the rice-fields of the South, and live upon the unrequited toil of four millions of our fellow-men, should not, upon their return, be viewed with favor by the friends of equal rights at the North, but should be destroyed by sportsmen as a sacrifice to outraged humanity. And no true anti-slavery taxidermist will, in our judgment, be found willing to stuff the skin of one of those mean and traitorous birds for any public or private ornithological show-case.

VIII.

Resolved, That one subject of great interest, well suited to occupy the attention of Massachusetts freemen and friends of liberty the current year, is this: Whether the great whips in Dock Square, Boston, which stand professedly as signs before the doors of whip-makers' shops, but are in the very sight of Faneuil Hall, shall be allowed to remain within that sacred precinct of liberty; and that we tender our thanks to those who are investigating the question whether the whips were not originally placed, and are not now maintained, there by the slave-power, in mockery of our Northern hatred of oppression.

IX.

Resolved, That, if it be true that the steel pen which signed the bill for the removal of a Judge of Probate for doing an accursed duty as U. S. Commissioner, was taken from the Council Chamber and is now in the possession of one who has driven it into the edge of his chamber-door casement, and every night hangs his watch upon it, at the head of his bed, with the infatuated notion that thereby, through some "most fine spirit of sense," the tick of a death-watch will disturb the political dreams of our Massachusetts rulers, we hereby declare that this is most chimerical and visionary, and that the great party of freedom in Massachusetts need not feel the slightest apprehension that our rulers have the least misgivings as to the morality of their conduct in the removal of said officer, nor that they fear political retribution for that deed;

nor do we believe that the death-watch will ever tick in the ear of freedom in Massachusetts.

X.

Resolved, That in the acquiescence of many at the North in the entire justice of a universal massacre, by the slaves, of their masters, including women and children, we recognize a state of preparedness for the proscription and banishment of all who do not come up to the high abolition standard; but that in carrying out that project, we ought first to seek the reclamation of the victims, and therefore that due inquiry ought to be made concerning the most effective modes of persuasion, as, for example, thumb-screws, racks, wheels, scorpions, water-dropping for the head, bags of snakes, tweezers, and steel-pointed beds, it being apparent that our agony for the slave cannot be satisfied except by his liberation, or by the forcible subjection to us of all who oppose it. And we do hereby request all the friends of freedom now travelling in despotic countries to make inquiry as to the most approved methods of persuading the mind by appeals to it through the sensibilities of the flesh, and to be prepared with this information against the time when the sublime march of abolition philanthropy shall arrive at the limits of forbearance with all the Northern advocates of oppression.

XI.

Whereas no one who holds slaves can be a Christian; and whereas Abraham, Isaac, and Jacob were slave-holders, Abraham himself having owned more slaves than any Southerner; and whereas a synonyme of heaven, in the New Testament, is " Abraham's bosom; " and whereas

3 *

no true friend of freedom can consistently have Christian communion with slave-holders,

Resolved, That we look with deep interest to the introduction among us of the principles of the Hindoo philosophy and religion (including the transmigration of souls), through tentative articles in our magazines ; by which there is opening to us a way of escape from that heaven one exponent of which is, to lie in the bosom of a slave-holder.

XII.

And in conclusion,

Be it Resolved, That Bunker Hill was since Mount Sinai, that Faneuil Hall is far in advance of the Tabernacle in the Wilderness ; and that our anti-slavery literature is immeasurably beyond epistles to Philemon and other inspired pro-slavery tracts.

CHAPTER V.

THE GOOD NORTHERN LADY'S LETTER FROM THE SOUTH.

"No haughty gesture marks his gait,
No pompous tone his word;
No studied attitude is seen,
No palling nonsense heard;
He'll suit his bearing to the hour,
Laugh, listen, learn, or teach,
With joyous freedom in his mirth,
And candor in his speech." — ELIZA COOK.

[My friend, A. Freeman North, having read the foregoing, returned it with a hasty note, in pencil, saying, "Please send me the Aunt's reply, if you have it, or can procure it." I accordingly sent it, and we have it here.]

MY DEAR NEPHEW, —

Your letter came while we had gone into the country for a fortnight. Hattie is much improved, and I trust will soon be well. I gave her your letter to read. She told me that she could not find it in her heart to wonder at you for it; for once she should probably have written very much in the same strain.

It was Easter Monday afternoon when our steamboat reached the wharf. We took an open carriage and drove toward the hotel. As we reached the centre of the city, the place seemed to be full of colored people, who evidently had just come out of their meeting-houses. This

was our first view of the blacks. Our driver had to stop
frequently while they were crossing the streets, and
we had full opportunity to enjoy the sight. Hattie exclaimed, after looking at them a few moments, —

"Why, Uncle, they are human beings!"

"What did you suppose they were?" said he.

"Uncle," said she, "these cannot be slaves. Where do
you suppose the yokes are?"

"Now, Hattie," said he, "you were not so simple as
to suppose that they wore yokes, like wild cows and
swine."

"Why," said she, "our papers are always telling about
their being 'reduced to a level with brutes,' and every
Sabbath since I was a child, it seems to me, I have
heard the prayer, 'Break every yoke!' Last Sabbath our
minister, you remember, said, 'Abraham was a slave-
holder, David a murderer, and Peter lied and swore.'
Why, Uncle, these black people look like gentlemen and
ladies! If slave-holders are like murderers and thieves,
these cannot be their slaves!"

"Ask that elderly gentleman," said your Uncle. He
was stopping for our carriage to pass, — a portly man,
with a ruffled shirt, and a rich-looking cane, the end of
which he kept on the ground, holding the top of it at some
distance from him.

"Please, sir, will you tell me if these are the slaves?"
said Hattie.

He looked round, while he kept his arm and the top
of his cane describing large arcs of a circle.

"They are our colored people, Miss," said he, ex-
changing a smile with your Uncle and me.

"Well, sir," said Hattie, more earnestly than before,
"are they slaves?"

He politely nodded assent, but was apparently interested by something which caught his eye. He then took out a snuff-box, and, looking round about him while opening it, said, —

"Some of them dress too much, Miss, — too much, altogether."

"Kid gloves of all colors," said Hattie, soliloquizing. "Red morocco Bibles and hymn-books. What a white cloud of a turban! Part of the choir, I take it, — those, with their singing-books. Elegant spruce young fellow, isn't he, Aunt? with the violoncello. Venerable old couple, there! over eighty, both of them. Well," continued Hattie, "I will give up, if these are the slaves."

"Don't make up your mind too suddenly," said your Uncle; "you will see other things."

"Uncle," said she, "what I have seen here in fifteen minutes shows me that at least one half of that which I have learned at the North about the slaves is false. Our novels and newspapers are all the time misleading us."

"And yet," said your Uncle, "perhaps everything they say may be true by itself; it may have happened."

"Why, Aunt," said she, "such a load is gone from my mind since looking upon these colored people that I feel almost well. Why, there's a wedding!" said she. "Driver, do stop! Uncle, please let us go in."

They left me, and went into a meeting-house, where a black bridegroom, in a blue broadcloth suit, white waistcoat, kid gloves, patent-leather shoes, and white hose, and an ebony bride, in white muslin caught up with jessamines, and a myrtle wreath on her head, had gone in, followed by a train of colored people. The white people, invited guests, it seems, were already assembled. The sexton told your Uncle that the parties were servants, each to a respectable family. This was a new picture to Hattie. She said that in looking back to the steamboat, an hour ago, the revelations made to her by what she had seen and heard, in that short time, all new, all surprising and delightful, afforded her some idea of the sensations of a soul after it has been one hour within the veil. We sat in the carriage, and saw the procession pass out, when the choir, who had been in the church before the wedding, practising tunes, resumed their singing.

"Now the idea," said Hattie, after we had listened awhile, "that they can forget that they are slaves long enough to meet and practise psalm-tunes!"

"You evidently think," said your Uncle, "that they would not sing the Lord's songs, if this were to them a strange land."

"They certainly have not hung their harps upon the willows by these rivers of Babylon," said Hattie.

"Why, some of our people at the North are to-day writhing in anguish, because of these slaves, and are imprecating God's vengeance, and praying that the slaves may get their liberty, even by violence, while the slaves themselves are practising psalm-tunes!" —

"And getting married," said your Uncle.

"Yes, Sir," said Hattie, "and this week our —— paper will come to us from New York loaded with articles about 'bondage' and 'sum of all villanies,' and 'poor, toil-worn slaves.' Toil-worn! I never saw such a lively set of people. Do see that little mite of a round black child, in black jacket and pants; he looks like a drop of ink; Oh, isn't he cunning! Little boy! what is your" ——

"Come, come!" said your Uncle, "you are getting too

much excited; you will pay for all this to-morrow with one of your headaches."

But a new surprise awaited us. The driver stopped opposite a large, plain-looking building, and told us that we had better step in. On entering, we involuntarily started back, for I never saw a house more densely filled; and all were blacks. It was a sable cloud; but the sun was in it. The choir were singing a select piece. The principal *soprano*, an elegant-looking black girl, dressed in perfect taste, held her book from her in her very small hand covered with a straw-colored glove. The singing was charming. We asked a white-headed negro in the vestibule what was going on.

" Why, it is Easter Monday, Missis."

" Is this an Episcopal church?"

" No; Baptist."

" What are all these people here for?" said your Uncle.

" Why, to worship, Sir, I hope. It's holiday."

" Do they go to church, holidays?"

" Why," said he, with a smile and bow, " some of the best of 'em, p'raps."

We returned to the carriage.

" Think," said your uncle, " of two thousand people at the North spending a part of ' Artillery Election Day ' in Boston, for example, in going to church!"

" Well," said Hattie, " if I were not to live another day, I would bless God for having let me live to see these things. I am so glad to find people happy who I had supposed were weeping and wailing."

We admonished her that she had not seen the whole of slavery.

A very interesting coincidence happened to us the next

day. We took tea at Rev. Mr. ——'s. A splendid
bride-cake adorned the table. As Hattie was admiring
the ornaments on the cake, the lady of the clergyman
smiled and said, —

"This is from a colored wedding."

Sure enough, that black bride whom we saw the day
before had sent her minister's wife this loaf. Said
Miss ——, "I was hurrying to get a silk dress made
last week, but my dressmaker put me off, because she
was working for Phillis B.'s wedding."

We both gave a glance at Hattie. She sat gazing at
Miss ——, her lips partly open, her eyes moistened, —
a picture in which delight and incredulity were in pleasant strife.

We have been in the interior a fortnight. One thing
filled me with astonishment, soon after I came here, namely,
to find widow ladies and their daughters, all through the
interior of Southern States, living remote from other habitations, surrounded by twenty, fifty, or a hundred slaves.
Hattie and I spent a week with a widow lady, whose head
slave was her overseer. There was not a white man
within a mile of the house. More than twenty black
men, slaves, were in the negro quarter. I awoke the
first night, and said to Hattie, —

"Do you know that you are 'sleeping on a volcano'?"

"What do you mean, Aunt? You frighten me."

"Well, it will not make an eruption to-night," said I.
"We will examine into it to-morrow."

At breakfast I asked the lady how she dared to live so.
I told her that we at the North generally fancied Southern people sleeping on their arms, expecting any night to
be murdered by their slaves.

"It ought to be so, ought it not?" said she, "according to your Northern theory of slavery; and it may get to be so, if your people persist in some of their ways. My only fear is of some white men who live about two miles off. I keep two of my men-servants in the house at night as a protection against white depredators."

"But," said Hattie, "there have been insurrections. Are you not afraid that your slaves will rise and assert their liberty?"

The lady smiled and was evidently hesitating whether to answer seriously or not, when Hattie continued, —

"Aunt! now I see what you meant by our sleeping on a volcano."

"Yes," said I, "we at the North often speak of you Southerners as sleeping on a volcano. Our idea is that the blacks here are prisoners, stealing about in a sulky mood, vengeance brooding in their hearts, and that they wait for their time of deliverance, as prisoners in our state-prison watch their chance to escape."

"Well," said she, "I believe I am the only slave on the premises. I am sure that no one but myself is watching for a chance to escape. I would run away from these people if I could. But what shall I do with them? I am not willing to sell them, for when I have hinted at leaving, there is such entreaty for me to remain, and such demonstrations of affection and attachment, that I give it up.

"Here," said she, "are seven house-servants, large and small, to do work which at the North a man and two capable girls would easily do. I have to devise ways to subdivide work and give each a share. My husband carried it so far that he had one boy to black boots and another shoes, and these two 'bureaus' were kept separate."

" Oh," said I, " what a curse slavery is to you ! "

" As to that," said she, " it is the negroes who are a curse, not their slavery. So long as they are on the same soil with us, the subordination which slavery establishes makes it the least of two evils. If there is any curse in the case, it is the blacks themselves, not their slavery. Were it not for their enslavement to us, we should hate them and drive them away, like Indiana and Illinois and Oregon and Kansas. Now we cherish them, and their interests are ours.

" Two distinct races," said she, " never have been able to live together unless one was subordinate and dependent. This, you know, all history teaches. Your fanatics say it should not be so ; they talk about liberty, equality, and fraternity, and put guns and pikes into the hands of the inferior race, here, to help them ' rise in the scale of being,' as they term it. What God means to accomplish in this matter of slavery I do not see.

" Suppose, merely for illustration," said she, " that cotton should be superseded. Vast numbers of our slaves might then be useless here. What would become of them ? We should implore the North to relieve us of them, in part. Then would rise up the Northern antipathy to the negro, stronger, probably, in the abolitionist than in the pro-slavery man ; and as we sought to remove the negroes northward and westward, the Free States would invoke the Supreme Court, and the Dred Scott decision, and then we should see, with a witness, whether the black man has ' any rights ' on free soil ' which the ' original settlers ' are bound to respect.' Think of bleeding Kansas, even, refusing to incorporate negro-suffrage in her constitution, when left free to follow the dictates of common sense, and a wise self-interest. I sometimes think that that one thing, as a philosophical fact, is worth all the trouble which Kansas has cost. It cannot be 'unholy prejudice against color.' It is human nature asserting the laws which God has established in it.

"I never," said she, "find abolitionists quoting the whole of the verse which says : 'and hath made of one blood all the nations of the earth.'"

"What," said I, "do they leave out?"

"'And hath fixed the bounds of their habitations,' are some of the next words," said she.

But you will tire of this. I will resume my story. I will only say that I told the lady that some of my gentleman friends would call her a strong-minded woman.

Your letter made me think of something which happened to a lady, a fellow-traveller of ours, a few weeks ago. She came here to visit a lady whose husband owns one hundred and fifty slaves. The morning after she reached the plantation, as she told me, she was awaked by the cracking of whips. She listened ; human voices, raised above the ordinary pitch, were mingling with the sounds. She lay till she could endure it no longer. Coming down to the piazza, she saw a white man mending a harness on a horse. "Those whips," said she, inquiringly, — "they have rather interfered with my peace. Any of the colored people been doing wrong?" He hesitated, and kept on fixing his harness, till, finally, he turned round, — for he had been standing with his back to her and, as she supposed, to hide his chagrin at being questioned on so trying a subject. "Truth is, Madam," said he, taking a large piece of tobacco and a knife from his pocket, and helping himself slowly, — "truth is, we have so much of this work to do, we have to begin early.

Sorry it disturbed you;" and he gathered up the reins and drove off.

The whips kept up their racket. "Here," said she to herself, "is the house of Bondage. How can I spend a month here?" She thought that she would peep round the house. Yet she feared that she should be considered as intruding into things which she had better not meddle with. But the screams became so fearful that she could no longer restrain herself. She rushed round the corner of the house, and came full against a black woman rinsing some fustian clothes in a tub near the rain-spout. "Do dear tell me," said she, "what they are doing to those people. Who is whipping them? What have they done?" The black woman stopped, and looked round without taking her hands from her tub, and then said, as she went on rinsing, " Lorfull help you, Missis, dem's de young uns scaring de birds out of de grain."

What bliss there was to her in that moment of relief! Six or eight little negroes were sauntering about at their morning work, each having a rude whip, with tape for a snapper, interrupting the hungry birds at their breakfast.

I expected to see a wretched, down-trodden, alms-house looking set of creatures; for the word *slave*, and all the changes which are rung on that word, made me think only of people who are convicts, such as you see in the state-prison yard at Charlestown, Mass. I never expected that they would look me in the face, but would skulk by me as a spy or enemy. A Christian heart is overjoyed to find what religion and society have done for these colored people. If one who had never heard of "slavery" should be set down here, the Northern idea of "bondage" would not soon occur to him.

In the Presbytery which includes Charleston, S. C.,

there are two thousand eight hundred and eighty-nine
church-members, and of these one thousand six hundred-
and thirty-seven, more than one half, are colored.   In
State Street, Mobile, there is a colored Methodist Church
who pay their minister, from their own money, twelve
hundred dollars a year.   Not long since they took up a
voluntary contribution for Home Missions, amounting to
one hundred and twenty dollars.   Their preacher was
sent by the Conference, according to rotation, into another
field, and the blacks presented him with a valuable suit
of clothes.

You see things here, good and evil, side by side, and
mixed up together, one thing counterbalancing another.
If you reason theoretically upon this subject, as you do
"about the moon," to quote from your letter, it is enough
to make one almost a lunatic, and I do not wonder that
some of our good people at the North, who pore over this
subject in this way, are on the borders of insanity.

My great mistake at the North with regard to this subject of slavery was, I reasoned about it in the abstract,
instead of considering it in connection with those who are
slaves under our laws, bound up with us in our civil constitution.   Things might be true or false, right or wrong,
in connection with the enslavement of a race who had
never been slaves, which cannot be applied to the colored
people of the South.   Hence, the arguments and the appeals founded on the wrongfulness of reducing you or me
to slavery are obviously misapplied when used to urge
the emancipation of these slaves.   Moreover, my thoughts
about slavery were governed by my associations with the
word *slave*, in its worst sense.   This is wholly wrong, and
it is the source of most of our mistakes on this subject.

Dreadful things happen here to some of the slaves in

the hands of passionate men. One slave who had run away was caught, and was beaten for a long time, and melted turpentine was then poured upon his wounds. He lingered for several hours. But the horror and execration which this deed met with were no greater at the North than at the South. It cannot be denied that slavery, as well as marriage, affords peculiar provocations and facilities for cruel deeds, — according to the doctrine of your friend and fellow-Sophomore. But in which section there is the more of unpunished wickedness, I am slow to pronounce, for I do not wish to condemn my own people, nor to justify others in their sins. An excellent minister in Cincinnati not long since preached a sermon on murder, in which he stated that "during his residence in that city, there had been more than one hundred murders, or an average of two a month, while in no instance had the perpetrator been executed." Reading lately of a husband at the North throwing oil of vitriol from a bottle, filled for the purpose, over his wife's face and neck, and of a Northern clergyman feeding his young wife, as she sat on his knee, with apple on which he had sprinkled arsenic, I questioned whether human nature were not about the same everywhere. The theoretical right of a master, in certain cases, to put his slave to death, without judge or jury, is controlled by the self-interest of the owner who, of course, does not recklessly destroy his own property. The slave-codes are no just exponent of the actual state of things in slavery. For example, — by law a master may not furnish his slave with less than a peck of corn a week. This has a barbarous look. But to see the slaves feasting on the fat of the land you certainly would not be reminded of the "peck of corn," except by contrast. There must be some legal standard, below which if an inhuman master falls in providing for his servant, he can be prosecuted. Hence the "peck of corn." By the will of an eminent citizen at the North, establishing courses of lectures for all coming time, the pay of each lecturer is to be determined by the market value, at the time, of a bushel of wheat. This is a fair standard for the unit of measure.

In arguing with one who should insist that the abuses in slavery are a reason for breaking up the institution in this country, I should feel justified in maintaining that there are as many instances of a happy relation between master and servant in the Southern country as there are happy marriages in the same number of households any-where. Let there be four millions of an inferior, de-pendent race mixed up with a superior race, anywhere on earth, and of course, while human nature is what it is, there will be hardships, wrong-doings, oppressions, and barbarisms. At the North, we get scraps of anguish in the newspapers relating to hardships at the South; and many pore upon them till they make themselves half-crazed. All the circumstances serving to qualify the narrative are sometimes withheld, and the stories are told with dramatic art. There is sorrow enough everywhere to furnish ma-terial for such kind of writing, especially to those who make it their calling, or find it for their interest, to pub-lish it. But the goings-on of life, at the South, with its alleviations and comforts, the practical mitigations of an oppressive system, theoretical evils qualified by difference of color, constitution, and history, and all the goodness and mercy which Christianity and a well-ordered state of society provide, we at the North do not see. Nor do our people consider that running away, and the complaints of the slaves, are partly chargeable to the discontent and restlessness of human nature; but we seem to take it for granted that every one who flees from the South is as though he had escaped from a prison-ship.

While at the North, I remember reading an article, signed with initials, in a prominent Massachusetts magazine, which contained this sentence: "Arsenic is universally in possession of the negroes; but it is considered the part of wisdom, where families are poisoned, that the fact should be kept as secret as possible." This was brought very powerfully to my mind one day on passing through King Street, in Charleston, and seeing for a painted sign over an apothecary's shop, a tall, benevolent-looking negro, in his shirt sleeves, behind a golden mortar, with the pestle in his hands, as though at work.

Now, I thought with myself, as I stood and enjoyed the sight, what a palpable and eloquent, though undesigned and silent, refutation that is, of all such Northern chimeras. If poisons are mixed with articles of food or medicine by the negroes with any noticeable frequency, the sign of a negro compounding medicines for public sale would surely be, to customers, the most detersive sign which an apothecary could erect over his premises. That little incident, and things like it, which are meeting you at every turn, show the state of things here to be in pleasing contrast to the horrors with which the imaginations of many of us Northerners are peopled. I find, in the "Charleston Mercury," a good cut of this "negro and golden mortar," and I send it to you as an appropriate answer to much of your letter.

Our landlord, driving us about the country the other day, and needing silver change, came to a gang of slaves in a field, and cried out, "Boys, got any silver for a five dollar gold piece?" Several hands went into as many

pockets, at once, and a lively fellow among them getting
the start, jumped over the fence, and changed the money.

I had been here a month when I received your letter,
and when I read it I at first laughed as heartily, I suspect, as " the pro-slavery Senior " did. Then I pitied
you, and I pitied myself for my own former ignorance,
and I pitied very many of our Northern people, and, not
the least, such persons as poor " Isaiah," who I know are
honest, but are grievously misled. The word slavery
is, to us, an awful word. Very much of our anti-slavery
feeling is a perfectly natural instinct. You cannot see
Java sparrows in a cage, nor even a mother-hen tied to
her coop, without a lurking wish to give them liberty. On
thinking of being " a slave," we immediately make the
case our own, and imagine what it would be for us to be
in bondage to the will of another. We cannot easily be
convinced that this is not exactly parallel with being one
of the slaves at the South, nor that to be a slave does not
have these things for its inseparable conditions, which, we
imagine, are always obtruding their direful visages; namely, " auction-block," " overseer," " whip," " chattelism,"
" separations," " down-trodden," " cattle." Hence it is
easy for orators and preachers to work on our sympathies.
There are scattered facts enough to justify any tale which
any public speaker chooses to relate. I confess that my
respect for many of our Northern people has not risen,
as I see them from this point of view. They ought not
to be so easily duped, so ready to believe evil, so quickly
carried away by partial representations, and so unwilling
to take comprehensive views of such a subject as this.
I condemn myself in speaking thus; I partly blame the
novel-writers, and the editors of party papers, and political leaders. But we ought at the North to understand

4

this subject better, to listen willingly to information from great and good men who have spent their lives among the slaves, and to discriminate between the evil and the good. The result may be that we shall not change our inbred views, nor cease to dissent from those who advocate slavery as a necessary means of civilization in its highest forms; but we shall certainly differ from those who declare it to be, practically, an unmitigated curse to all concerned. I am often made to wish that the Southerners could be relieved of our Northern hostility and its effects upon them, just to see them laboring, as they then would, to correct certain evils which ought to be redressed. We are all apt to neglect our duty, more or less, when we are suffering abuse.

Educate this people, some years longer, in the way in which they are going on, and they cannot be slaves in any objectionable sense. Tens of thousands of them, now, are not slaves in any such sense, and they never can be; they could not be recklessly sold at auction; the owners would revolt at it, and those in want of servants would meet with great competition in obtaining such as these. A church-member who should separate husband and wife for no fault, would be disciplined at the South as surely as for inhumanity at the North. But oh, we say at the North, only to think, that all those fine-looking people whom Hattie saw from the barouche, that Monday afternoon, were liable on Tuesday morning to have their kid gloves and finery taken from them, and to be marched off to the auction-block! Hence our commiseration. And it is a most groundless commiseration.

One thing is especially impressed on my mind. There being sins and evils in slavery, as all confess, there are men and women here who are perfectly competent to manage them without our help. There is nothing that seems to me more offensive than our self-righteousness, as I must call it, at the North, in exalting ourselves above our fathers and brethren of all Christian denominations at the South; as though there were no conscience, no Christian sensibility, no piety here, but it must all be supplied from the North. When I hear these Southern ministers preach and pray, and see them laboring for the colored people, and then think of our designation of ourselves at the North, " friends of the slave," and remember that all our anti-slavery influence has been positively injurious to the best interests of the slave at the South, I have frequently been led to exclaim, What an inestimable blessing it would be to this colored race, and to our whole land, if anti-slavery, in the offensive sense of that word, could at once and forever cease! and I have as often questioned in my own mind whether slavery has not been, and is not now, the occasion of more sin at the North than at the South, and whether we at the North are not more displeasing in the sight of God for the things which are said and done there, in connection with anti-slavery, than the South with all the sins and evils incident to slave-holding. I am coming to this belief.

The people who most frequently excite my commiseration are the free blacks. They are " scattered and peeled." The Free States dread their coming; they cannot rise in the Slave States. Even the slaves look down upon them, sometimes. "Who are you?" said a slave to a free black, in my hearing; "you don't belong to anybody!" Some States have given them notice to quit, within a specified time, or they must be sold. Some here insist that slavery is the only proper condition for the blacks, and they would reduce them back to bondage.

Others remonstrate at this as cruel. Surely it is a choice of evils for them, to be free, or to be slaves, if they remain here. There is one thought that affords a ray of consolation, — they are better off, in either condition, than they once were in Africa. It is unquestionable to my mind that their relation to the whites, even in bondage, is, as the general rule, mercy to them, while they are on the same soil with the whites. Allow it to be theoretically wrong to be a slave, — it is, under existing circumstances, protection and a blessing, compared with any arrangement which has yet been proposed. I have not sufficient patience to argue with those, North or South, who contend for slavery as a normal condition. I should be called at the North "pro-slavery;" but the North is in a passion on this subject. I am not, and I never can be, an advocate for this relation in itself, but as a present necessity.

I once heard a speaker at an anti-slavery meeting at home say, "They tell us how elevated the blacks are, how intelligent, how pious; that shows how fit they are for freedom, how wrong it is to hold such people in bondage. As much as you raise the slaves in our opinion, you deepen the guilt of the slave-holder."

This used to dwell much on my mind. I see the thing differently now. You remember your Uncle Enoch, from Madras, who made your first Malay kite. I remember a fable which he told you when he was flying the kite for the first time. "A kite," he said, "high in the air, reasoned thus : If, notwithstanding this string, I fly so high, what would I not do, if I could break away! It gave a dash and became free, and was soon in the woods." I do not mean to strain the comparison; but, certainly, a *string* has raised, and now keeps up, the colored race, here. How they would do, if the string were cut, let wiser heads than mine decide. They cannot have my scissors, at present.

The way to be friends of the slave, I now see, is to be the real friends of their masters, and to pray that the influences of truth and love may fill their hearts. Where this is the case, the slaves, as a laboring class, are better off than any separate class of laboring people on earth, both for this world and the next.

As to setting them free at once and indiscriminately, it would be as unjust to them as it originally was to steal them from Africa. So it appears to me. What God means to do with them, no one can tell. That He has been doing a marvellous work of mercy for the poor creatures is manifest. They were slaves at home; they have changed their situation to their benefit. I have made up my mind to leave this great problem — the destiny of the blacks — to my Maker, and, in the mean time, pray in behalf of the owners, that they may have a heart to act toward them according to the golden rule. I am glad that I am not oppressed with the responsibility of ownership. Those who assume it should be encouraged by us to treat their charge as a trust committed to them for a season. I do not argue, much less plead, for the continuance of this system; it may be abolished very soon, but that is with Providence. I have acquired no feelings toward the institution which would not lead me to rejoice in emancipation the moment that it would be for the good of the colored people.

You are looking for my letter to furnish you with details of horrors in slavery. Wherever poor human nature is, there you will find imperfection and sin; and of course power over others is always liable to great abuses. If I were to follow the plan of those who collect the horrors of slavery and spread them out before our Northern friends, but should gather merely the beautiful and touching incidents which I meet with, and which are related to me, I could make people think that slavery is not an evil.   But I have not seen an intelligent Southerner who, admitting all that we had said about the happiness of the slaves as a class, did not go far beyond me in declaring that the presence of a subject, abject race, cannot fail to be an evil.   There is not an ultraist at the North, whom, if he had their confidence, and were not put in antagonism to him, the Southerners could not make ashamed, and put to silence, by telling him evil things about slavery, which he had never contemplated, and by admitting most fully things which he would expect them to deny.   But they are placed in a false position by his clamor and anger, which set them against him and his doctrines.   They say, " Allowing all that the North asserts, here are the colored people on our hands; what are we to do with them ? "   Not one of the Northern " friends of the slave," nor all of them together, have ever proposed a feasible plan with regard to the disposal of the slaves, which would be kind or even humane to the blacks.   Moreover, theoretical arguments against slavery, and representations of it, from many quarters, are so palpably wrong, that replies to them and refutations are counted by us at the North as defences of " oppression ; " which they were never designed to be.   I am surprised at the extent and depth of real anti-slavery feeling at the South.   Sometimes I question whether Providence is not permitting the antagonism of the North and South to continue just to compel the South to hold these colored people in connection with themselves for heir good, until God's purposes of mercy for them are

accomplished, and " the time, times and half a time " of
their captivity is fulfilled. If Northern resistance to
slavery had ceased, perhaps the South would have rid
herself of the blacks sooner than would have been for
their good.

I hope that you will not think me " a strong-minded
woman " in what I here repeat to you of the opinions and
expressions which I have gathered in listening to the conversation of intelligent people on this subject. I write
these things for your instruction, and also as memoranda
for my own future use.

It is a cherished idea with many excellent people that
the time will come when there will not be a slave in this
land, nor on the earth. If they mean by this that the
time will come when every man in every face will see a
brother and a friend, it is certainly true. But if they
mean by it that ownership in man will come to an end,
their opinion and prophecy are as good as those of men
who should undertake to differ from them, and no better;
while both would be entirely presumptuous in being positive on such a subject. Some people seem to think that,
in the good time coming, it is as though we should dwell
out-of-doors, among flowers and fruits, with few wants,
these being supplied by the spontaneous offerings of nature.

Others, however, suppose that we shall still need some
to shovel, take care of horses, work over the fire the
greater part of the day in preparing food, go of errands,
and, in short, be a serving class. They suppose that the
same sovereign God which distributes instincts, and wisdom, variously, to animals, and gifts of understanding to
men, will, in the same sovereign way, create men and
women with such degrees of capacity and susceptibility as will lead inevitably to their being superiors and

inferiors, and that this will be, as it is now where love and kindness reign, the source of the greatest happiness to all concerned.

This being so, none of us will venture to say that no one of the existing races of men will, to the end of time, be of such gentle, dependent natures as to find their highest happiness and welfare in being, generally, in the capacity of servants. Some of all races, we do not object, may be servants to the end of time. No one will say to his Maker that it will be unjust for Him to put a whole race of men forever in that serving condition, making them, according to their capacity, most happy in being so. For "Who hath been His counsellor?" That the Africans are under a cloud of God's mysterious providence, no one denies. I will not dictate to my Maker when He shall remove that cloud, while I still endeavor to mitigate the effects of it upon my fellow-creatures, the blacks. I do not know that he may not perpetuate, to the end of time, a relationship of dependency to other races in this African race. I know nothing about it. But I always feel impelled to say these things, when I hear good men confidently predicting that ownership in man will soon and forever come to an end. I reply, It may be in the highest measure necessary to the happiness of the human family, at its best estate, that one race, or that races, should be in the relation of inferiors, finding their very best advantage in the relative place which a sovereign God has assigned them in the scale of intelligence, by holding that relation to the end of time. Of course it would cease to be a curse ; it would become one of those subordinate parts in the great orchestral music of life which subdue and soften it for the highest effect. If any one gets angry at such an idea, I leave him to his folly; for he is angry without a cause at me, who have, in this idea, expressed no wish that it may be true; and he is angry that his Maker should do a thing which contradicts his pet notions about "freedom." But the singular fact of slavery in this land, continued and defended under all political changes, and now having the prospect of being more firmly established than ever by means of our great national commotion on this subject, is enough to make a serious mind reflect whether it be wholly the work of Satan, or whether the providence of God be not concerned in this great and difficult problem.

It is certainly remarkable that religion, which once gained such a footing in Africa, so soon and entirely died out there, but that the Africans, transported to our land, are of all races the most susceptible to religious influences. If we should visit a foreign missionary field, and learn that the mission had been blessed to the extent which has characterized the labors of Christians at the South for their slaves, of whom, according to the "Educational Journal," Forsyth, Ga., there are now four hundred and sixty-five thousand connected with the churches of all denominations, we should regard it as the chief of all the works of God in connection with modern missions. It is this providential and Christian view of slavery which quiets my mind. Now, suppose that, contemplating a foreign missionary field where such results should be found, one should object: "But there are evils there; people do not all treat their dependants as they ought; hardships, cruelties, and some barbarisms remain;" — we should not, I apprehend, proceed to scuttle such a ship to drown the vermin. But I can see that Satan must be in great wrath to find himself spoiled of so many subjects. One stronger than he has brought

4 *

here hundreds of thousands, who, in Africa, would have
perished forever, but who are now civilized and Chris-
tianized. Satan would be glad, I think, to see American
slavery come to an end. We have no right to go and
steal people in order to convert them; the salvation of
these slaves will not, in one iota, extenuate the guilt and
punishment of those who were engaged in the slave-trade.
But "the wrath of men shall praise Thee." In the writings of anti-slavery men I do not remember to have met
with cordial acknowledgments of what religion has done
for the slaves at the South. They coldly admit the fact,
but often they speak disparagingly of the negro's religion,
which is full as good as that of converts in our foreign
missionary fields, as good, judging from some things in
Paul's Epistle to the Ephesians, as that of some converts
to whom he wrote. Our Northern anti-slavery people
cannot bear to have anything good discovered or praised
in connection with slavery.

My own hopeful persuasion is, that great and marvellous works of Divine Providence and grace are in reserve
for the African people in their own land, and that we are
to prove to have been their educators. Most sincerely
do I hope, however, that the number of scholars and
future propagators of religion and civilization, imported
here from Africa, will not need to be increased, considering that one hundred and fifty per cent. of deaths by
violence take place in procuring a given number of
slaves. This is but one objection; others are sufficiently
obvious. Both parts of that passage of Scripture are
exceedingly interesting : " Princes shall come out of
Egypt; Ethiopia shall stretch out her hands unto God."
Egypt, the basest of kingdoms, shall yet send forth first-
rate men ; and Ethiopia, even, shall be the worshipper

of God. I hope that these prophecies, though fulfilled once, are yet to have their great accomplishment. This is my persuasion, and I trust that every nation will be independent; but I shall not discard the Bible, if my interpretation and hope should fail. Ethiopia is certainly stretching out her hands unto God in our Southern country.

Hattie received some papers for children from a young friend at the North, last week. After attending the colored Sabbath-school in ———, and teaching a class of nicely-dressed, bright little " slave " girls, and hearing the school sing their beautiful songs, with melodious voices, such as, I can truly say, I never heard surpassed at the North, and after looking upon the teachers, who represented the very flower of Southern society, the superintendent being a man who would adorn any station, you cannot fully conceive with what feelings I read, in one of Hattie's little papers from the North, these lines, set to music for the use of Northern children :

> " I dwell where the sun shines gayly and bright,
> Where flowers of rich beauty are ever in sight;
> Here blooms the magnolia, here orange-trees wave;
> But oh, not for *me*, — I'm a poor little slave.

> " They say ' Sunny South ' is the name of my home;
> 'Tis here that your robins and blue-birds are come,
> While snows cover nests up, and angry winds rave;
> *They* may rest here, — not *I*; *I'm* a poor little slave.

> " Here beautiful mothers, 'mid splendors untold,
> Their fairy-like babes to their fond bosoms fold;
> My mammy's worked out, and lies here in the grave;
> There's none to kiss *me*, — I'm a poor little slave.

> " I've heard mistress telling her sweet little son,
> What Jesus, the loving, for children has done;
> Perhaps little black ones he also will save;
> I ask him to take *me*, a poor little slave! "

No wonder, Gustavus, that you write such letters as your last, fed and nourished as you are on such things as this. I took it with me that evening to a missionary party at the house of Judge ———. I read the lines. The ladies said nothing for a time, till at last one said to me, " Such things have helped us in seceding." The Judge took the lines, looked them over, and, smiling, handed them back to me, saying, " Madam, is Massachusetts a dark place ? " " Yes," said a young gentleman, " and the dark places of the earth are full of the habitations of cruelty." " Oh," said I, " how prejudiced you all are !" Whereupon they all laughed. "Now," said I, "you think, no doubt, that the author of such a piece is malign. I know nothing of its origin, but I venture to say it was written by one whose heart overflows with love to everybody, but who is ' laboring under a delusion.' " I did not tell them of the " delusion " which you were " under," in the Senior's room, but I said, " I have a nephew in a New England college who has the Northern evil very badly. But he is so very kind. Set him to write poetry about the South and he would produce just such lamentable stanzas." Nothing will cure these fancies, about oranges and magnolias not blooming for the little negroes, so well as to bring these good people where they can see them pelting one another with oranges, such as these poets never dreamed of, and making money by selling magnolias to passengers at the railway stations.

" Here beautiful mothers, 'mid splendors untold," etc. I went with the wife of a planter to her " Maternal Association " of slave-mothers. She gathers the fifteen mothers among her servants once a fortnight, and spends an afternoon talking to them about the education of their

children, and reading to them ; and when she knelt with
them and prayed, I cried so all the time that I hardly
heard anything. Oh what a tale of love was that Maternal Association !   " Here beautiful mothers 'mid splendors untold," etc. ; — those words kept themselves in my
thoughts. Now tell this to some great " friend of the
slave," in Massachusetts, and what will he say ? — " All
very good, I dare say; hope she will go a little further,
and give those fifteen their liberty."   I sometimes say,
" Must I go back to the North, and hear and read such
things ? "

Yes, it is such things as these, simple and inconsider-
able as you may deem them, which are dividing us irrec-
oncilably, and breaking up the Union. It is not Messrs.
——, nor their frenzy, but it is Christian brethren who
allow their Sabbath-school children, for example, to say
and sing, " I've heard mistress telling her sweet little
son, what Jesus, the loving, for children has done," making
the impression that such a Christian mother leaves a colored child in her house, without instruction, to draw the
inference, if it will, that Jesus, perhaps, will love a " poor
little slave ! "   There are no words to depict the feeling
of injustice and cruelty which this conveys to the hearts
of our Christian friends at the South.   " Let us go out of
the Union ! " they cry, in their blind grief ; but where will
they go ? for while our Northern people write and pub-
lish and sing and teach their children to sing such things,
we can have nothing but mutual hatred, and perhaps ex-
terminating wars. We must change. If our Northern
people would discriminate, and, while retaining all their
natural feelings against oppression and man-stealing,
would admit that " ownership in man " is not necessarily
oppression nor man-stealing, they would do themselves

justice and contribute to the peace of the country. " But
O !" they say, " look at the iniquitous *system*. If separating families, and destroying marriage, and liberty to chastise at pleasure, and to kill, are not *sin*, what is sin?" So
they impute the *system*, and everything in it, to the people
who live under it. How a system can be a sin, it would
puzzle some of them, who say that all sin consists in action, to explain. And when they came to look into the
system itself, they would find, that if slavery is to exist,
some laws regulating it are, of necessity, self-protective,
and must be coercive. Even in Illinois, it is enacted that
a black man shall not be a witness against a white man.
But if the slaves could swear in court, every one sees
that the whites must be at the mercy of their servants.
The testimony of the honest among them is procured,
though indirectly, and it has weight with juries; but it is
a wise provision to exclude them as sworn witnesses. So
of other things, which theoretically are oppressive, but
practically right; while many things in the system which
are rigorous are as little used as the equipments in an
arsenal in times of peace.

When you quote John Wesley's words and apply them
to the South : " Slavery is the sum of all villanies," you
unconsciously utter a fearful slander. Whatever may
have been true of British slavery, in foreign plantations,
in Wesley's day, the good man never would utter such
words about our Southern people could he see and enjoy
that which gladdens every Christian heart. If slavery
be, necessarily, " the sum of all villanies," as you and
many use the expression, the relation cannot exist without making each slave-holder a villain, in all the degrees
of villany. You will do well to look into the cant
phrases of " freedom," before you indulge in the use of

them. The bishops and clergy of the noble army of
Methodists in the South would not sustain their great
chief in applying the phrase in question to the actual
state of things in the Southern country. Wesley used
those words concerning slavery in foreign colonies; he
had not seen it mixed up with society in England, as it
is in the South.

Taking the blacks as they are, and comparing them
also with what they would be in Africa, or if set free, to
remain in connection with the whites, slavery is not a
curse. To be free is, of course, in itself a blessing. But
it depends on many things whether, under existing circumstances, being a slave here is practically a curse.
Our people generally insist that it must be, and therefore
that it is. Here they are mistaken, as I now view the
subject. The British people and the French, looking at
the blacks in a colony, settle the question of emancipation in their own minds without much difficulty. But it
would be found to be a different thing to emancipate
the colored race, to live side by side with the English
people in the mother-country. In that case, a contest
between the two races for the possession of power, and
innumerable offences and practical difficulties, would, in
time, lead to the extermination, or expatriation, of one
of the two races, or to their intermarriage, if the universal history of such conjunction of races is any guide.

I do not wonder that the good lady with the "marsh-
mallow" exclaimed so at your groundless commiseration
of the sick among the slaves. You have no more idea
of the practical relation between the whites and the
blacks, the owners and the slaves, than most of the English people, who have never been here, have of our Fed-
eral and State relations.

_I will tell you an incident which I know to be literally true.

A lady from a free state was visiting at the South. Calling upon a married lady, a near relative of one who has been Vice-President of the United States, she found her with a little sick black babe at her breast.

The Northern lady started with astonishment. I am not informed whether she was what is called among us a "friend of the slave;" the eminent lady friend whom she visited certainly was such, in the best sense. The Northern lady's feelings of repugnance would not be found to be peculiar to her among our Northern people. The little babe died on the lap of the Southern lady.

So you see that there are more things here than are dreamed of in your philosophy. When you stigmatize the Southerners as oppressors, my only consolation for you is that you know not what you do. Imagine, now, the Rev. Mr. Blank, at the North, relating that little incident : " Behold and see this monstrous picture of infinite hypocrisy : The Slave-power with a slave at its breast ! Yes, rather than lose one or two hundred dollars' worth of human " property," a distinguished lady slave-holder will give her nourishment to a slave-infant. So they fatten the accursed system out of their own bodies and souls." Such is a fair specimen of this man's frenzy ; and there are multitudes all over the Free States who will listen to such language and applaud it. But how cruel it is, how low and wicked ! I pray Heaven to deliver you from being an abolitionist in the cast of your mind, your temper, and spirit. Nothing gives me such an idea of the world of despair as when I read ultra anti-slavery speeches. I see how the lost will hate God's mysterious providence, and revile it; and how they will fight with each other, and pour out their furious invective and sarcasm and vituperation, and scourge one another with their fiery tongues, as they now do, when some one of the party appears to falter. If there were not something truly good in connection with slavery amid all its evils, I think such men would not oppose it.

Pray, who are these gentlemen, and who are their extremely zealous anti-slavery friends of more respectable standing, that they should have such immense instalments of sympathy and pity for the "poor slave"? Their neighbors are as susceptible as they to every form of human sorrow; they know as much, their judgments are as sound, their motives are as good as theirs. Had these zealous people made new discoveries, or, were the subject of slavery new, we might give them credit for being on the hill-tops, while we were in the vales. This passionate sympathy, on the part of some, for "the downtrodden," as they call the negroes, is not like zeal for a theological, or a political, or a scientific, doctrine, which would justify its adherents in rebuking the error and indifference of others; for if slavery be as they represent it, the proofs of it must be as self-evident as starvation. What if a class of men among us should rage against those who do not contribute largely to the Syrian sufferers, as the zealous anti-slavery people reproach and even revile those who do not see slavery with their eyes? We should then say, "Friends, who are you, that you should claim to have all the virtuous sensibility?"

But more than this, — I doubt, I venture to deny, and that on philosophical grounds, the true philanthropy of these people. For true love and kindness always create something of their own kind where they have full power. Are there any words or acts of love, kindness, gentleness, mercy, toward others, in the speeches and doings of the zealous anti-slavery people?

I wish that you had been with me, one evening, in a corner of the Methodist meeting-house, where I sat and enjoyed the slaves' prayer-meeting. I had been filled with distress that day by reading, in Northern papers, the doings and speeches at excited meetings called to sympathize with servile insurrection. In this prayer-meeting the slaves rose one after another, went in front, and repeated each a hymn, then resumed their seats, while some one, moved by the sentiments of the hymn, would lead in prayer. A white gentleman presided, according to custom, and I was the only other white person present. Going to that meeting with the impressions upon my heart of the terrible excitements which you were witnessing at home, and saying to myself, "O my soul, thou hast heard the sound of the trumpet and the alarm of war!" you cannot imagine what my feelings were when the largest negro that I ever saw rose and stood before the desk, and repeated the following hymn by Rev. Charles Wesley. The first lines, you may well suppose, startled me, and made me think that the insurrection had reached even here.

> " Equip me for the war,
>   And teach my hands to fight;
> My simple, upright heart prepare,
>   And guide my words aright.
>
> " Control my every thought,
>   My whole of sin remove;
> Let all my works in thee be wrought,
>   Let all be wrought in love.
>
> " Oh, arm me with the mind,
>   Meek Lamb! that was in thee;
> And let my knowing zeal be join'd
>   With perfect charity.

" With calm and temper'd mind
  Let me enforce thy call;
And vindicate thy gracious will,
  Which offers life to all.

" Oh, may I love like thee,
  In all thy footsteps tread;
Thou hatest all iniquity,
  But nothing thou hast made.

" Oh, may I learn the art,
  With meekness to reprove;
To hate the sin with all my heart,
  But still the sinner love."

You must read this hymn to " Isaiah," and tell him
about the prayer-meeting. While the " friends of the
slave," as you call them, are holding such humiliating
meetings as you describe, in behalf of the slaves, and are
vexing themselves and chafing under the imagination of
their unmitigated sorrows and " oppression," the slaves
themselves, all over the South, are holding prayer-meet-
ings, and are blessing God that they are " raised 'way up
to heaven's gate in privilege." As I sat in that prayer-
meeting I could almost have risen and asked the prayers
of the slaves in behalf of many at the North who are
making themselves and others nearly insane on their behalf. But I thought of my former ignorance and prejudice, and said, " And such were some of you."

I will tell you some of the little incidents which meet
one every day, and which give you impressions respecting the relations between the whites and blacks, full as
instructive as those received in any other way.

Crossing a public street, which is steep, in the city of
———, a truckle-cart came by me at great speed, drawn
by a white boy, with another white boy pushing, and
seated in it, erect and laughing, was a fine-looking black

boy of about the same age as his white playmates.
Around the corner of another street there came by me,
with a skip-and-jump step, two white girls, about thirteen
years old, and between them — the arms of the three all
intertwined — was another girl of the same age, as black
as ebony. On they went jumping, and keeping step, and
singing.

I had not been accustomed to such sights in Beacon
Street, on my visits to Boston. " Friends of the
slave," as we most surely are, and some of us being
decorated with that name by way of distinction, signifi-
cant of our all-absorbing business " to raise the black
man at the South to the condition of a human being,"
when we get them there we are not greeted in the streets
with pictures of white and black children on such terms
as appeared in these two casual incidents. Nothing at
first struck me with greater wonder at the South than to
see the most fashionably dressed ladies in the most public
streets stop to help a black woman with a burden on her
head, if she needed assistance, or to hold a gate open for
a man with a wheelbarrow.

One white boy cried to another across a street, " Come
along, it's most time to be in school." The other answered, in a petulant tone, " I a'n't going to school."
A tall, white-headed negro was passing ; his black sur-
tout nearly touched the ground ; he had on his arm a
very nice market-basket, covered with a snow-white napkin, and in his right hand a long cane. Hearing what
the last boy said, he came to a full stand, put down
his basket, clasped his long cane with both hands, and
brought it down on the brick sidewalk with three quick
raps, and then a rap at each of these points of admiration : " What ! what ! what ! " said he, drawing himself

up to express surprise, and calling out with magisterial
voice; "Go to school! my son! go to school! and
larn! a heap!" the cane making emphasis at every
expression. The white boy retreated under the impression of a well-deserved, though kind, rebuke. He did
not call the old man "nigger," nor in any way insult
him.

But here is an incident of a different kind.

Standing to talk with a man who had charge of my
baggage, in the passage-way between the baggage-room
and the colored passengers' apartment, I saw a white
man with a pert, flurried manner and coarse look ascend
the steps of the cars, and behind him a tall graceful
black man, a little older than the other, with signs of
gentleness and dignity in his appearance. As he stooped
and turned, his air and carriage would have commanded
attention anywhere. The white man, seeing him enter
the wrong door, cried out to him with an impudent voice,
ordered him back, pointed him to the proper room, and
told him to go in there and make himself "oneasy," with
a laugh at his own attempt at inaccurate talk as he cast
a glance at some white men standing by. The black man
was his slave. The natural and proper order of things
was reversed in their relation to each other.

I looked at the black man as he took his seat, and,
without being observed, I kept my eye on his face. He
cast his eye out of the window, as though to relieve a
struggle of emotions, but a calm expression settled down
upon his features.

A Southern gentleman, a slave-holder, witnessing the
scene with me, said, —

"Disgusting! There, madam, you have one of the
great evils of slavery, — irresponsible power in the hands

of men who are not fit to be intrusted with authority over others. No man, I sometimes think, ought to be allowed to hold slaves till he has submitted to examination as to character, or brings certificates of a good disposition. I know that man. His father was from —— [a New England State.] He is what we call a torn-down character. His neighbors all " —— but the signal was given for starting, and the conversation was broken off.

My first thought was, How glad I would be to set that man free from such bondage! The next thought was, Where would I send him to be free from "the power of the dog?" I had been reading, in a Boston paper, a lecture delivered in Boston, by a distinguished "friend of the slave," against Mr. Webster and Mr. Choate, before an "immense audience." I thought, How much better it is to be a Christian slave, even to this master, than to sit in the seat of the scornful, applauding such a lecture!

The poor slave was having his probation and discipline, as we all have ours, and he was suffering, as we all do in our turns, from an impudent tongue. Little did he think that a fellow-creature, looking at him at that moment, was reminded, by his meekness under insult, of Him, our example, who, under such provocation, opened not his mouth, and that I was made to remember, as I stood there and received instruction from him, that the best alleviation and cure of anguished sensibility under ill-treatment is in this same silence, and in thoughts of Jesus.

After the cars had started, I took my Bible from my carpet-bag, and read these passages : "Servants, be subject to your masters with all fear; not only to the good and gentle, but also to the froward. For this is thankworthy, if a man for conscience toward God endure

grief, suffering wrongfully." Then this is enforced by
the example of our incarnate God and Saviour, who is
held up to Christian slaves as their example; and in this
connection, not only in this passage, but elsewhere in
speaking to slaves, the Apostle brings in the most sublime truths relating to redemption. You will be struck
with this in reading what is said to slaves, that in several
cases, the train of thought proceeds directly from their
condition and its duties, to the most sublime and beautiful
truths of salvation. How divinely wise did these exhortations to slaves appear to me, that morning, in contrast
with the spirit of the Northern abolitionist, and his talk
about "Bunker Hill," "'76," and his "grandfather's old
gun over the mantel-piece," and his injunctions to slaves as
to the duty of stealing, and even murdering, if necessary,
to effect their liberty. This is not the spirit of the New
Testament. The idea of submission on the part of
"servants" to "masters," of "pleasing them well in all
things," of "fear and trembling," "not purloining but showing good fidelity in all things," is not found in the Gospel
of the abolitionist. He complains that we do not send
the true Gospel to the South. There are passages in the
Epistles addressed to slaves, which, if faithfully regarded,
would make fugitive slave laws for the most part needless. No wonder that the New Testament, with its exhortations to meekness and patience under suffering, and
the duty of those who are "under the yoke," and of
masters as being "worthy of honor," and the caution
that the slave do not take undue liberty where his master
is a believer, nor assert the doctrine of equality in Christ
as a ground for undue familiarity, or disobedience, is
repudiated by the vengeful spirit of the abolitionist.
How well the Apostle understood him! "If any man

teach otherwise," that is, contrary to these injunctions
as to the duty of slaves who have believing masters, "he
is proud, (that is the leading feature of his error) he
is proud, knowing nothing, but doting about questions and
strifes of words, whereof cometh envy, strife, railings, evil
surmisings." What an anomaly it would be to have an
abolition convention opened with reading a collect of
Paul's inspired directions to masters and slaves.

But we never hear anything quoted from the Bible on
the subject but "break every yoke!" "let the oppressed
go free!" "undo the heavy burdens!" I was telling a
slave-holder of the frequency with which we hear these
expressions in public prayer. "I could join in every
one of them," said he; "I am for breaking every yoke,
South and North, unbinding every heavy burden, and
destroying every form of oppression. But they must
be actual, not theoretical, nor imaginary."

This gentle slave in the cars, we will suppose, refuses
opportunities to escape, but complies with the exhortations of the New Testament, "enduring grief, suffering wrongfully." His master is at last touched by his
meekness, his "not answering again." I should relate
only that which I know to have happened, should I say,
that one day this master is filled with distress on account
of sin. He goes out into the cotton-field and finds
Jacob.

"Jacob," he says, "I am a great sinner. Jacob, I feel
that I am sinking into hell. Jacob, pray for me. I mean
to turn about, if I live."

"Dat's jest what I've sought de Lord for, massa, dis
six months coming New Year. Let's go up into de loft;
it's whar I've wrastled for you in prayer."

He leads the way. The floor of the loft is covered

with cotton-seed. A wheelbarrow is in the middle of the floor. Jacob takes off his jacket, and with it brushes the cotton-seed away from one side of the wheelbarrow, lays the jacket down for his master to kneel upon, and goes to the other side. Like Jacob at Peniel, he has power over the angel, and prevails; he weeps and makes supplication unto him. The master breaks out in prayer. He rises and says, —

"Jacob, forgive me if I've been unkind to you; I've seen that you are a Christian; now if you want to leave me for anybody else, say so."

"Thank you, massa; only sarve de Lord with gladness for all de good things he has done for you, and I'll sarve you de same. Please go home and tell missis; she told me to pray for you; 'twill finish up her joy."

This is better than running away and going to Canada. Those Christians who send the Gospel to the South by missionaries and religious tracts, to promote such scenes as this, do a better work than though they withheld missionaries and tracts from one half of the nation, and called it "Standing up for Jesus."

I am sometimes inclined to put down all that I see and hear, good and bad, and publish a book to satisfy my truly candid but mistaken friends at the North as to the real truth on this subject. But I have in mind the way in which similar works have already been received and treated by an unreasoning, passionate North. I have amused myself sometimes in imagining what certain writers would say to some of the incidents which I have related in this letter. Let me attempt to show you the spirit and manner of our Northern reviewers when one ventures to state favorable things relating to slavery. I will take some of the incidents already related in this letter

5

and let these men review them. I am perfectly familiar
with their style, from having been employed in helping
your uncle prepare the notices of new publications for
the " —— Review." Here, then, I will give you first a
supposed notice of my little book, should I make one, from
a Northern religious newspaper, quoting, in all cases, the
identical expressions from articles which I have read : —

" ' The authoress, it seems, is yet in her Paradise of
slavery.' Her ' opulent friends ' and the slave-holders generally, it would appear, got up little tableaux for her, to
impose on her good-nature.   Knowing the times when
she took her daily walks, they put the fattest and sleekest
black boy whom they could find, into a truckle-cart, and
made two of the sons of the ' most opulent ' citizens race
down hill with him.   Slavery, therefore, is not the bad
thing she and we had supposed.   The female teacher of
a school in the neighborhood of her daily walk was
suborned, most probably, by the ' opulent ' ladies of the
place, to practise another pleasing trick.   Two white
girls and a black girl were made to practise running with
their arms interlocked, and one day, as our friend came
in sight, they were pushed out to astonish her with one
instance of white girls hugging a negro slave-child.   No
doubt our friend, on seeing these three together, solilo-
quized as follows : —

> " See Truth, Love, and Mercy in triumph descending,
>   All nature now glowing in Eden's first bloom."

The old negro, respectable and well off, was one of those
rare exceptions to surrounding degradation which you now
and then see in Southern cities.   The poor slave in the
cars, gentle, timid, quivering, was the true exponent ot
slavery.   Had our authoress filled her book with such
illustrations exclusively, she would have written more

truthfully, more for her reputation with the real 'friends of the slave,' and, we confess, more in accordance with our taste."

A writer in a very respectable publication at the North, already referred to, gave us several years ago a curious piece of criticism on some publication which he regarded as too favorable to slavery. His pages, some of them, were crowded with daggers, in the shape of exclamation marks, — two, three, four, and, in one instance, five, at the end of quotations from the book under review. It was he that made the assertion about the " arsenic," as being " universally in the hands of the slaves."

I shall now let him review my little stories. I quote many of his words : —

" 'To show the ignorance and simplicity of our travelling' lady, we give the following,— and what will the North say to this new argument in favor of slavery ? namely, a truckle-cart! a black boy riding !! two white boys giving him a ride!!! and three girls, one of them black! arm in arm!! romping. 'It is not the fault of this writer, that she cannot understand a principle;' 'she is a New England Orthodox,' — 'and a fair specimen of the limitations of that type of mankind.' 'But does not the lady know,' why negro boys are put in truckle-carts? 'If not, any of her Southern friends could have told her.' We can tell her; 'we have lived at the South.' These white boys were sent on an errand with their cart, and to increase its momentum down hill, and, withal, to tease and worry a fellow-creature, with a skin not colored like their own, they made this poor slave-boy get in. She should have seen the poor creature trudging home, up hill, under a Southern sun, after the little white tyrants had done with him, unless it was the case, which we more than half suspect, that the ride was a stratagem to convey the poor child to the auction-block. 'How the merry dogs,' the white boys, must have laughed at this Northern lady's complacent looks at them. She had no tears for the poor old white-headed negro, who, hearing the word 'school' from the lips of his white young masters, had such a rush of sorrow come over his soul at the thought of the midnight ignorance in which the slave-driver's whip had kept him, that he actually dropped his burden in the public street, and uttered incautious words, for which, no doubt, old as he was, he caught a terrible flogging. Why, in the name of humanity, did not the authoress load her pages, as she might so easily have done, with scenes like that in the cars? There is slavery! patent! undisguised!! In the other cases it is slavery, indeed, but covered with the pro-slavery lady's snow-white napkin."

Here is a review of me and of my little stories, by a distinguished New England divine, and author. He has written much on slavery. Having prepared notices of some of his writings on this subject, I am familiar with his turns of thought and modes of expression. I have great regard for him, and always read him with pleasure and profit, not excepting when he writes as follows, in doing which he has the approbation of large numbers among the Northern clergy of all denominations, except the Episcopalians, — who, more than other Northern ministers, are remarkably free from ultraisms.

"Concerning the truckle-cart, 'we would say this,' that unquestionably 'the moral power' of the incident was all which the writer assumes, but its 'logical sequences' 'we utterly deny.' Slavery is evil, and only evil, and that continually ; now, to infer that agreeable relations can subsist between the children of masters and the children of slaves under the 'immense, malignant, and all-pervading influence of slavery,' abhorred of Heaven and all good men, does violence to all sound principles of reasoning, and is at war with 'the manifest rules of Providence.'

"And as to the three girls 'we are prepared to say' that the author 'did not look deep enough' into the philosophy of human motives under the controlling power of slavery. For slavery makes men improvident, and their children also; (see 'Judge Jay,' 'Weld on Slavery,' etc.) These white girls, therefore, probably had no money in their pockets; it was the time of recess; they were hungry; the black child we presume had money in her pocket, for by the authoress's own showing (in the story of a slave changing a gold piece for the landlord), slaves may have money of their own. Had our authoress followed her trio down to the confectioner's, there she might have seen these white children cajoling the poor black, and making her treat them; in preparation for which they affected to put their arms around her; but, in the true diabolical spirit of slavery, it was only to devour.

"We have no space to enter philosophically into the instruction afforded us by the old negro and the school-boys; but there is deep meaning in it, which the true friends of the slave, who may read it, will do well to ponder. The old negro is the prophetic representation of his down-trodden race, crying with bewildered accents, he heeds not where, 'Go to school! boys; go to school!' Let a united North echo back his words, suiting their political action to them, and saying to the colored children, with an authority which shall shake the very pillars of the Union, 'Go to school, boys! go to school!'

" Nor can we, for the tears which dim our sight, speak as we would of the wretched master and his amiable slave in the cars.   The sketch reminded us of the best in 'Uncle Tom.' We need books filled with such pictures, to electrify the slumbering sensibilities of the North.   Wanton candor in speaking of slavery, is the most unpardonable of sins.   There is a time to tell the whole truth ; but the wise man says, There is ' a time to keep silence.' "

I did not pretend, Gentlemen Reviewers, that my little, pleasing incidents were arguments in favor of slavery ; you should not have been so alarmed ; you are really rude ; I almost feel disposed to say to you, for each of my tales, as the Rosemary said to the Wild Boar, —

> "Sus, apage! haud tibi spiro; "

which, not having a poetical friend near to translate for me, I venture to render as follows : —

> " Thus to the Boar replied the Rosemary:
> O swine, depart! I do not breathe for thee."

In noticing the manner in which many Northern writers, some of them amiable men, receive the candid views and statements of travellers and visitors at the South, I have been made to think of a company of the owls, such as you see in Audubon, listening to the reading of David's one hundred and fourth Psalm, in which he describes nature.   Not a smile of satisfaction ; on the contrary, if you

> " Molest the ancient, solitary reign "

of prejudice in their minds against the South, they either mope, or make a sad noise.   With regard to others, are there any limits to their anger and denunciations ?   You

may, without difficulty, imagine how this appears to the
Southerner, who knows the truthfulness of the representations which excite this passionate resentment, and how
much the character of the North for ordinary candor
falls in his esteem, and how little disposed he is to heed
their admonitions, and how absurd their demands upon
his ecclesiastical bodies to suffer their remonstrances,
appear, together with their subsequent withdrawal of
fellowship for the reason publicly assigned; namely, that
the South will not let them admonish her " in the Lord."
Indeed, whatever may be true of slavery, the South
looks on the great body of zealous anti-slavery people as
being in as false and unnatural a state of excitement as
the Massachusetts people were in the times of witchcraft.
A great delusion is over the minds of many at the North,
like one of our eastern sea-fogs. It always makes a
Southerner merry, when listening, in New York or Boston, for example, to a lecture, if the speaker concludes a
sentence with some allusion to " freedom," and the people
clap and stamp. That the blood should tingle in our
veins at so slight a cause, makes him think that we are
certainly in need of something worthy of our great ex-
citability, and that we are thankful for small favors in
that way. He does not think less than we of liberty
where an occasion makes that name and idea appropriate ; but that the condition of his slaves should reconse-
crate for us all the old battle-cries of freedom, seems
to him pitiably weak. It shows him how incompetent
we are to deal with the acknowledged evils of slavery ;
and there are those at the South who are stirred up by
us to take extreme views of an opposite kind, which good
people there very generally deplore.

A Southern lady here tells me that some time since,

being on a visit at the North, she received through the
post-office anonymous letters with extracts from newspapers containing little items of woe, declared to have
been experienced at the South, with here and there de-
lirious abuse of slave-holders and frenzied words about
freedom. She could have matched every one of them,
she said, with wife-murders at the North, during her visit.
In dealing with people like the slaves, of course men of
brutal passions, provoked by their stupidity and negli-
gence, or exasperated by their crimes, and, in cases of
ungovernable anger, venting their displeasure upon their
negroes under slight or merely imaginary affronts, give
occasion to tales of distress which are nowhere mourned
over more deeply than at the South. These cases are
the natural results of a superior and inferior class of
society, standing in the relation, the one to the other, of
proprietor and dependant, and such evils are not peculiar
to this institution. Human nature is the same everywhere. The South is willing to have the abuses of irresponsible power among them compared with abuses, dis-
comforts, disadvantages elsewhere. Grant that an owner
may abuse his liberty ; ownership leads to more of care
and protection than of abuse and cruelty. The slaves
are here ; the question is not, What would be the best
possible condition for these people under the sun, but,
What is best for them, being on this soil. " Set them all
free," is the answer of some. Half the ministers at the
North every Sabbath pray for the slaves thus : " Break
every yoke ; let the oppressed go free." If this means,
Give the slaves their liberty, this would be their most
direful calamity ; they would be chased away from every
free state, in process of time, and the Dred Scott decision
would be invoked, even in Massachusetts, by its present

most bitter opposers, and in its most misrepresented forms, as a defence of the American white race against the blacks. "Set them free and hire them!" is the reply of others. This, among other effects, would make them a far more degraded people than they now are. Slavery keeps them identified with the whites; they are more respectable and respected by far, in this relation, than they can be, in the circumstances of the case, if they are detached from the whites. There is no expression which conveys a more absolute error than this, and we often meet with it: "He ceased to be a slave, and became a man." I read lately the report of a lecture at the North, by an eminent gentleman, of great moral worth, and highly respected. He said, "A man cannot be, voluntarily, a slave, without having his manhood crushed out of him." That might be true in our case; but having seen manhood forced into benighted natures here, and splendid specimens of man as the result, I was, by this remark, reminded again of the delusiveness which there is sometimes in the best of logic. You gave us a good specimen in your admirable illustration of no water in the moon. A comparison of the slaves with the free negroes of the North, and in Canada, and with the free colored population in some of the Slave States, will satisfy any impartial spectator that manhood is full as conspicuous in the slaves, as a body, as in the free negroes.

Here are two extracts from Northern papers, which, true or false, awaken compassion in every human bosom toward the free colored people. Indeed, allowing these statements, so unfavorable to them, to be mostly false, it reveals the antipathy of the white to the colored race when the blacks come to seek equality with the whites.

5 *

Let these free blacks be mixed up in large proportions
with society in England and Scotland, and if Canadians
feel as they are here represented, we may be sure that
the present tone of the British people with regard to
American slavery and the blacks, would also be modified.   But here are the extracts : —

"GETTING SICK OF THEM. — The colored persons of
Toronto, having had a meeting to denounce Colonel John
Prince, a member of the Canadian Parliament, for speaking
against them, he publishes a reply, in which he says, —

" 'It has been my misfortune, and the misfortune of my
family, to live among those blacks (and they have lived upon
us) for twenty-four years.   I have employed hundreds of them,
and with the exception of one, named Richard Hunter, not
one of them has done for us a week's honest labor.   I have
taken them into my service, fed and clothed them, year after
year, on their arrival from the States, and in return have generally found them rogues and thieves, and a graceless, worthless, thriftless set of vagabonds.   This is my very plain and
simple description of the darkies as a body, and it would be
indorsed by all the Western white men, with very few exceptions.' "

"UNDERGROUND R. R. RETURN TRAINS. — The 'Cleve-
land Plaindealer' states that every steamboat arriving at that
place brings back from Canada families of negroes, who have
formerly fled to the Provinces from the States.   They are prin-
cipally from Canada West.   They describe the life and condition of the blacks in Canada as miserable in the extreme.
The West is, therefore, likely to have large accessions to its
colored population.   The Canada folks do not want them, and
have shown a disposition in their Parliament, and otherwise, to
discourage their coming to, or remaining in the Provinces.   In
some instances, the question of ejecting those now resident
there, has been discussed.   Our Western States will be likely
to experience a similar attack of the *black vomito*, when they

shall have become satisfied with this peculiar Southern luxury. In some localities the superabundant free negro population has already become a burden, while in others they are under severe restrictions, which amount almost to an exclusion from the limits of the state.

" Should this exodus from Canada continue to any great extent, it would throw such a burden upon those states which have adopted the most liberal policy towards the negro, that it would occasion a reaction in the public sentiment which would compel them to abandon their abolition doctrine and practice, for their own self-protection. We should then hear of fewer attempts to abduct slaves from the slave-holding states; and abolitionists would be content to allow slaves to remain under the care and protection of their masters. Even though at heart sympathizing with the oppressed and task-worn negro, and yearning towards him with all the love of the professed philanthropist, he would still be permitted to toil and bleed; for now that the route to Canada has been closed, there is no alternative but to take them to their own bosoms."

Compare with this the condition of the free blacks in South Carolina. The amount of property held by them is $1,600,000; their annual taxes, $27,000; and the free blacks own slaves to the amount of $300,000 in value.

The above statements teach us that any attempts to force the Southern slaves away from their present relation, are in violation of the laws of Providence concerning them. If they become free in a natural way, and can provide for themselves, or be provided for, it is well; otherwise, the South, and their present relation to the white race, are the bounds of their habitation fixed for them by an all-wise God, till his purpose concerning them as a race shall be made manifest. The people of the Free States ought to thank God that the South is willing to keep the colored people. Instead of inflaming our passions against the abstract wrongfulness of holding fellow-men in bondage, we should consider that theoretical justice to the slaves as a whole would be practical inhumanity. The destiny of the colored race here is a dark problem. But it is not for us to penetrate the future. When God is ready to finish his purposes with regard to their continuance with us, He will open a way for their liberation; in the mean time it is our duty to protect them from their own improvidence and from the neglect and degradation which they would suffer at the hands of the Free States. Instead of aiding slaves to escape, or rejoicing when we hear of runaways, I say we should feel grateful, on our own account, and for the slaves, that the South is willing to harbor them, and we ought to consider that the very best thing to be done for them is to encourage the South in treating them well, mitigating their trials and sorrows, and, in short, complying with the Apostle's doctrine and exhortations as to the duty of masters.

But we have a way, at the North, of delivering over our Southern brethren to supposed terrible liabilities in their relation to the slaves. "They are sleeping on a volcano;" "they keep weapons under their pillows;" "they are always in fear." And when a servile insurrection takes place, many close their eyes and lift their hands, and say, "Perhaps the day of retribution is come! They have been 'sinning against the Northern conscience;' they have been resisting our well-meant efforts for their good; we would not stir up the slaves against them," (some kindly say,) "but if they rise, did not Jefferson say, 'There is not an attribute of the Almighty that would take part with the whites?'" Thus we prefer to take Jefferson's opinion on this subject, though hundreds as good and wise as he, and quite as

decided in their acceptance of the Christian religion, differ totally from him.   In strictly political matters, many
of the same people who love to quote Jefferson against
modern slave-holders, are of opinion that time and experience give modern statesmen some advantages in their
judgments.   As to Jefferson's oft-quoted remark, above
cited, it appears to me that if the Almighty has anywhere set the seal of his divine blessing, clear and broad,
it is on the Christian influence of our Southern friends
upon this colored race.

It is humiliating to me, in looking back to the North,
to see how injudicious and weak we are in pouring out
our sympathy upon a fugitive slave, without discrimina-
tion.   The lecture before the Boston audience, already
mentioned, contains a perfect illustration of Northern
credulity in the case of fugitive slaves.   The lecturer
tells us that while reading the printed report of Mr.
Everett's Oration at the inauguration of the Webster
statue, a fugitive slave appeared at his door, and, baring
his breast and back, showed him the marks of the branding-iron, and the scars from the lash.   At the sight, he
says, the paper dropped from his hand.   He " thought
of Webster and the Fugitive Slave Law."

Now this negro was, just as likely as not, one of those
characters whom we call jail-birds.   If so, and he had
lived at the North, instead of branding-iron and stripes,
he might have had parti-colored pants, and manacles, and
a record of ten or twenty years in the state's prison.   But
because he ran away from the South, he straightway
became, as a matter of course, a martyr and a saint.
Perhaps he was, truly, a saint ; and perhaps he was
not.

Looking out of the window in a hotel the other day,

we saw two white men leading up a black man with a leather bridle around his neck.

"Here, Hattie," said your Uncle, "here is slavery; now you have it in full bloom."

The poor fellow was crying and protesting and begging to be released. Your Uncle stepped out and spoke to a very respéctable gentleman whom he met on the piazza. He could not refrain from expressing some feeling at the sight of a fellow-creature so literally "reduced to the level of the brutes." I did not hear the whole of the conversation, for my attention was diverted by two roosters who just then flew at each other and were assailed by a troop of black urchins who tried to scare them apart, pulling their tail-feathers and uttering ludicrous cries.

"You are from the North, sir, I take it," said the gentleman, in reply to your Uncle.

"I am, sir," said your Uncle. "Do you often bridle your slaves in this way, in these parts? I am seeking for information on the subject of slavery."

"I shall be happy to give you any," said the gentleman. "I am here as a magistrate."

"I am one at home," said my husband.

"One of these white men who led the negro," said the gentleman, "was riding on horseback, and was attracted to a by-place by the screams of a child, and found this black man attempting violence upon a black girl ten years old. He knocked the fellow down and held him, and called for help. A white man who came up took the bridle from the horse, to secure the villain with it. They have with difficulty kept the negroes from putting him to death."

"We are all ready, sir," said a sheriff to the gentleman.

" Will you walk into the hall ? " said the magistrate to
your Uncle.

But the stage-coach was waiting for him, and we were
soon on our way. Your Uncle was silent for nearly fifteen minutes, when he said, —

" What is that passage, Hattie, about answering a matter before you understand it ? "

I gave Hattie my Bible, and, after a while, she read :

" He that answereth a matter before he heareth it, it is
folly and shame unto him. The spirit of a man " ——

" That will do, child," said your Uncle, " I wanted only
that one verse."

I should be glad to transfer some of this Southern ease
and beauty of manners to the North. I wish that we
could see more of these Southern ladies and gentlemen
there. They stay away very much, because they cannot
bring servants with them. Whole families would rejoice
to visit our Northern shores and mountains for summer
residences, were it not for this. When our passions sub-
side, and we can look at this subject fairly, we shall
repeal the statutes which prevent a Southerner from
residing in a free state for a season, with his or her servant. The people of Massachusetts, for example, can
easily appreciate the hardship of being kept away from a
clime which they would visit for health or recreation, by
the fear of being set upon by a mob of whites and blacks
seeking to drag a wet-nurse, for example, before a court
to be interrogated whether she does not wish to leave
us. How long will our warm-hearted, hospitable people allow such things? The answer, from ten thousand
tongues, will be, So long as Southern people imprison
colored seamen from the North ! — If Southern slaves

should come here and make trouble between our domestics and us, and we should forbid their coming, the cases would be more nearly parallel. — Moreover, it will be said that the manner in which people from the North have in many instances of late been treated at the South, does not encourage the hope and prospect of amicable intercourse. This is certainly so ; and therefore what have we to look for but everlasting hatred and strife ? and that whether we be one nation or two confederacies.

A distinguished Southern gentleman came home from his visit to the North, where he had received great attentions, and he filled his hearers with his enthusiastic admiration of us for our wonderful ingenuity in all the arts of life.

"It is astonishing," said he, "how they work everything into shape, and create instruments for their purposes. But," said he, "there is one thing in which they are deficient. They are omnipotent with matter, but they do not know how to govern men. If they did," said he, "there would be no chance for us in any form of contest with them."

I was much entertained, and I said to him that I supposed his remarks would need qualification on both sides ; but I was greatly impressed, as I often am here, with the secret, strong attachment which there is in Southern hearts to the North as a part of the country, irrespective of its anti-slavery views and feelings. Its climate and institutions and arts and scenery are adapted to their diversified wants. "The North and the South, Thou hast created them." God made the North for the South, and the South for the North, and our acts of non-intercourse are in violation of his will. We are in a war of "conscience," inflamed by doctrinal error on our part.

It allows no "conscience" to the other side. The state of our "consciences" at the North is jury, judge, and executioner. There is no "conscience," we think, in Southern churches, ministers, judges, citizens, except that which is defiled. Probably there is not on earth this day a greater despot, or one more prepared for inquisitorial proceedings, than "Northern Conscience."

No doubt I should be contented and happy to be a slave-holder, had I been born and bred here, but I rejoice that I belong to a free state. I love to think of my capable girls, my "help," at home, who make the household go like clock-work, instead of having a swarm of servants who do only half as much, and only half as well. I am glad, too, that my children live in a climate favorable to labor, and are not born to be waited upon. But I am ashamed of those who erect these things into an invidious comparison, and with a supercilious, reproachful spirit. God, who made us of one blood, has fixed the bounds of our habitations. I love these Southerners as I never loved new acquaintances before. But I prefer a state of society free from slavery : yet this makes me love those to whom God has given a South country, and imposed upon it a necessity, at present at least, to employ the African race as cultivators of the soil. It has often disturbed my feelings to hear some people inveigh reproachfully against the Southern country, as comparing unfavorably with neighboring free states. Going up the Ohio River one day, a Northern gentleman pointed to some poor-looking lands in Kentucky on the one hand, and some flourishing fields of Ohio on the other. "There, ladies and gentlemen," said he, "is slavery," pointing to Kentucky, "and there," turning to the other side, "is freedom."

" Now," said an intelligent Ohioan, " if you will excuse
me for saying it, I regard that as clear humbug. What
is cultivated on either side? The products of Kentucky,
if raised in Ohio, would give the same look to her lands.
It is not slavery and freedom that make the difference; it
is the difference between large staples sown over large
territories, and smaller staples raised on smaller fields.
Kentucky's soil would be exhausted just as fast under
free labor, so long as she cultivated her present crops."

I long to see some clear running water. Our streams
and brooks in New England are not appreciated till one
comes to this part of the land. I long to see some good
grass. I yearn for some hills. I would sail again along
our rock-bound coast; Oh for a walk on its beaches, to see
the tunnellings of the sea in the rocks, and the spouting-
horns. But what a relief it is to be in a section where
the Christian religion is so generally accepted, and the
swarms of errorists and sectarians which abound elsewhere are comparatively unknown. Here, the lowest
class, in which error would be prolific, is under instruction, to a great degree. I see now why it is that false
views about slavery are a great stimulant to heretical
views and feelings; — they are a convenient substitute
for the love and zeal which true Christianity supplies. The
human mind, where it is accustomed to act freely, must
be impelled by some master-passion; and when true religion does not supply it, error stands ready to satisfy the
demand.

On the whole, I am persuaded that our Northern people behave full as well under the anti-slavery excitement
as Southerners would if their consciences were perverted
like ours, and we were the objects of their opposition.
I think that a change will come over us. At the North,

you have heard the wind, at midnight, after a warm
rain, in winter, haul out to the north-west, and you know
what a piping time we then have of it, and how the clear
cold air, the next morning, and the bright sun, excite
and cheer us. There has been with us for a long time
at the North, in our political and religious atmosphere, a
warm, foggy, unwholesome drizzle of weak, fanatical feeling, with now and then gusts of wind and scud, — a kind
of weather most abhorred by mariners. But we hope that
the wind is changing, and that "fair weather cometh out
of the North." God will not suffer us to live long, we
earnestly hope, in this condition of misunderstanding and
hatred, for it would be contrary to his established laws
that we should long continue to be one nation with such
feelings toward each other. The change will be in the
North. Slavery will come to be regarded as not in itself
a sin; and the evils incident to it will be left for those
immediately concerned to bear them or seek their removal. Or, if we become divided, the Southern section may extend its conquests into the whole southern
part of the American continent, and spread the institution of slavery over that vast domain. God may have
purposed that the good which has flowed to the African
race in this land by its connection with us, shall be extended
to millions more, not by importation, we may suppose,
but by propagation here. I say this to show that fanatical opposers of slavery may be employed under God as
the instruments of extending slavery to the very limits of
habitable land in the southern parts of our continent.
We have tried in vain at the North, for thirty years, to
abolish slavery. It is time either to cease, or to try some
entirely different influences.

But I must close my long letter. When you write

again, I have no doubt that you will have seen some
things in a new light. Tell me more about your studies.
I was interested in your way of describing things. I only
wondered that, with your occasional sense of the ludicrous, you should not have been aware of the impression
which you yourself must have made on others. Burns's
" giftie," " to see oursel's," etc., we all, more or less, need.
I told Hattie the other day that I thought some parts
of your letter did you very great credit, but that the
monomania of the North has fallen upon you, and that
you have it, as it seemed to me, in one of its worst forms.
Some it makes fierce, others, flat, according as the victim
is, naturally, more or less amiable.

Your mother gave you in charge to me in her last
sickness, and I must do all in my power for your best
good. I have, therefore, told you some things which I
have seen and considered. These you must now add to
the facts of your " inductive philosophy." Your defini-
tion of " pro-slavery," and " friends of oppression," is a fair
illustration of a prevailing state of mind at the North : —
" Pro-slavery — i. e., do not agree with me in my manner of viewing and treating the subject." This you will
correct. Excuse my freedom, but you have no father
nor mother now, to advise and guide you, and you must
let me be your Mentor in some things. I shall keep
your letter and let you see it perhaps ten years hence.
Be careful what newspapers you read. Those which
abound with low, opprobrious language about the South
and Southerners, avoid. There are some low Southerners about here who go around buying up refractory and
vicious negroes ; they are the dregs of society ; but I
have listened, with others, at the North, to men, on the
subject of " freedom," who, I think, would take kindly to

this business, and they would be as hearty in it as they are now in vilifying it. The "Legrees" are not confined to the South. Do not incline your ear to those who systematically inveigh against slavery, making it their principal business. You will invariably find that there is something false and wrong in their principles as well as spirit. Be careful to what influences you commit your thoughts and your taste.

You need not become a friend of oppression; you need not approve of "auction-blocks," and "separation of families;" slavery can exist when these are done away. Until you are appointed and commissioned as a minister of righteousness to Southern Christians and ministers, I advise you to blot slavery out of the list of topics about which you are called to express the least concern. The South will work out the problem for herself, with the help of that God who has evidently appointed her to do a great work for the African race, and all the more perfectly and speedily as our Northern people let her entirely alone as to the moral relations of the subject.

You subscribe yourself, "Yours for the slave;" I shall subscribe myself, "Yours for preaching the Gospel to every creature."

With the strongest love,

Your affectionate Aunt.

CHAPTER VI.

QUESTIONS AND ANSWERS.

" The sages say dame Truth delights to dwell,
    Strange mansion ! in the bottom of a well.
    Questions are, then, the windlass and the rope
    That pull the grave old gentlewoman up."
                                        PETER PINDAR.

MY friend, Mr. North, having read the foregoing letters, wrote me a note requesting me to come and
spend an evening with him and his wife, and answer
some questions occasioned by these letters.   The lady
was earnest that I should do so.

After being seated before a cheerful fire in my friend's
house, while it was raining violently, so that we felt defended from all interruption, my friend said, —

" Here, first of all, is the Southern lady's letter to her
father, which, I suppose, belongs to him, and which you
may wish to send back."

" I do," said I.

" But, please," said Mrs. North, " let it be published.
Add to it the incident of the Southern lady nursing the
sick babe of a slave."

" O my dear," said her husband, " that would create a
false impression.   It would be a pro-slavery tract.   It
would abate Northern zeal against the ' sum of all villanies.'   Something should go forth with such representa-

tions to correct their influence in the Free States. What would become of the cause of freedom should such stories make their impression upon the minds of our people ? "

" You might," said I, " make a heading of an auction-block, or slave-coffle ; add the last pattern of a slave-driver's whip ; picture a panting fugitive on his way to the North ; give us a ship's hold, with a black boy just detected among the stowage. You would thus, perhaps, keep these beautiful, touching illustrations of loving-kindness in slave-holders from having the least effect."

" It is very important," said he, seriously, " to keep up a just abhorrence of slavery here at the North, because " ——

" Excuse me," said I, " but what do you mean by an abhorrence of slavery ? "

" Why," said he, " is not the Christian world agreed that ' slavery is the sum of all villanies ' ? "

" By no means, in the United States," said I ; " you might with as real truth say that here slavery is the sum of all the loving-kindnesses."

" Is not that letter of the Southern lady to her father," said he, " as rare a thing almost as a white crow ? "

" O husband," said Mrs. North, " what an opinion you must have of Southern society ! "

" Is not Gustavus," said I, " a perfect representative of the North, on the subject of slavery ? Does not ultra anti-slavery find or make everybody, as the Aunt says, either fierce or flat ? "

" You do not believe so," said he.

" Neither do you believe," said I, " that where Christianity has exerted the same influence on the hearts of men and women as on yours, and all the humanizing and elevating influences of society prevail, that letter is a rare product."

" I cannot believe," said he, " that one can own a fellow-creature, hold God's image as property, and be a true Christian. This lady is an exception which does not destroy the general rule."

" My dear sir," said I, " you are an abstractionist. You make the best possible condition under the sun your standard, to which you would make all men and things conform, instead of allowing for the vast inequalities, the necessities, the mutual dependence, the long historical conditions of men, as individuals and races. A race or class of human beings may be in such a condition, that being 'owned' by a superior race will be, in their circumstances, a real mercy and a great blessing."

" O my dear sir," said he, " I weep over the degradation of your moral sense. ' Owning a fellow-creature ! ' I would not hold property in a human being ' for all the wealth that sinews bought and sold have ever earned.' "

" Thousands of men and women," I replied, " as good in the sight of God as you or I, think otherwise. There is nothing in the relation of ownership to a human being which in itself is sinful, or wrong."

" If it is your purpose," said he, " to argue in favor of oppression, perhaps we had better not pursue the conversation."

" Uncharitableness, false judgments, self-righteousness," said I, " condemning a whole people for the sins of a few, are as truly ' oppression' as anything can be. I plead for no wrongs ; I justify no selfishness in the relation of master and servant ; I regard the golden rule of Christ as the law by which slave-holding should be regulated in every instance."

"I never expected," said he, "to live long enough to hear of the golden rule being applied to slavery! It would be like applying light to darkness, truth to falsehood, holiness to sin."

"By what rule," I inquired, "do you think the lady is habitually governed who wrote the letter which has interested you so much?"

"Why," said he, "there are good people under every iniquitous system. These exceptional cases are not the rule of judgment with regard to the nature and effect of a system."

"Can you not imagine one man owning another," said I, "under circumstances, and with motives, and in a temper and spirit which will make the relation most desirable?"

"I go further back," said he, "and I deny that it is right for one human being to own another."

"Has not God a right," said I, "to place one human being over another as his owner?"

"Has God a right," said he, "to countenance theft and oppression?"

I said to him: "I might follow your example, and answer you by asking, Has God a right to countenance war? But I will relieve all your disagreeable apprehensions as to our conversation at once, by saying that I am not to argue in favor of oppression. If holding a slave is oppression, it is a sin. And if it be inconsistent with the golden rule, it is a sin."

"If that be your doctrine," said he, "we shall soon agree. Now apply the golden rule to slavery. Are there any circumstances in which you would yourself be willing to be 'owned'?"

"Certainly," I replied.

6

He rose, and put some lumps of coal upon the fire with the tongs, and said, " I presume you mean what you say, and that you do not wish to trifle with the subject."

" Mr. North," said I, " would you be willing that any one should make you head-cook in a hotel, engineer in a steamboat, or keeper of a floating light ? "

" No, Sir," said he.

" You would, Mr. North," said I, " under given circumstances. You would petition for such places, get recommendations for them, and count yourself perfectly happy, if you succeeded in obtaining them.

" Now look at the slaves. They are a foreign race, we are their civil superiors, and unless we amalgamate, we intend to remain so. While we are in this relation, it is a privilege to the blacks to have owners, but they must use their ownership according to the golden rule. When this is done, the condition of the blacks, in their present relation to us, is happy."

" How often," said he, " do you suppose that it is done ? "

" That," said I, " is another and a very interesting question, which we will consider soon. You took the ground, as I understood you, that the law of love would prevent any one from holding a fellow-creature as a slave. I reply that it would be in perfect accordance with it, as the blacks at the South are now situated, for the whites to be their humane owners. But pray what do you mean by ' owning ' a human being ? "

" I mean," said he, " having the right to abuse them, domineer over them, work them as cattle, sell them, and — "

" Did this Southern lady," said I, while he paused for more words, " ever acquire a right with her ownership to treat Kate so ? "

"Her laws," said he, "give her a right to punish her; and such irresponsible power is fearful. She could whip her to death and "——

"And be punished for it," said I, "as surely as you would be for whipping a servant to death."

"She is at liberty to punish more severely than the case warrants," said he, "and then she can shield herself under the laws."

"I presume," said I, "a Northern parent never gives a hasty box on the ear, never strikes one passionate blow in the chastisement, never shakes a child a single trill beyond the due harmony of parental affection, never scourges it with the tongue to momentary madness! What a dreadful thing parental authority is! Would it not be well to abolish the authority of parents over children! Indeed, would it not be well to go further, and interdict the public lands of the United States from being settled; for as surely as men live there, every form of wickedness will, in its turn, be perpetrated. How much better the calm and holy silence of the woods and fields, than if the tumultuous passions of men should roll over them!"

"But, my dear sir," said he, "I maintain that oppression is inseparable from the holding of a slave. I insist that this Southern lady, if all her feelings and conduct toward her servants are like her letter, is an exception among her people."

"No, Sir," said I, "she is the general rule among all decent people, and there is as much sense of decency and propriety there as with us, as many good people, kind, humane, generous, and it is as rare a thing for a servant to be ill-used there, as for our apprentices, and servants, and even our children. How kind and good you would be, Sir, if Providence should place a human being under you as his owner, for the mutual good of both of you."

"Dear me," said he, "I should try to feel and act just as I suppose those Southerners do who, you say, are fairly represented by this lady's letter about the slave-babe."

"Mr. North," said I, "suppose that the State should make you the absolute owner of some of those boys who set fire to the Westboro' and Deer Island institutions. In consideration of your personal responsibility for them, there is ceded to you all right and title to their services, and absolute control over them, subject, of course, to the laws against misdemeanors and crimes against the person. My only point is this: Where would be the sinfulness of that relation? All that would be sinful about it would be in your neglect or violation of your duty as a master."

"How glad all this makes me feel," said he, "that I am not troubled with slaves. If we do not like our servants or apprentices, we can get rid of them."

"Then," said I, "you surely ought to pity those who are bound to their slaves and have to put up with a thousand things which you say we can escape by changing our help."

"But," said he, "can they not sell off their slaves when they please?"

"Suppose, however," said I, "that they happen to be humane, as Mr. North is, and as we all are in the Free States! and that they are unwilling to turn off a poor helpless creature for her faults, to be sold, and to go they know not where!"

"Slavery," said Mr. North, "is surely a great curse. I am so glad that I live under free institutions."

"Who made us to differ from the South in this

respect? How came those blacks there? Whose ships, whose money, imported them? You remember that it was by the votes of Free States, that the importation of slaves was continued for eight years beyond the time when the Southern States had voted in the Convention that it should cease. And now what would you have the South do with the slaves, to-day?"

"Set them all free," said he, "'break every yoke; proclaim liberty to the captives, the opening of the prison-doors to them that are bound.'"

"Allow me," said I, "to smile at your simplicity, for you are very child-like, not to say childish, in your feelings. You would have the colored people universally go free. Do you really think that Kate is worse off in being what you call a slave, than that young, free black woman who keeps a stall and sells verses and knives near our Park?"

"O dear sir," said he, "liberty is a priceless boon; liberty"——

"Liberty to what?" said I.

"Why," said he, "liberty not to be sold, nor to be beaten, nor to be subject to the wicked passions of a master."

"Would you rather," said I, "have your daughter a servant in a Southern family, brought up as a playmate with the children, a sharer in many of their gifts, a partner with their parents, as the children grew up, in the pride and joy of the parents, an honored member of the wedding party when a daughter is married, one of the principal mourners when the bride departs, identified with the history of the family, provided for in the will, a support guaranteed to her by law in sickness and old age, and that, too, not in a pauper establishment, but in her owner's home, and when the parents die, if she survives, taken by some branch of the family or neighbor from regard to her and to them; her moral and religious character improved under their training, a respectable standing in society conferred upon her by her connection with them, her religious privileges sacredly secured to her, any insult redressed as though it were the family's personal affair; she a partaker of their food and of all their comforts, and followed to her grave with respect and love; or, for the sake of 'priceless liberty,' 'heaven's best gift to man,' would you prefer to see her seated under the iron fence of a park, an old umbrella tied to the pickets for her shelter, and she, in rain and sunshine, selling 'Old Dan Tucker,' 'Jim Crow, Illustrated,' and pea-nuts, and sleeping you know not where? Which lot would you choose for a child? Which is best for this world and the next? In one case, she is 'owned,' she is 'a slave;' and in the other, she is a free woman."

"You have no right," said he, with some warmth, "to take the best condition in slavery, and the very worst in freedom, and compel me to choose."

"'Best condition in slavery!'" said I; "is there any 'best' in being a slave, in not being free? Does it admit of degrees? Is not being 'owned' such a curse, such an unmixed iniquity in its essence, that to compare its best estate with the worst in freedom, is like comparing the best devil with the most inferior saint? Is not a devil's nature incapable of comparison as good, better, best, with anything which is not, in its nature, devilish? According to your conversation just now, it seemed as though being 'owned' always implied an unmitigated transgression; and now when I inquire whether you would prefer degradation to the iniquity of being 'owned'

in comfort and usefulness, respectability and happiness,
you shrink from the question. If freedom in the abstract is the best thing under the sun, of course you will
prefer it to everything else. No happy condition, no
happy prospect for this life, and the life to come can, in
your view, make being 'a slave,' as you call it, capable of
being compared with this abstract privilege of being free.
In this you and your friends labor under a huge mistake, and it poisons all your views and feelings about
slavery. When you denounce slave-holders and slavery, and depict the condition of the slave in your awful
colors, they at the South know that in hundreds of thousands of instances, as it regards masters and slaves, all
that you say is practically false; you are carried away
by your zeal against a theoretical wrong.

"Now suppose that instead of starting with the theoretical wrong and getting only such facts as illustrate it,
you should travel through the South to pick up such
letters as you consider this, respecting Kate, to be; — what
a pleasing view might be presented of the slaves' condition in cases without number!"

"But," said he, "there are terrible evils underlying
these fair features of slavery."

"True," said I, "but why, in the name of truth and
love do you never hear such a letter as this read on
the platforms of Northern abolition societies? What
mingled groans and hisses and shrieks for freedom, and
then what an emptying of the demoniacal epithets there
would be, if such a letter should be offered. One case
of whipping would have more effect than a thousand
such letters, in your assemblies and newspapers. No
one from the continent of Europe would infer from those
meetings that such beings as Kate and her little babe,

and this lady and her husband and father, existed even in fiction, but that slave-holders are Legrees, and the slaves their victims. What a beautiful effect it would have on us and on the South, if touching tales of loving-kindness between masters and slaves, instances of perfect happiness in that relation, should be cited, and then you should enter your candid, but decided opposition to the system, to its extension, to its evils where it exists. How soon we should all be found working together, so far as we might, for the amelioration of the colored race here, with a view to the extinction of slavery in every form of it in which it is an evil, or a greater evil than anything which might properly be substituted."

" Well," said Mrs. North, " husband, what do you say to that ? "

" I like it," said he.

" But now," said I, " the language of the place of despair is exhausted in describing and denouncing the South. If a man among us lifts up his voice to say good things about Southerners, one universal hiss goes up from all your conventions and anti-slavery prints. He may be seeking the same end with you, namely, the peaceful removal of slavery, with due regard to the highest good of all concerned ; but let him utter a word in arrest of your unqualified condemnation of slavery as it actually is, and there are no persecutors, nor scourges, nor intolerance on the earth, more fierce and cruel than you and your denunciations."

" Take it patiently, husband," said Mrs. North, " you know that you deserve it."

" I know from this," said I, " if from nothing else, that your theory is wrong. The truth does not excite such passions in those who love and seek to promote it. We see that, in cases without number, the present condition of the slaves is a blessing for both worlds, and that if all who possess slaves were, as many are, slavery would cease to be any more of a curse than any dependent condition in this world. There must always be those who will do every sort of menial work. The great Father of all, who himself says that he has 'deprived' the ostrich 'of wisdom, neither hath he imparted to her understanding,' so arranges the capacities of some that their happiness consists in leaning upon superior intelligence and capability.

"The serving people, in some districts of country, are volunteers from all races; at the South, they consist of one inferior, dependent race, who for ages have been slaves in their own country, and would be such even now, if they were there. We will not shut the door of hope forever upon any part of the human family, as to their elevation among the tribes of men, but this race has, for a long period of its history, evidently been undergoing a tutelage and discipline at the hand of Providence. There is some marvellous arrangement of Providence, it seems to me, designing that this black race shall lean upon us. Let the same number of any other immigrant race have gone from us to Canada as of this colored race, and the world would have heard a better report from them ere this. They thrive best in connection with us as their masters, whether it be right or wrong for us to be in such relation to them."

"But now," said he, — in a persuasive tone, and evidently wishing to turn the drift of the remarks, — "just set them free, and hire them; we shall agree then. The slaves will be as well off, and so will their masters."

"Mr. North," said I, "being owned is, in itself, irre-
6 *

spective of the character of the master, a means of protection to the negro. Somebody then is responsible for
him as his guardian and provider, and is amenable to the
State for his sustenance. You can easily see that, let
the colored people come to be a hireling class, and their
interests and those of their masters are disjoined. There
would be conflicts and oppressions among themselves ; they
would fall into a degraded, serf-like condition ; but now
each of them partakes of his master's interests, and rises
with him. I am not here pleading for slavery in the
abstract, but, the blacks being on the soil, it is far better
for them to be owned than to be free. Why are the
Southwestern States, one after another, passing laws, or
framing their constitutions, to shut out from their borders
free negroes, — people in the very condition into which you
would reduce by wholesale all the blacks in the South ?
I pray you look and see that you are an abstractionist,
setting what you deem a theoretical wrong against a
practical good, and under the circumstances, a real mercy."

" But," said Mr. North, " slavery impoverishes the soil,
makes the whites shun labor, feeling it to be degrading,
and it keeps the white children from industrial pursuits,
and " ——

" Please stop," said I, " my dear Sir, and think of what
you are saying, and be not carried away by that popular
flood of cant phrases. Now you know that God has given
our Southern friends a south country, nearer than ours
to the tropics. Out-of-door labor there is injurious to the
white people, as you know. They are not to be blamed
for this. God has not given them strength to endure exposure to the sun. Had they a northern climate, in
which the labor required by the mechanic arts could be
performed with safety and comfort, do you not suppose

that they would have the same aptitude and relish as we for handicraft? Their children cannot be brought up to manual labor to the extent that ours are, because the God of heaven has ordained their lot in a land less favorable than ours to toil. His providence, making use of the sins of men, has placed the blacks here; you and the rest of the world, who depend upon their cotton, are willing enough to use it in its countless forms, while you reproach your Maker, as I think, for having caused it to be raised as he has seen fit to do."

"But Oh," said Mr. North, "free labor is more profitable than slave labor. You well know how it affects the soil, and that the great price of slaves will in time make the system oppressive to the masters, especially if they are all as considerate as you say they are about selling."

"The good Aunt has replied to you as to the soil, and we need not distress ourselves about the price of slaves; that will regulate itself. You well understand," said I, "that I am not arguing in favor of slavery *per se*, nor for the slave-trade, nor for the extension of slavery; but I contend that where slavery now exists, no one has yet proposed a scheme which is better than the continuance of ownership, the blacks remaining on the same soil with their present masters. Nor do I mean to say that the present system must inevitably continue forever. We must leave future developments in other hands. Of course there are difficult problems on such a subject as this. Intelligent Christian gentlemen at the South say that the best schemes which have been proposed by Europeans for the substitution of apprenticed negroes for slaves would make the condition of the negro as far worse than our slavery as the condition of a degraded negro here is below that of his master. Who will care for him when he is old, or sick? Granting this apprentice scheme to be arranged without oppression or sin of any kind, I hold that the condition of our slaves owned by masters and mistresses, is better than such a hireling condition, though it have the appearance of liberty."

"Why so?" inquired Mr. North.

"The slaves are not treated as hired horses are liable to be treated," I replied. "We know how a man is likely to treat his own horse, compared with the horse which he hires. Men nurse their slaves when they are sick; they provide for them when they are old. By their care and responsibility for them, and in relieving them from responsibility, they pay them wages whose market-value, if it could be reckoned in dollars, would be higher wages than are paid to the same class of laborers in the land. There are not four millions of the lower class of the laboring people in any one district of the earth whose condition is to be compared with that of the Southern slaves for comfort and happiness."

"I presume," said Mrs. North, "that you would not regard exemption from responsibility as in itself a blessing. You know how it educates us, how it sharpens the faculties, how it makes a man more of a man; therefore is it, after all, any kindness to the slaves, that they are relieved from responsibility?"

"I thank you," said I, "for that question. Does it concern us that our domestic servants are relieved, for the time, of all responsibility for house-rent, taxes, political duties?

"Every condition of poverty and toil has its peculiar hardships and sorrows. But putting together, respectively, all the advantages and the disadvantages of our slaves, he who looks upon a population with enlarged views of liabilities and of the inevitable results in the working of different schemes of labor, and is not so weak or morbid as to dwell inordinately on real and imaginary wrongs and miseries, which, after all, if real, are compensated for by advantages or surpassed by aggregated smaller evils in other conditions, must admit that, the colored people being here, their being owned is the very best possible thing for their protection, and the surest guarantee against all their liabilities to want in hard times, sickness, and old age.

" Speaking of hard times leads me to say, that if you could put four millions of laboring people in the Free States, for a winter or during commercial distresses and the stagnation of every kind of business, in a position where, while they were still active and useful, a single thought or care about their sustenance would not visit them, you would be deemed a philanthropist and public benefactor. There will not be the same number of people in the laboring class throughout our land next winter, in any one section, whose comfort and happiness will exceed that of our slaves."

" Oh, well," said Mr. North, " all this may be true, but this does not reconcile me to slavery. Our horses here at the North will all be comfortably provided for, notwithstanding any money pressure. But I would rather be a human being and fail, every winter, than be a horse."

" Husband," said Mrs. North, " do you consider that a parallel case? Mr. C. is not arguing, as I understand him, that slavery is better than freedom. He is not persuading us to be slaves rather than free. He takes these four millions of blacks as he finds them, in bondage, and he asks, What shall we do with them? You say, Set them free. He says, They are better off, as a race, in their present bondage, than they would be if made free, to remain here. Not that they are better off than four millions of colored people, who had never been slaves, would be in a commonwealth by themselves."

" I thank you, Mrs. North," said I, " for your clear and correct statement of my position. And now I will take up Mr. North's parable about the horses, and apply it justly. Let hay and grass be exceedingly scarce, and I had rather take my chance with an owner and be a horse, in a stable, and at work, than a horse roaming in search of food, chased away everywhere. The comparison is between horse and horse, and man and man."

" You make me think," said Mrs. North, " of an interesting passage in a late magazine, written by a lady. She was on a voyage to Cuba. She arrived at Nassau. She says, ' There were many negroes, together with whites of every grade ; and some of our number, leaning over the side, saw for the first time the raw material out of which Northern Humanitarians have spun so fine a skein of compassion and sympathy. You must allow me one heretical whisper, — very small and low. Nassau, and all we saw of it, suggested to us the unwelcome question whether compulsory labor be not better than none.'" [1]

" There is," said I, " this great question of right, with some, as to slavery : As the State has a right to interpose and send vagrant children to school, has the world a right to interpose, in certain cases, and send certain races to labor for the good of mankind? This was the question which broke upon the lady's mind. It is very interesting to see the question thus stated, and to notice the graceful touch of apology, and of playfulness, in the manner of stating it. There was risk, and even peril, in making the suggestion, but, withal, some moral courage. Still a lady may sometimes venture where it might not be safe for a gentleman to go.

[1] *Atlantic Monthly*, May, 1859, p. 604.

"But the question between us is not, 'Freedom or slavery,' in the abstract, nor, Whether it is right, in any case, to reduce a people to slavery; but, What is best for our slaves? All your proofs that freedom is better than slavery in the abstract, are nothing to the point."

"It is the foulest blot on our nation in the eyes of the world," said Mr. North, "that we have four millions of human beings in bondage."

"Have you read 'Uncle Tom's Cabin?'" I inquired.

"Ask me," said he, pleasantly, "if I know how to read. Every lover of liberty and hater of oppression has read 'Uncle Tom.'"

"That is very far from being true," said I; "but still, you like Uncle Tom as a character, do you?"

"You astonish me," said he, "by making a question about it. He is the most perfect specimen of Christianity that I ever heard of."

"Among the martyrs," said I, "have you ever found his superior?"

"No, Sir!" was his energetic answer.

"Now," said I, "what made Uncle Tom the paragon of perfection?"

"What made him?" said he.

"Yes," said I, "what made him the model Christian? You do not reply, and I will tell you. SLAVERY MADE UNCLE TOM. Had it not been for slavery, he would have been a savage in Africa, a brutish slave to his fetishes, living in a jungle, perhaps; and had you stumbled upon him he would very likely have roasted you and picked your bones. A system which makes Uncle Toms out of African savages is not an unmixed evil."

"But," said he, "it makes Legrees also."

"I beg your pardon, Sir," said I, "it does not make Legrees. There are as many Legrees at the North as at the South, especially if we include all the very particular 'friends of the slave.' Legree would be Legree in Wall Street, or Fifth Avenue; Uncle Tom would not be Uncle Tom in the wilds of Africa."

"And so," said he, "it is right to fit out ships, burn villages in Africa, steal the flying people, bestow them in slave-ships, and sell them into hopeless bondage!"

"So you all love to reason," said I, "or seek to force that conclusion upon us. No such thing. If God overrules the evil doings of men, this is no reason for repeating the wrong. I am insisting that slavery as it exists in the South has been a blessing to the African. This does not warrant you in perpetrating outrages on those who are still in Africa.

"But the result has been, through the mercy of God as though we had taken millions of degraded savages out of Africa, and had made them contribute greatly to the industrial interests of mankind.

"We have raised them from heathenish ignorance and barbarism to the condition of intelligent beings. Look at them in their churches and Sabbath-schools. Slavery has done this. See the colored population of Charleston, S. C., voluntarily contributing, as they do, on an average, three dollars apiece, annually, for the propagation of the Gospel at home and abroad. See the meeting-house of the African Church at Richmond, Va., a place selected for public speakers from the North to deliver their addresses in it to the citizens of Richmond, because it is more commodious than any other public building in the city. Think of the membership of slaves in Christian Churches; of the multitudes of them who have died in the faith and hope of the Gospel. Slavery has done this. The question is whether slavery has been, or is, such a curse, on the whole, to the African race, that we must now set free the whole colored population? Please let us keep to the point. The reopening of the slave-trade is a question by itself.

"It seems that God had chosen to redeem and save large numbers of the African race by having them transported to this Christian land. Philanthropists would not be at the cost and trouble of all this. God has, therefore, used the cupidity of men to accomplish his purposes, and he punishes the wicked agents of his own benevolent schemes. His curse has for ages rested on the African race, and the laws of nature have, to a great degree, interposed to prevent Christian efforts in their behalf. God saw fit to change the prison-house, and prison yards and shops of this race from one continent to another, and New England merchantmen, in part, have been allowed to be the conveyers. In the process of transferring these future subjects of civilization and Christianity, vast misery is endured, as in opening a way by the sword for the execution of his decrees, great slaughter is the inevitable attendant. I look at the whole subject of slavery in the light of God's providence. And I do not see that his providence yet indicates any way for its termination consistent with the interests of the colored people.

"As to the extension of slavery, in this land, if the Most High has any further purposes of mercy for the African race in connection with us, he will not consult you nor me. He will open districts of our country for them ; if my political party refuses to be the instrument in doing this, from benevolent motives, or from any other cause, He will make that party to be defeated, it may be by a party below us in moral principle, as we view it. This question of slavery, its extension and continuance, is therefore among the great problems of God's provi-

dence. I shall do all that I properly can to prevent it,
and to encourage, and, if called upon, to aid my brethren
now in immediate charge of the slaves, to fulfil their solemn trust ; but anything like impatience and passion at
the existence of slavery, I hold to be a sin against God.
I pity those good men whose minds are so inflamed by
the consideration of individual cases of suffering as not
to perceive the great and steadfast march of the divine
administration.   Politicians and others who get their
places, or their bread, by easy appeals to sympathy for
individual cases of suffering, are the causes of much
misplaced commiseration and of a low, uninstructed view
of the great interests involved in slavery.   Yet these very
men who, for selfish purposes, stir up the passions of our
people, by dwelling on cases of hardship in slavery, are
greatly disappointed when Napoleon III., at Villafranca,
prematurely terminates a war of unparalleled slaughter.
They would have preferred, for the cause of constitutional liberty and for its possible influence against the
Pope, that the fighting had continued a month longer ;
we hear no pathetic remonstrances from them on the
score of the killed and maimed, the widows and orphans
and the childless, of homes made desolate, by this additional month of battle.   Such is man, so inconsistent, so
blinded by party prejudice, so ready to maintain that
which, in a change of persons and places, he will denounce.   He will be wholly blinded by individual acts
of suffering to all that is good in a system ; and again,
the good to be effected by a war will blind him to the
hundreds of thousands of dead or mutilated soldiers, with
five times that number of bleeding hearts, rifled by the
sword of their precious treasures."

I saw that I had prolonged my remarks to an undue

length. We sat in silence for a little while, looking into
the fire, and listening to the rain against the windows,
when Judith called Mrs. North to the door ; and, after
some whispering between them, Mrs. North said to her,
    " Oh, bring them in ; our company will excuse it."
    The cranberries, it seems, were not doing well over the
fire in Judith's department, and she had hesitatingly proposed that they should be promoted to the parlor grate
where, after due apologies, they were placed. They soon
began to simmer ; then one would burst, and then another,
we pausing unconsciously to hear them surrendering themselves to their fate, while one mouth, at least, watered at
the thought of the delicious dish which they were to furnish ; the rich, ruby color of their juice in the best cut-
glass tureen, and the added spoonful, as a reward for not
spilling a drop on the table-cloth the last time they were
served, coming to mind, with thoughts of early days.
And here I was discussing slavery. Now, while the
cranberries were over the fire, making one feel domestic
and also bringing back young days, it was impossible to
be disputatious, had we been so inclined. The Northern cranberry-meadow and the Southern sugar-planta-
tion seemed mixed up in my feelings on this subject,
qualifying and rectifying each other. Perhaps the sooth-
ing presence of the cranberry saucepan was timely ; for,
without any design, a phase of our subject next presented itself which was not the most agreeable. I broke
the silence, and said, —
    " Mr. North, what do you think is the mission of the
abolitionists as a party, and of all who sympathize with
them ? "
    " Why," said he, " to abolish slavery, to be sure. What
else can it be ? "

" You are mistaken," said I. " The real mission of
the abolitionists, thus far, is, To perpetuate slavery till
Providence has accomplished its plan. You know what
Southern synods, and general assemblies, and many of
the ablest men at the South have said about slavery;
how they deplored it, and called upon Christians to seek
its extinction. The South would probably have tried to
abolish slavery ere this, if left to themselves. But they
would have failed; and Providence prevented the useless effort. The influence of those sentiments which prevailed in the General Assembly of 1818 would have
been to remove all the objectionable features of slavery,
at least, preparatory to its final extinction, if that could
be reached. It looked as though Churches generally
would, in obedience to the General Assembly, have made
it, in certain cases, the subject of discipline. Abolition-
ism, however, began about that time. It had the effect
to make the South defend themselves and slavery too.
Providence saw that the South was weary of the system,
and wished to throw it off. But the years of the captivity
appointed of God had not come to an end. Purposes of
mercy for the African race had not been accomplished ;
the South must be made willing to hold these poor people
for the 'time, times, and half a time,' ordained of God.
To encourage them, the God of Nature makes the great
Southern staple, cotton, to be in greater demand for the
supply of the world; the cotton-gin is invented, and immediately the slaves are thereby assisted to retain that
hold upon the South which was about to be broken off.
All this seems to me designed, as it certainly has the
effect, to perpetuate slavery until Providence shall indi-
cate measures for the removal of the colored people
among us. This may be delayed for centuries to come.

In the mean time, we at the North, by keeping up our
agitation of the subject, have impressed the South with
the importance of being united against us; but if any of
our schemes of emancipation had divided them, it would
not have been for the good of the slaves. So the abolitionists have been fulfilling their destiny by fighting
against Providence to help perpetuate slavery till the
Most High shall disclose his will concerning it."

"And helped the South," said Mr. North, "perpetuate
violations of the marriage relation, and to separate families, and to countenance all the sins in slavery!"

"Yes, to some degree," said I; "for should we treat
them with common candor and truthfulness, make them
feel that we appreciate the perplexities of the subject,
admit for once, and act upon it, that they are better and
more competent 'friends of the slave' than we, it would
be the surest way to put a stop to every evil in slavery.
Now they have little power over a certain class of men
among them, who, when measures are proposed for the
relief of the slaves, raise the cry that they are abolitionists, and excite an odium which deters them from doing
many things which would otherwise be attempted."

"They might all certainly join," said Mr. North, "one
would think, to prevent the violation of the marriage con-
tract by the slaves, and the sundering of the marriage tie
by the auctioneer."

"Now," said I, "there are two allegations, and I will
answer them. As to the violation of the marriage covenant by the slaves, are you aware how many divorces
for the same cause are granted in your own state yearly?
You will find, on inquiry, that 'freedom' has nothing to
boast of in this respect. As to the auctioneer, and the
separation of the marriage tie by him, how often do you

think that an honest black man, for no crime, is taken from his wife and sold, or she from him? How often, do you suppose, are families divided and scattered at the auction-block? If you will inquire, you will find that the cases are extremely rare; that in some large districts it has not occurred for several years; and that in other cases, where it has occurred, regard has been had to the neighborhood of the purchasers, so that members of the same families have been within reach of one another. You seem to think that a great feature, and the most common effect, of slavery is to separate families. Such is the general belief at the North. Let me remind you that there is no form or condition of service in the world which has more effect than slavery to keep families together."

"Well," said Mrs. North, dropping her work in her lap, "I never thought of that before."

"Why," said I, "where will you find in the Free States husband and wife and children living together as servants in the same family?"

Said Mrs. North, "It is rather uncommon with us to find two sisters living together as help in a family. At least, it is always spoken of and noted as pleasant and desirable."

"What would Northerners think," said I, "of gathering the old parents and all the brothers and sisters of their domestics together, in small tenements near their own dwellings? He who should do this would be regarded as a very great saint. So that you may as well say that slavery is a system by which a serving class is kept together in families, as to say that its purpose and effect is to break up families."

"Just think," said Mrs. North, "of the serving class

in our families here at the North, — how they are separated by states, by oceans, from one another!"

"Be careful, Mrs. North," said I, "how you even hint at such mitigations in slavery, for you will be denounced as a 'friend of oppression' if you discern anything in the system but 'villanies.' You never hear such a feature of slavery, as that of which we have just spoken, recognized here at the North by our zealous anti-slavery people."

"Do you not think," said she, "that if we were candid and less passionate, and viewed the subject as anti-slavery men at the South do, we should exert far more influence against slavery?"

"If we exerted any," I replied, "it would be 'far more' than we do now. If we would only cease to 'exert influence' in that direction, and begin to learn that the people of the South are as Christian, benevolent, and good in every respect as we, this first, great lesson, which we all need to learn, would do us all great good. Self-righteousness is the great characteristic of the Northern people with regard to the South. Fifteen States declare that they are justified before God in continuing the system of slavery. The other States would be ashamed to condemn those fifteen States for immorality in the discussion of any other subject; but here they assume that one half of the American nation is convicted of crime. I take the ground that, if the Churches and the ministry of those fifteen States say, With all the evils of slavery, it is right and best that we should maintain it, I will so far yield my convictions as not to feel that they are less righteous than I."

"Oh," said Mr. North, "but they have been born and educated under the system. Of course they must be blinded by it, and their moral sense perverted."

"There," said I, "Mr. North, is the 'Northern Evil' again. Oh, what a shame it is for intelligent people to decry Southern Christians in this way, and to erect their own moral sense into such self-complacent superiority!

"You will see in your church one excellent brother, whose heart is filled with anguish at the thought of the 'poor slave.' One sits by him who knows full as much on this and on all subjects as he, who feels that the people at the South are perfectly qualified to manage this subject, and that we have no need to interpose. He thinks that if one wishes to be excited with compassion at the sorrows and woes of men, a short walk will bring him to certain abodes such as no Southern slave would be allowed by any human master to inhabit. If he would benefit men as a class, our own sailors need all his philanthropy. But the good anti-slavery brother is possessed with the idea that the Southern slave is the impersonation of injustice and misery, and that those who stand in the relation of masters are guilty of crimes, daily, which ought to shut them out of the Church.

"I have often thought that the most appropriate prayers in our public assemblies, with regard to slavery, would be petitions against Northern ignorance and passion with respect to Southern Christians. It is we who most need to be prayed for. When I think of those assemblies of Christians of all denominations in the South, with a clergy at their head who have no superiors in the world, and then hear a Northern preacher indicting them before God in his prayers, what shall I say? The verdict of a coroner's inquest, if it were held over some of his hearers at such a time, might almost be, Died of disgust."

"Now I desire to know," said Mr. North, "if we are never to pray in public about slavery? Is it not the great subject before the country, and are not all our interests in Church and State deeply involved in it ? "

" While we believe," said I, " that holding slaves is a sin, I take the ground that praying for the Southerners is a false impeachment. When we are rid of this error, we do not feel their need of being prayed for any more than 'all men,' for whom Paul says, 'I will that men pray everywhere,' — 'lifting up holy hands without wrath or doubting.' Our 'hands' must be 'holy' when we lift them up for 'all men,' including Southerners ; there must be no 'wrath' in our prayers, — which I am sorry to say is too easily discerned in prayers against the South ; and there must be no 'doubting' in the petitioners whether their feelings and motives are right before God. There is as much in the relation of officers and crews in our merchant vessels, to say the least, to enlist the prayers of ministers, as in slavery. But this relates to ourselves, and has not the enchantment of a distant sin.

" You must bring yourself to believe, Mr. North, that Southern hearts are in general as humane and cultivated as ours. This, it is true, is a great demand upon a Northerner."

" But oh," said he, (we happening to be alone just then,) " the cruelty of compelling virtuous people, members of Churches, to commit sin, under pain of being sold."

" Mr. North," said I, " how do you dare to open your lips on that subject, — you, with myself, a member of a denomination in which men, eminent in our pulpits, have — so many of them of late years — fallen. One would think that we would never cast a stone at the South on that subject.

" Some among us seem to think that the power and the opportunity to commit sin must necessarily be followed

7

by criminal indulgence. They do themselves no credit in this supposition. They also leave out of view a natural antipathy which must be overcome, sense of degradation, probability of detection, loss of character, conscience, and all the moral restraints which are common to men everywhere; and they only judge that all who exercise authority over an abject race must, as a general thing, be polluted.

"As to opportunities for evil-doing at the South compared with the North, no one who walks the streets of a Northern city, by day or night, with the ordinary discernment of one who sets himself to examine the moral condition of a place, will fail to see that we need not go to the South to find humiliating proofs of baseness and shame. There is less solicitation at the South; here it is a nightly trade, without disguise. At the South the young must go in search of opportunity; here it confronts them. The small number of yellow children in the interior of the Cotton States, on 'lone plantations,' is positive proof against the ready suspicions and accusations of Northern people. Let all be true which is said of 'yellow women,' 'slave-breeders,' and every form of lechery, he is simple who does not believe that the statistics of a certain wickedness at the North would, if made as public as difference of color makes the same statistics at the South, leave no room for us to arraign and condemn the South in this particular. Their clergy, their husbands, their young men, if they are no better, are no worse than we. But there is nothing in which the self-righteousness created by anti-slavery views and feelings is more conspicuous than in the way in which the South is judged and condemned by us with regard to this one sin. Had the pulpits of the South afforded such dreadful instances of frailty, for the last ten or fifteen years, as we have had at the North, what confirmation would we have found for our invectives against the corrupting and 'barbarous' influence of slavery!

"How the morbid fancy of a Northerner loves to gloat over occasional instances of violence at the South, and is never employed in depicting scenes of betrayal and cruelty which our policemen in large cities could recount by scores."

"I saw," said Mr. North, "in a recent paper, that a slave in Washington County, N. C., was hanged by the sheriff in the presence of three thousand spectators, for the murder of a white man, whom he shot with a pistol because he suspected him of undue familiarity with the wife of the black man. Poor fellow! no doubt he swung for it because he was a slave. He must let his marriage rights be invaded by the whites, and bear it in silence, or die."

Said I, "What a perfect specimen of Northern anti-slavery feeling and logic have we in what you now say. If a man, on suspicion of you, takes the law into his hands and shoots you with a pistol, does he not deserve to die? He does, if he is a white man; perhaps, if he be a slave, that excuses him! Even where a man is known to be guilty of the crime referred to, and the husband shoots him, he is apt to have a narrow escape from being punished. As to bearing such violations of one's rights in silence under intimidation, there is no more power in intimidation to save a villain at the South from disgrace and abhorrence in his community, than at the North."

"But he can evade prosecution under the statute," said Mr. North, "more easily at the South than here."

"When you have served on the grand jury a few terms," said I, "you will be more charitable toward

Southerners. Human nature is the same everywhere. It makes, where it does not find, occasion for sin.

" Now you will not understand, in all that I have said, that I am pleading for slavery, that I desire to have this abject race among us, that Southerners are purer and better than we. We are both under sin. We all have our temptations and trials ; each form of society has its own kind of facilities for evil ; but the grace of God and all the influences which bear on the formation and the preservation of character, are the same wherever Christianity prevails."

" Well, after all," said he, " it must be a semi-barbarous state of society, where such a system is maintained."

" I shall have to send you," said I, " to the ' Hotel des Incurables.' I think that your judgments are more than semi-barbarous. If you please to term even the Southern negroes ' semi-barbarous,' you may do so ; but you are bearing false witness against your neighbor.

" My dear friend," said I, " sum up all the evils of the laboring classes, of foreigners and the lower orders of society. Take their miseries, vices, crimes, with all the blessings of freedom and everything else. Get the proportion of evil to the good. Remember that these classes will continue to exist among us. Then take the slaves, the lower order at the South, as foreigners are with us, and say if, on the whole, the proportion of evil among the slaves is any greater than among the corresponding classes elsewhere. Do not be an optimist. Acknowledge that society, in this fallen world, must have elements of evil, by reason at least of imbecility, want of thrift, misfortune, and other things. You will not fail to see that slavery with all its evils is, under the circumstances, by no means, the worst possible condition for the colored people."

"Well," said he, "I will think of all you have said. I do not wish to be an ultraist, nor to shut my eyes against truth. You will wish to go to bed; there are some further points on which I would know your views, and we will, if you please, resume the subject to-morrow."

CHAPTER VII.

OWNERSHIP IN MAN. — THE OLD TESTAMENT SLAVERY.

"Therefore all things whatsoever ye would that men should do to you, do
ye even so to them; FOR THIS IS THE LAW AND THE PROPHETS."

HOLY WRIT.

THE rain still poured down in the morning, making it
    agreeable to us that we had the prospect of an unin-
terrupted forenoon for our conversation.

So when we found ourselves together again in the
course of the forenoon, by the fire, we opened the discussion.

Mr. North inquired what I understood by the term
"owning a fellow-creature."

"I understand by it," I replied, "a right to use, and to
dispose of, the services of another, wholly at my will.
That will must be subject to the whole law of God,
which includes the golden rule. I do not mean by it
that a man owns the body of a man in such a sense that
he can maim it at will, or in any way abuse it. Ownership in men is power to use their services and to dispose
of them, at will."

"Now," said he, "who gives you a right to go to
Africa or to a slave auction and to say to a human being,
'I propose to own you.' How would you like to have a
black man come to you in a solitary place and say, 'My

dear Sir, I propose to own you. Henceforth your services are subject to my will.' ? "

"As to Africa," said I, "and making slaves of those who
are now free, we cannot differ. As to the other part of
your question, I will carry the illustration a little further,
and in doing so, will answer you in part. How would
you like to have some Michael O'Connor come to you
and say, 'Mr. North, I propose to hire you and pay you
wages as my body-servant, or my ostler.' Why should
you not consent? If you do not, why should you hire
Mike himself to serve you in either of those capacities?
What has become of the golden rule, if you hire a man
to do work for you which you would not be hired to do?

"You are feasting with a company of friends; and
your domestics, below, hear your cheerful talk, and feel
the wide difference between your state and theirs. Why
do you not go down and say, 'Dear fellow-creatures, go
up and take our places at table, and let us be servants'?
Does the golden rule require that? Inequalities in
human conditions are a wise and benevolent provision
for human happiness, so long as men are dependent on
one another, as they are and ever must be. Some are
so constituted by an all-wise God that they are happier to be in subordinate situations. Mind is lord; and
they, seeing and feeling the superiority of others, gladly
attach themselves to them as helpers, to be thought for
and protected, and to enjoy their approbation. There is
nothing cruel in this, unless it be cruel not to have made
all men equal. There are important influences grow-
ing out of these relationships of superiors and inferiors,
— gentleness, kindness, benevolence, in all its forms,
on the one hand, and on the other, respect, deference,
love, strong attachments and identification of interests.

" As to the remaining part of your question, let me ask, What nation or tribes are capable of such bondage as the Africans at home inflict and bear ? We never had a right to go and steal them, nor to encourage their captors in their pillage and violent seizure of the defenceless creatures ; nor do I think that all the blessings which multitudes of them have received, for both worlds, in consequence of their transportation from Africa, lessens the guilt of slave-traders; nor are these benefits any justification of the trade, nor do they afford ground for its continuance. Nothing can justify it. Such is the voice of the human conscience everywhere except where covetousness or controversy prevail.

" But finding these colored people here, the question upon which you and I differ, is, What is our duty with regard to them ?

" You say, Set them all free. I reply, The relation of ownership on our part toward them is best for all concerned. You say, It is wrong in itself. To say this, I think, is to be more righteous than God."

" Then you maintain," said he, " that the Most High, in the Bible, countenances all the atrocities of American slavery."

" What a strange way," said I, " of arguing, do we very generally find among anti-slavery men, when their feelings are enlisted, as they are so apt to be. They take unwarrantable, extreme inferences from what we say, and oppose these as logical answers to a statement or argument. ' Auction block ' and ' Bunker Hill,' are sufficient answers with them to most of our reasoning on this subject. But let us look at this point in a dispassionate manner.

" But," said I, " before I begin I wish to be distinctly

understood as holding this doctrine; namely, The Bible
does not justify us in reducing men to bondage at our
will.   God might appoint that certain tribes should be
slaves to others ; but before we proceed to reduce men to
slavery, our warrant for it must be clear.

"If, however, slavery is found by a certain generation
among them, and it is not right and just nor expedient to
abolish it, may we not safely ask, How did the Most
High legislate concerning slavery among the people to
whom he gave a code of laws from his own lips?

"Learning this, we must then consider whether circumstances in our day warrant, or require, different rules
and regulations.

"But our inquiry into the divine legislation respecting
slavery, will disclose some things which draw largely
upon one's implicit faith in the divine goodness; and
if a man is disposed to be a sceptic and his anti-slavery
feelings are strong, here is a stone on which, if that anti-
slavery man falls, he shall be broken, but if it falls on
him, it shall grind him to powder.

"You will acknowledge this, if you will allow me to
speak further on this subject.

"Did you ever notice," said I, "with what words Christ
concludes his enunciation of the golden rule?   They are
a remarkable answer to our modern infidels, who im-
pugn the Old Testament as far behind the New in its
moral standard.   After declaring that the rule by which
we should treat others is self-love, the Saviour says, —
'for this is the Law and the Prophets.'   So there was
nothing in the Law and Prophets inconsistent with the
golden rule.   The golden rule therefore marks the history of divine legislation, from the beginning; and if God
appointed slavery, he ordained nothing in connection with

7 *

it which was inconsistent with equal love to one's self
and to a neighbor.

" This deserves to be considered by those who, finding
slavery in the Old Testament appointed by God, begin,
as it were, to exculpate their Maker by saying that the
Hebrews were a rude, semi-barbarous people, and that divine legislation was wisely accommodated to their moral
capacity. Now it is singular, if this be so, that the Mosaic
code should be the basis, as it is, of all good legislation
everywhere. The effort to make the Hebrew people
and their code appear inferior, in order to excuse slavery,
is one illustration of the direful effect which anti-slavery
principles have had in lowering the respect of many for
the Bible, and loosening its hold upon their consciences.
Now it is to me a perfect relief on this subject of slavery
in the Old Testament, to know that God appointed nothing in the relation of his people to men of any class or
condition which his people in a change of circumstances,
might not be willing should be administered to them. If
slavery was ordained of God to the Hebrews, it must,
therefore, have been benevolent. If we start with the
doctrine that 'Slavery is the sum of all villanies,' no
wonder that we find it necessary to use extenuating words
and a sort of apologetic, protecting manner of treating
the divine oracles. After all it is evidently hard work,
with many anti-slavery men to maintain that reverence
for the Old Testament and that confidence in God which
they feel are required of them. So they lay all the responsibility of imperfection in the divine conduct, to the
' semi-barbarous Hebrews ! ' — a people by the way,
whose first leader combined in himself a greater variety,
and a higher order, of talent, than any other man in history. As military commander, poet, historian, judge,

legislator, who is to be named in comparison with the man Moses?

"We must come to the conclusion," said I, "that the relation of ownership is not only not sinful, but that it is in itself benevolent, that it had a benevolent object; for its origin was certainly benevolent."

"What was its origin?" said Mrs. North; "I always had a desire to know how slavery first came into existence."

"Blackstone tells us," I replied, "that its origin was in the right of a captor to commute the death of his captives with bondage. The laws of war give the conqueror a right to destroy his enemies; if he sees fit to spare their lives in consideration of their serving him, this is also his right. Thus, we suppose, slavery gained its existence.

"True, its very nature partakes of our fallen condition; it is not a paradisiacal institution; it is not good in itself; it is an accompaniment of the loss which we have incurred by sin. In that light it is proper to speak of the Most High as adapting his legislation to the depraved condition of man; but that is no more true of slavery than of redemption; everything in the treatment of us by the Almighty is an exponent of our departure from our first estate."

"Now," said Mrs. North, "all this is a relief to me; for I have always been sorely tried by remarks seemingly impugning the divine wisdom and goodness, whenever slavery in the Bible has been under discussion."

"Please give us an outline," said Mr. North, "of the Hebrew legislation on this subject." He handed me a Bible.

"I will try and not be tedious," said I, "and will repeat

to you in few words the principal points of the Hebrew
Code, with regard to involuntary servitude.

"Slavery is the first thing named in the law given at
Sinai, after the moral law and a few simple directions as
to altars. This is noticeable. In the twenty-first chapter of Exodus, and in the twenty-fifth chapter of Leviticus, we find the Hebrew slave-code. The following
is a summary of it: —

"1. Hebrews themselves might be bought and sold by
Hebrews; but for six years only, at farthest. If the
jubilee year occurred at any time during these six years,
it cut short the term of service.

"2. Hebrew paupers were an exception to this rule.
They could be retained till the year of jubilee next en-
suing.

"3. Hebrew servants, married in servitude, if they went
out free in the seventh, or in the jubilee year, must go
out alone, leaving their wives which their masters had
given them, and their children by these wives, (if any,)
behind them, as their masters' possession. If, however,
they chose to remain with their wives and children, the
ear of the servant was bored with an awl to the door-
post, and his servitude became perpetual.

"4. Hebrew servants might also, from love to their
masters, in like manner and by the same ceremony, become servants forever.

"5. Strangers and sojourners among the Hebrews,
'waxing rich,' were allowed to buy Hebrews who were
'waxen poor,' and who were at liberty to sell themselves to these sojourners or to the family of these strangers. The jubilee year, however, terminated this servitude. The price of sale was graduated according to the

number of years previous to the jubilee year. The kindred of the servant had the right of redeeming him, the price being regulated in the same way.

"6. In all these cases in which Hebrews were bought and sold, there were special injunctions that they should not be treated 'with rigor,' the reason assigned by the Most High being substantially the same in all cases, namely, 'For unto me the children of Israel are servants; they are my servants whom I brought forth out of the land of Egypt: I am the Lord your God.'

"7. Liberal provision was to be made for the Hebrew servant at the termination of his servitude. During his term of service, he was to be regarded and treated 'as an hired servant and a sojourner.'

"8. Bondmen and bondmaids, as property, without limitation of time, and transmissible as inheritance to children, might be bought of surrounding nations. The children of sojourners also could be thus acquired. To these the seventh year's and the fiftieth year's release did not apply.

"Now, Mr. North," said I, "let me proceed to try your faith somewhat. I will see whether your confidence in divine revelation is sound, for nothing at the present day has overthrown the faith of many like the manifest teachings of the Bible with regard to slavery. You have felt that the Hebrew code is better than ours, so far as it relates to slaves who were Hebrews. As to the slaves from the heathen, we infer that they met 'with rigor,' or at least were liable to it; for God continually enjoins it upon the Hebrews that they shall not use rigor with their brethren.

"Now let me mention some things which will try your faith in revelation, if you are an abolitionist.

" The Hebrews were allowed to sell their servants to other people.

" Thus they traded in flesh and blood. This was prohibited in the case of a Hebrew maid-servant, whom a man had bought and had made her his concubine. If she did not please him, it was said that — ' to sell her unto a strange nation he shall have no power.' The inference is that they sold their Gentile slaves, if they pleased, ' to a strange nation.' Again. When a father or mother became poor, their creditor could take their children for servants. Thus you read : ' Now there cried a certain woman of the wives of the sons of the prophets unto Elisha saying, Thy servant my husband is dead, and thou knowest that thy servant did fear the Lord ; and the creditor is come to take unto him my two sons to be bondmen.' This was according to the law of Moses, in the twenty-fifth of Leviticus ; ' bondmen,' however, meaning here a servant for a term of years. See also the New Testament parable of the unforgiving servant.

" This was hard, it will seem to you and to all of us, that if one became poor in Israel, his children could be attached. Thus the idea of involuntary servitude, where no crime was, prevailed in the Theocracy.

" But we come now to something which draws harder upon our faith.

" We find the Most High prescribing, Exodus xxi. 20, 21, that a master who kills his servant under chastisement shall be punished (but not put to death) ; and if the servant survives a day or two, the master shall not even be ' punished ' for the death of his slave !

" The reason which the Most High gives is this : ' *For he is his money* ' !

" A human being, ' money ' ! An immortal soul,

'money'! God's image, 'money'! And this the reasoning, these the very words of my Maker! Is it not
astonishing, if your principles are correct, that there has
been no controversy for ages against this? and that the
Bible, with such passages in it should have retained its
hold on the human mind? 'He is his money'! It
would have been no different had it read: 'He is his
cotton.' You see that the Most High recognized 'ownership,' 'property in man.' Why is it said, 'He is his
money'? Poole (Synopsis) says, — 'that is, his possession bought with money; and therefore 1. Had a power
to chastise him according to his merit, which might be
very great. 2. Is sufficiently punished with his own
loss. 3. May be presumed not to have done this purposely or maliciously.'

"Either and all of which explanations, or any other
which can be given, only bring more clearly to view the
idea of 'money' as a reason why the master is not to be
punished, for causing the death of a slave by whipping,
if the slave happens to continue a day or two, no matter
under what mutilations and sufferings.

"Furthermore. We find the Most High decreeing
perpetual bondage in certain cases, and more than all,
as we have seen, *the forcible separation of husband and
wife* among slaves. Let me turn to Exodus xxi. and
read : —

"'1. Now these are the judgments which thou shalt set before them.

"'2. If thou buy an Hebrew servant, six years he shall
serve : and in the seventh he shall go out free for nothing.

"'3. If he came in by himself, he shall go out by himself:
if he were married, then his wife shall go out with him.

"'4. If his master have given him a wife and she have

borne him sons or daughters, *the wife and her children shall be her master's*, and he shall go out by himself.'

"I have not finished my reading," said I ; " but what do you say to that, Mr. North ? "

" Read on," said he.

" ' 5. And if the servant shall plainly say, I love my master, my wife, and my children, I will not go out free :

" ' 6. Then his master shall bring him unto the judges, he shall also bring him to the door, or unto the door-post, and his master shall bore his ear through with an awl, and he shall serve him forever.'

" God decreed, therefore, that the marriage of a slave in bondage, in those days, was dissoluble, as no other marriage was.   Divorces among the Hebrews, allowed for the hardness of their hearts, were not parallel to the forcible separation of a slave from his wife under the hard necessity of choice between perpetual bondage with a wife, or freedom without her. The merciful God who kindly enacted, ' No man shall take the nether nor the upper millstone to pledge : for he taketh a man's life to pledge,' and that a garment pawned should be restored before sundown, that wages should not be withheld over night, yes, the God who legislated about bird's-nests ordained the dissolution of the marriage tie between slaves in certain cases, unless the slave husband was willing for his wife's sake, to be a slave forever !

" What do you say to this, Mr. North ? " I asked again.

Said Mrs. North, " I begin to see the origin and cause of infidelity among the abolitionists."

" Tell me," said Mr. North, " how you view it."

" On stating this, once," said I, " in a public meeting, I raised a clamor.   Three or four men sprung to their feet, and one of them, who first caught the chairman's eye, cried out, his face turning red, his eyes starting from their sockets, his fist clenched, 'I demand of the gentleman whether he means to approve of all the abominations of American slavery! Is he in favor of separating husbands and wives, parents and children? Let us know it, Sir, if it be so. No wonder that strong anti-slavery men turn infidels when they hear Christian men defending American slavery from the Bible. No wonder that they say, "The times demand, and we must have, an anti-slavery constitution, an anti-slavery Bible, and an anti-slavery God." Mr. Moderator, will the gentleman answer my question, — Do you mean to approve all the atrocities of American slavery, on the ground that the Bible countenances them?'

"I was never more calm in my life. I replied, 'Mr. Chairman, taking for my warrant an inspired piece of advice as to the best way of answering a man according to his folly, it would be just, should I reply to the gentleman's question, Yes, I do. But the gentleman, I perceive, is too much excited to hear me.'

"He had flung himself round in his seat, put his elbow on the back of it, and his hand through his hair; he then flung himself round in the opposite direction, and put his arm and hand as before, and he blew his nose with a sound like a trombone.

"I then said, 'Mr. Chairman, if all that the gentleman meant to ask was, Do you find any countenance under any circumstances, for the relation of master and slave in the divine legation of Moses, — and this was all which, as a fair man, not carried away by a gust of passion, he should have asked me, — my answer was correct and proper. If he wished to know my views of what is right and proper as to the marriage relation of our slaves, he should have put the question in a different shape. But first, Sir,' said I, 'if he dislikes the twenty-first chapter of Exodus, his controversy must be with his God, not with me. Sinai was, let me remind him, more of a place than Bunker Hill. I am not a friend of "oppression" any more than the gentleman; but I trust that had I lived in Israel, I should never have thought of being more humane than my Maker.'

"I then proceeded to say that (as before remarked to you) we are not warranted by the Bible to make men slaves when we please; nor, if slavery exists, are we commanded to adopt the rules and regulations of Hebrew slavery.

"But we do learn from the Bible that property in man is not in itself sinful, — not even to say of a man, 'He is my money.'

"Were it intrinsically wrong, God would not have legislated about it in such ways; for granting, if you please, the untenable distinction about his 'not appointing' slavery, but 'finding it in existence' and legislating for it, what necessity could there have been for making such a law as that relating to the boring of the ear, rather than giving the slave his wife and children and suffering them all to go free?

"No, Mr. North," said I, continuing our conversation, "I cannot oppose the relation of master and slave as in itself sinful; for then I become more righteous than God. But I must inquire whether it is right, in each given case, to reduce men to bondage: shall that be, for example, the mode in which prisoners of war shall be disposed of? or a subjugated people? or criminals? or, in certain cases, debtors? 'In doing so, there is no intrinsic sin;

the act itself, under the circumstances, may be exceedingly sinful; but the relation of ownership is not necessarily a sin. This, I hold, is all that can be deduced from the Bible in favor of slavery: The relation is not in itself sinful."

" But," said Mr. North, " we sinned in stealing these people from Africa; all sin should be immediately forsaken; therefore, set the slaves free at once."

I replied, " Let us apply that principle. You and I, and a large company of passengers, are in a British ship, approaching our coast. We find out, all at once, that the crew and half of the passengers stole the ship. We gain the ascendency; we can do as we please. Now, as all sin must be repented of at once, it is the duty of the passengers and crew to put the ship about, and deliver it to the owners in Glasgow! Perhaps we should not think it best to put in force the ' ruat cœlum ' doctrine, especially if we had had some ' ruat cœlum ' storms, and it was late in the season. But then we should actually be enjoying the stolen property — the ship and its comforts — for several days, with the belief that benevolence and justice to all concerned required us to reach the end of the voyage before we took measures to perform that justice, which, before, would have been practical folly.

" Now, please, do not require this illustration to go on all fours. All that I mean is this: A right thing may be wrong, if done unseasonably, or in disregard of circumstances which have supervened.

" But to go a little further, and beyond mere expediency: Can you see no difference between buying slaves, and making men slaves? While it would be wicked for you to reduce people to slavery, is that the same as becoming owners to those who are already in

slavery? In one case, you could not apply the golden
rule; in the other, the golden rule would absolutely compel you, in many instances, to buy slaves. Go to almost
any place where slaves are sold, and they will come to
you, if they like your looks, and, by all the arts of persuasion, entreat you to become their master. Having
succeeded, step behind the scenes, if you can, and hear
them exulting that they 'fetched more' than this or that
man. Is there no difference between this and reducing
free people to slavery?"

"Say yes, husband," said Mrs. North, "or I must say
it for you."

"So that, let me add," said I, "in opposing slavery, I
am necessarily confined to the evils and abuses committed in the relationship of master. But, even in doing
this, why should I be meddlesome? We have a most
offensive air and manner in our behavior towards Southerners, in connection with their duties as masters. It
is perfectly disgusting. I may oppose slavery, on the
grounds of political economy or for national reasons.
But if I mix up with it wrathful opposition to the sin,
so called, or the unrighteousness of holding property in
man, it has no countenance in the Bible. If I speak of
it publicly, as a system fraught with evil, I must discriminate; or they whom I would influence, knowing that I
am mistaken, will regard me as an infatuated enemy,
who will effect more injury than I can repair. As to
Mr. Jefferson's testimony, there are as good and conscientious men at the South in our day as Thomas Jefferson. Mr. Calhoun was as worthy a witness in all
respects."

"Now tell us," said Mrs. North, "your sober convictions, apart from this Northern controversy, about

that twenty-first chapter of Exodus, where God directs
that slaves, in certain cases, shall be slaves forever; and,
moreover, in certain cases, that slave husbands may have
their wives and children withheld from them, and the
husbands leave them forever. How do you reconcile this
with the justice and goodness of God?"

I said to her, "To make the case fully appear, before
we converse upon it, hear this passage, Leviticus xxv.
44–46 : — 'Both thy bondmen, and thy bondmaids, which
thou shalt have, shall be of the heathen that are round
about you; of them shall ye buy bondmen and bondmaids.' So, in the next verses, 'The children of the
strangers that do sojourn among you, of them shall ye
buy, and of their families that are with you, which they
begat in your land; and they shall be your possession:
And ye shall take them as an inheritance for your children after you, to inherit them for a possession; they
shall be your bondmen forever; but over your brethren,
the children of Israel, ye shall not rule one over another
with rigor.'

"Here, and in all the divine legislation on this subject, a distinction is made between Hebrews who became
slaves, and slaves who were foreigners, or of foreign extraction, though resident in Israel. Slaves of Hebrew
extraction might go free after six years, and upon the
death of the owner; and in every jubilee year they must
all return to freedom, and be free from every disability by
reason of bondage, except where the ear was bored.

"Not so with the slaves of foreign extraction; nor
even with the Hebrew whose ear was bored, provided
his wife was given him in slavery, and he had elected to
live with her rather than be free. Not even upon the
death of the owner could such slaves be manumitted, as

was the case ordinarily with regard to Hebrew slaves ; but property in these Gentile slaves, and in Hebrew slaves reduced to the same condition, God ordained should be an 'inheritance,' passing down forever from father to child.

"No jubilee trumpet was to cheer their hearts. Think what the jubilee morning must have been to those slaves in hopeless bondage, if bondage were necessarily such as many fancy. Our abolitionists represent the bells and guns of our Fourth of July to be a hideous mockery in the ears of the slaves ; and multitudes of our good people ludicrously fancy them as most miserable on that day, by the contrast of their enslaved condition with our boasted Independence. Let us borrow this fancy, and apply it to the Hebrew slave.

"The jubilee trumpets, and all the joyous scenes of the fiftieth year in Israel, caused multitudes of slaves in Israel, we will suppose, to reflect, This Jehovah, God of Israel, has doomed us to hopeless bondage. We are guilty of having been born so many degrees south or north, east or west, of these Hebrews. We, by God's providence, are Gentiles. Our chiefs sold us, and these Hebrews bought us. We were betrayed ; we were driven out of our homes ; unjust wars were made upon us, to make us captives, that we might be sold. And 'the Lord's people' bought us, by his special edict (Lev. xxv. 44). Our brother-servants, unfortunate Hebrews, get released in the jubilee year, except these poor creatures who were so unfortunate as to be married in slavery, and, not being willing to be divorced, had their ears fastened, with the ignominious 'awl,' to their master's door-post. God could have ordained that they, with their wives and children, and we, with ours, should have release in the fiftieth year. But, no! our bondage is forever, and so is theirs; and our children and their children are to be servants forever. But we hold it to be a self-evident truth that all men are born free and equal, and have an inalienable right to life, liberty, and the pursuit of happiness. Slavery is the sum of all villanies. Our master's will is our law; we are subject to his passions; we are chattels; we 'are his money.' This is the language of your God, — the God whom you worship; and not only so, but you circumcise us to worship Him!

"Some benevolent Levite, jealous for the character of his Maker, replies, 'But God did not institute slavery; He found it in existence, and he only legislates about it, and regulates it.'

"A thousand groans are the prelude to the withering answer which the slaves make to this apology for oppression.

"'He broke your bonds, it seems,' they cry, 'in Egypt, and in the Red Sea. Did He "find slavery" on the opposite shore of the Red Sea? Why did he not merely "legislate for it, and regulate it?" No, He enacted it. How dare you apologize for your God with such a miserable pretext? He made the ordinance separating a husband from wife and children, unless the husband would submit to the indignity of having his ear bored and to the doom of perpetual bondage, in case his wife was a Gentile. If he goes away, he must leave his wife and children. Great indulgence have you in multiplying wives; that is winked at "for the hardness of your hearts;" but the poor Hebrew must abandon his wife and family if he chooses freedom! They are his master's "property," "his money," and God gave the servant these children, knowing that they would be the "property" of another, and that he would have no unencumbered right to them; and down through all ages they and their descendants must be servants. And now you tell us, "God did not institute" this! He only "found it!" He "regulated it!" Come, blow up your trumpet, reverend Levite! Go, worship the God of whom you feel half ashamed. Do not ask us to worship and love a Being who is bound by the laws of fate so that he cannot do otherwise, if he would, than make one of us a slave forever, while the man who grinds with me at the same mill, goes with his wife and children, forever free!'"

"Those remarks have the true Boston tone," said Mrs. North.

"Yes," said I, "there were brave men before Agamemnon, Horace tells us. There is slavery forever," said I, "or the separation of husband and wife, father and children, unless the man would be a slave forever. What 'partings' there must have been! What struggles in those who concluded to take the fatal 'awl' through their ears, before they could make up their minds to be slaves forever. See the hardship of the case. If the man 'loves his wife and children,' he may be a slave; that love would make him spend and be spent for them in freedom, in his humble home, amid the sweets of liberty; but no; if he loves his wife he must take the bitter draught of slavery with his love. But if he hates her and his children, he may be free! What a bounty on conjugal fickleness, on unnatural treatment of offspring!"

"Was there no Canada?" said Mrs. North, biting off her thread. "O, I recollect; Hagar went there. I wonder if the angel who remanded her was removed from office, on his return to heaven."

"Come, wife," said Mr. North, "there is such a thing

as being converted too much. Please, Sir, will you answer the question as to the consistency of all this with the divine wisdom and goodness ? "

" That," said I, " is not the question which you wish to ask."

" I do not understand you," said he ; " please to explain."

" You wish to ask," said I, " how I reconcile these things with your notions of wisdom and benevolence."

" Why," said he, " I have my ideas of divine wisdom and goodness, and I wish to make these things square with them."

" And that," said I, " is just the rock on which you all split. Your ideas of the divine goodness must be based on a complete view of the revealed character and conduct of God. But you and your friends say, ' this and that ought to be, or ought not to be,' and you try your Maker by that measure. Now I say, ' he that reproveth God, let him answer it.' Are not the things which I have quoted, parts of divine revelation, as much as the flood and the passover ? "

" I see that they are," said Mr. North.

" Do you believe that God is a spirit infinite, eternal, unchangeable, in his being, wisdom, power, holiness, justice, goodness, and truth ? "

" I do," said he.

" You believe this notwithstanding the apostasy, the destruction of Sodom and Gomorrah, the flood, and the extirpation of the Canaanites."

" I do," said he, " so long as I receive the Bible as the Word of God."

" I think," said Mrs. North, " that the loss of the ' Central America' with her four hundred passengers,

8

tries my faith in God full as much as a heathen's having his ear bored to spend his days with his wife and children among God's covenant people."

"Then you do not worship the Goddess of Liberty, Mrs. North," said I. — " 'Art thou called being a servant? Care not for it. But if thou mayest be made free, use it rather.' "

"That," said she, " seems to express my idea about bondage and freedom. Of course it is not, theoretically, a blessing to be a slave. It may be, practically, to some. But what strikes me oftentimes is the utter inability of an abolitionist to say to a slave, under any circumstances, 'Care not for it.' His doctrine, rather, is, 'Art thou called being a servant? If thou hast a Sharpe's rifle, or a John Brown's pike, use it rather.' Or, ' Art thou called being a servant? If thou canst run for Canada, use it rather.' Paul had not an abolitionist mind, that is very clear. But," she continued, " do relieve my husband and enlighten me also, by giving us your views about the Old Testament slavery, which I presume you can do without seeming to arraign the character of God."

I replied, "This is a sinful race, and we are treated as such. Slavery is one of God's chastisements. Instead of destroying every wicked nation by war, pestilence, or famine, he grants some of them a reprieve, and commutes their punishment from death to bondage. Those whom he allowed to be slaves to his people Israel were highly favored; they enjoyed a blessing which came to them disguised by the sable cloud of servitude; but in their endless happiness many of them will bless God for the bondage which joined them to the nation of Israel.

"I look upon our slaves as being here by a special

design of Providence, for some great purpose, to be dis-
closed at the right time.   Unless I take this view of
it, I am embarrassed and greatly troubled; 'perplexed,
but not in despair.'   The great design of Providence
in no wise abates the sin of those who brought the slaves
here, nor does it warrant us in getting more of them.
While this is true, I cannot resist the thought that God
has a controversy with this black race which is not yet
finished.   I believe that God withholds from them a
spirit and temper suited for freedom till he shall have
finished his marvellous designs.   His destiny with the
Jew, as a nation, to the present day, is another illustration of his mysterious providence with regard to a
people.

"As to the enactment which made the Hebrew servant a slave for life, thus dooming even one of the covenant people to perpetual bondage, if he had married in
slavery, I see in it several things most clearly.

"You will have noticed that in every case in which a
Hebrew was made a servant, poverty was the ground
of it.   'If thy brother be waxen poor,' he could sell himself, either to a Hebrew or to a resident alien.   He and
his children could also be taken for debt.   This seems
to us oppressive.

"Let a family among us be reduced, from any cause,
to a condition in which they cannot maintain themselves,
and what follows?   The children find employment, some
of them in families, in various kinds of domestic service.
Indented apprenticeships in this commonwealth are within the memory of all who are forty or fifty years of age.
We remember the very frequent advertisements: 'One
cent reward.   Ran away from the subscriber, an indented apprentice,' etc.   The descriptions of such fugitives,

all for the sake of absolving the master from liability for the absconding boy, and sometimes the hunt that was made, with dogs to scent his tracks, when his return was desired, are far within the memory of the oldest inhabitant.

"In Israel, this descent of a family from a prosperous to a decayed state, and the consequent servitude, were used by the Most High to cultivate some of the best feelings of our nature. It touched the finest sensibilities of the soul. Let me read from the fifteenth of Deuteronomy : —

"'And if thy brother, an Hebrew n woman, be sold unto thee, and serve thee six years, then in the seventh year thou shalt let him go free from thee.

"'And when thou sendest him out free from thee, thou shalt not let him go away empty.

"'Thou shalt furnish him liberally out of thy flock, and out of thy floor, and out of thy wine-press : of that wherewith the Lord thy God hath blessed thee thou shalt give unto him. And thou shalt remember that thou wast a bondman in the land of Egypt, and the Lord thy God redeemed thee : therefore I command thee this thing to-day.

"'And if it shall be, if he say unto thee, I will not go away from thee ; because he loveth thee and thine house, because he is well with thee,

"'Then thou shalt take an awl and thrust it through his ear unto the door, and he shall be thy servant forever. And also with thy maid-servant thou shalt do likewise.

"'It shall not seem hard unto thee when thou sendest him away free from thee : for he hath been worth a doubled hired servant to thee, in serving thee six years ; and the Lord thy God shall bless thee in all that thou doest.'

"Is not this very beautiful and touching, Mrs. North ?"
She said nothing, but hid her face in her little babe's

neck, pretending to kiss it. But Mr. North wiped his eyes. "There is not much barbarism in that," said he.

"The golden rule," said I; "for this is the law and the prophets.

"The people to whom these touching precepts were given by the Most High, and who were susceptible to these finest appeals, are, as we have said, sometimes represented as a semi-barbarous people, so gross that God was obliged to let them hold slaves! Now, could anything be more civilizing, refining, elevating, than such relationships as this limited servitude of poor Hebrews created? What scenes there must have been oftentimes, when the six years were out, and the servant was about to depart, laden with gifts! And what a scene when, with strong attachment to the family, the servant declined to be free, and went to the door-post to have his ear pierced with the awl, to be a servant, and not only so, but to be an inheritance forever!

"Is this 'the sum of all villanies,' Mr. North?" said I. "Yet it is 'slavery.' 'Auction-blocks,' 'whippings,' 'roastings,' 'separations of families,' are not 'slavery.' They are its abuses; slavery can exist when they cease. I pray you, is such slavery as the God of the Hebrews appointed, in such cases as these, 'forever,' an unmitigated curse?

"Now," said I, "go through our Southern country, and you will find in every city, town, and village just such relationships between the whites and the blacks as must have existed where these Hebrew laws had effect. Think of the little slave-babe, and the Southern lady's letter, which have given occasion to all our conversation. The Gospel, as it subdues and softens the human heart, will make the relationship of involuntary servitude every-where to be after this pattern. Instead of exciting ha-tred and jealousy, and provoking war between the whites and blacks, I am for bringing all the influences of the Gospel to bear upon the hearts of the white population, to convert them into such masters as God enjoined the Hebrews to be, and such as the Apostle to the Gentiles enjoined upon Gentile slave-holders as their models. And I am filled with sorrow and astonishment as I see some of the very best and most beloved men among us at the North withholding missionaries and tracts from the Southern country, and — as Gustavus's aunt said some of these do — calling it ' standing up for Jesus ! '

" Now," said I, " if such were the injunctions of the Most High as to the manner in which the Hebrews should treat their Hebrew slaves, it is easy to see that such a habit with regard to them would serve greatly to mitigate the sorrows of bondage on the part of Gentile slaves. And thus the curse of slavery, like sin, and even death, is made, under the influences of religion, a means of improvement, a source of blessing. Let but the sun shine on a pile of cloud, and what folds of beauty and deep banks of snowy whiteness does it set forth, and, at the close of day, all the exquisite tints which make the artist despair are flung profusely upon that mass of va-por which but for the sun were a heap of sable cloud.

" The minister," said I, " who, Hattie tells us, classed ' Abraham the slave-holder ' with the ' murderer,' and the ' liar and swearer,' knew not what he did. People who laugh and titter at the ' patriarchal institution,' need to peruse the laws of Moses again, with a spirit akin to their beautiful tone ; and those who say that to hold a fellow-

man as property is 'sin,' are not 'wiser than Daniel,' but
they make themselves wiser than God.

"All who sustain the relationship of owner to a human
being," said I, "do well to read these injunctions of the
Most High, as very many of them do, applying them to
themselves.   And it is also profitable to read how that a
violation of these very slave-laws was, in after years, one
great cause of the divine wrath upon the Hebrews.
You will find, in the thirty-fourth of Jeremiah, that, not
content with having Gentile slaves, the Hebrews violated
the law requiring them to release each his Hebrew slaves
once in seven years.

"'I made a covenant with your fathers,' God says, 'in
the day that I brought them forth out of the land of
Egypt, saying, At the end of seven years let ye go every
man his brother an Hebrew which hath been sold unto
thee.   But ye turned and polluted my name, and caused
every man his servant to return, and brought them unto
subjection.   Ye have not hearkened unto me in pro-
claiming a liberty every one to his brother; — behold,
I proclaim a liberty for you, saith the Lord, to the sword,
to the pestilence, and to the famine.'

"Thus it is evident that the relation of master and
servant was originally ordained and instituted by God as
a benevolent arrangement to all concerned, — not 'winked
at,' or 'suffered,' like polygamy, but ordained, — that it
was full of blessings to all who fulfilled the duties of the
relation in the true spirit of the institution ; and, moreover, it is true that there are few curses which will be
more intolerable than they will suffer who make use of
their fellow-men, in the image of God, for the purposes
of selfishness and sin ; while those who feel their accoun-
tableness in this relation, and discharge it in the spirit of

the Bible, will find their hearts refined and ennobled, and the relationship will be, to all concerned, a source of blessings whose influences will bring peace to their souls when the grave of the slave and that of his owner are looking up into the same heavens from the common earth."

CHAPTER VIII.

THE TENURE.

" One part, one little part, we dimly scan
Through the dark medium of life's fevering dream ;
Yet dare arraign the whole stupendous plan
If but that little part incongruous seem ;
Nor is that part, perhaps, what mortals deem ;
Oft from apparent ill our blessings rise." — BEATTIE, *Minstrel.*

MR. North then said, " Let us change the subject a
little.   Please to tell us why, in your view, any
slave who is so disposed may not run away.   Would you
not do so, if you were a slave, and were oppressed, or
thought that you could mend your condition ?   Where
did my master get his right and title to me ?   God did
not institute American slavery as he did slavery among
the Hebrews.   If I were a slave to certain masters,
South or North, I should probably run away at all hazards.   I should not stop to debate the morality of the
act.   No human being would, in his heart blame me.   It
would be human nature, resisting under the infliction of
pain.   We catch hold of a dentist's hand when he is drawing a tooth.   Perhaps there may be found some moral
law against doing so ! "

" But we are apt," said I, " to take these exceptional
cases, and make a rule that includes them and all others.
I have been present when intelligent gentlemen, North-

8 *

erners and Southerners, have discussed this subject in the most friendly manner, though with great earnestness. Once I remember we spent an evening discussing the subject. I will, if you please, tell you about the conversation.

"I must take you, then, to an old mansion at the South, around which, and at such a distance from each other as to reveal a fine prospect, stood a growth of noble elms, a lawn spreading itself out before the house, and the large hall, or entry, serving for a tea-room, where seven or eight gentlemen, and as many ladies were assembled.

"A Southern physician, who had no slaves, took the ground that all the slaves had a right to walk off whenever they pleased. He did not see why we should hold them in bondage rather than they us, so far as right and justice were concerned. Some of the slave-holders were evidently much troubled in their thoughts, and did not speak strongly. My own feelings at first went with the physician and with his arguments; but I saw that he was not very clear, nor deep, and his friends who partly yielded to him, seemed to do so rather under the influence of conscientious feelings, than from any very well defined principles. This is the case with not a few at the South, and it was very common in Thomas Jefferson's days. But the large majority, who were of the contrary opinion, got the advantage in the argument, and it seemed to me went far toward convincing the physician, as they did me, that he was wrong.

"The company all seemed to look toward a judge who was present, to open the discussion with a statement of his views. He did so by saying, for substance, as follows : —

"'I will take it for granted,' said he, 'that we are

agreed as to the unlawfulness of the slave-trade, past and present. We find the blacks here, as we come upon the stage. We are born into this relationship. It is an existing form of government in the Slave States.

" ' Ownership in man is not contrary to the will of God. I also find it written that " Canaan shall be a servant. Hear these words of inspiration : " Cursed be Canaan ; a servant of servants shall he be unto his brethren. And he said, Blessed be the Lord God of Shem ; and Canaan shall be his servant. God shall enlarge Japheth, and he shall dwell in the tents of Shem ; and Canaan shall be his servant." As the Japhetic race is to dwell in the tents of Shem, for example, England occupying India, so I believe the black race is under the divine sentence of servitude. Moreover, being perfectly convinced of the wrongfulness and the infinite mischief to all concerned of the forcible liberation of our slaves, I am assisted in set-tling, in my own mind, the question as to the right of individual slaves to escape from service, and our right to continue in this relationship, conforming ourselves in it always to the golden rule.

" ' If it be the right of one, under ordinary circum-stances, to depart, it is the right of all. But the govern-ment under which they live, in this commonwealth, rec-ognizes slavery. The constitution and the general gov-ernment protect us in maintaining it. The right of our servants to leave us at pleasure, which could not of course be done without violence, on both sides, implies the right of insurrection. It is impossible to define the cases in which insurrection is justifiable, but the general rule is that it is wrong. Government is a divine ordinance ; men cannot capriciously overthrow or change it, at every turn of affairs which proves burdensome or even oppressive. God is jealous to maintain human government as an important element in his own administration. Men justly in authority, or established in it by time, or by consent, or by necessity, or by expediency, may properly feel that they are God's vicegerents. He is on their side; a parent, a teacher, a commander, — in short, he who rules, is, as it were, dispensing a law of the divine government, as truly as though he directed a force in nature. Hence, to disturb existing government is, in the sight of God, a heinous offence, unless circumstances plainly justify a revolution; otherwise, one might as well think to interfere with impunity and change the equinoxes, or the laws of refraction. It is well to consider what forms of government, and what forms of oppression under them, existed, when that divine word was written : "Let every soul be subject unto the higher powers. For there is no power but of God : the powers that be are ordained of God. Whosoever therefore resisteth the power, resisteth the ordinance of God ; and they that resist shall receive to themselves damnation." This was written in view of the throne of the Cæsars.

" ' But it is very clear that when a people are in a condition to establish and maintain another form of government, there is no sin in their turning themselves into a new condition. In doing so, government, God's ordinance, evolves itself under a new form, and provided it is, really, government, and not anarchy, no sin may have been committed by the insurrection, or revolution, as an act. The result proved that government still existed, potentially, and was only changing its shape and adapting itself to the circumstances of the people. If a man or body of men assert that things among them are ready for such new evolutions, and so undertake to bring them about,

they do it at their peril, and failing, they are indictable
for treason; they may be true patriots, they may be conscientious men; the sympathies of many good people may
be with them, but they have sinned against the great law
which protects mankind from anarchy.

" ' To apply this,' said the Judge, ' to our subject, —
When the time comes that the blacks can truly say, " We
are now your equals in all that is necessary to constitute
a civil state, and we propose to take the government of
this part of the country into our hands," we should still
make several objections, which would be valid. The
Constitutions of the States and of the United States must
be changed before that can be done, and we will presume that this would involve a revolution. Moreover,
this country belongs to the Anglo-Saxon race, with which
foreigners of kindred stocks have intermingled, and they
and we object to the presence of a black race as possess-
ors of some of the states of the Union, even if it were
constitutional. We do not propose to abandon our right
and title to the soil, without a civil war, which would
probably result in the extermination of one or the other
party. If you are able to leave us at pleasure, the proper
way will be to do it peaceably, and on just principles, to
be agreed upon between us.

" ' No such exigency as this,' said the Judge, ' is possible. It would be prevented or anticipated, and relief
would be obtained while the necessity was on the increase
and before it reached a solemn crisis.

" ' One of three ways will, in my opinion,' said he,
' bring a solution to this problem of slavery.

" ' One is, the insurrection of the slaves, the massacre
of the whites, and the forcible seizure and possession of
power by the blacks throughout the South. This would

be a scene such as the earth has never witnessed. I have no fear that it can ever happen.   But,' said he, addressing me, ' I presume that I know, Sir, how your people in the Free States, to a very considerable extent, think on this point.   I will speak, by-and-by, of the other two ways in which slavery may find its great result.   One, I say, is, by insurrection and then the extermination of the black race ; for that would surely follow their temporary success if I can trust my apprehensions of the subject.'

" ' Please, sir,' said I, ' let me hear what you think is ' very considerably ' the sentiment at the North on this subject of insurrection.'

" ' I presume sir,' said he, ' if the slaves should, some night, take possession of us, and demand a universal manumission, and we should refuse, and fire and sword and pillage and all manner of violence should ensue, and our persons and property should be at their will, vast multitudes of your people, including clergymen, would exclaim that the day of God's righteous vengeance had come, and they would say, Amen.'

" ' So we interpret Thomas Jefferson's idea,' said I.

" ' I think, Sir,' said he, ' that very many reasonable people of the North are of opinion that all the attributes of God are against any such procedure.

" ' In the large sense in which nations speak to each other when they are asserting their rights, there is no objection to the first clause in the Declaration of Independence ; but when you come to the people of a state, and one portion of that people rise and assert their right to break up the constitution of things under which they live, there is no more pertinency in that clause in the Declaration than there would be in giving us the reason for a revolution that all men are not far from five or six feet high. What they say may be true in the abstract, but it does not prove that men, having come into a state of society, involuntarily, if you please, have all the freedom and equality which they would have, if they were each an independent savage in the wilderness. Society is God's ordinance, not a compact. We have, all of us, lost some of our freedom and equality in the social state; now how far is it right that the blacks, being here, no matter how or why, should lose some of theirs? and how far is it right that we should take and keep some of it from them, whether for the good of all concerned, or for the good of ourselves, their civil superiors? — whose welfare, it may be observed, will continually affect theirs.'

"The Judge said that he believed that God had, in his mysterious providence, and of his sovereign pleasure, making use of the cupidity of white men, placed these blacks here in connection with us for their good as a race, and for the welfare of the world. He said that his mind could feel no peace on the subject of slavery, unless he viewed it in this light. In connection with the great industrial and commercial interests of our globe, and as an indispensable element in the supply of human wants, this abject race had been transported from their savage life in Africa, and had been made immensely useful to the whole civilized world. 'We agree, as I have said,' he continued, 'as to the immorality of those who brought them here; but he is not fit to reason on this subject, being destitute of all proper notions with regard to divine providence, who does not see in the results of slavery, both as to the civilized world and to negroes themselves, a wise, benevolent, and an Almighty Hand. Here my mind gets relief in contemplating this subject, not in abstract reasoning, not in logical premises and deductions, but by resting in Providence.   There are mysteries in it, —as truly so as in the human apostasy, origin of evil, permission of sin, which confound my reasonings as to the benevolence of God ; in which, however, I, nevertheless, maintain my firm belief.   Here was the great defect in Mr. Jefferson's views of slavery.   In the highest Christian sense, he was not qualified to understand this subject ; he reasoned like one who did not take into view the providence and the purposes of God, even while he was saying what he did of there being "no attribute in the Almighty that would take part with us" in favor of slavery.   Standing as I do by this providential view of the great subject, the assailants of slavery at the North seem to me, some of them, almost insane, and others, even ministers of the Gospel, shall I say it ? more than unchristian ; —there is a sort of blind, wild, French Jacobinical atheism in their feeling and behavior ; while as to the rest, good people, they are misled by what Mr. Webster, in one of his speeches in the Senate, called "the constant rub-a-dub of the press," — "no drum-head," he says, "in the longest day's march, having been more incessantly beaten than the feeling of the public in certain parts of the North."   I cannot reason with these men,' continued the Judge, 'for I confess, at once, that I cannot demonstrate, either by logic or by mathematics, a modern quitclaim or warranty in holding slaves.   In combating their illogical and unscriptural positions, I seem to them to be an advocate of the divine right of oppression, —which I am not.   That it is best, however, and that it is right, for this relation to continue until God shall manifest some purpose to terminate it consistently with the good of all concerned, I am perfectly convinced and satisfied.   I believe that it has reference to the great plan of mercy toward our world, and that when the object is accomplished, the providence of God will, in some way, make it known. It may be the case, no candid man and believer in revelation and divine providence will deny it to be possible, that this dispensation with regard to this colored race will continue for long ages to come, in the form of bondage. That they are now under a curse, and have been so for centuries, is apparent. When the curse is to be repealed, God only knows. I like to cherish the idea that some development is to be made of immense sources of wealth in Africa, that we have an embryo nation in the midst of us, whom God has been educating for a great enterprise on that continent, and when, like California and Australia, the voice of the Lord shall shake the wilderness of Africa, and open its doors, it may appear that American slavery has been the school in which God has been preparing a people to take it into their possession.

"'EMIGRATION, then,' said he, 'is the second of the three ways in which this problem of slavery may have its solution.

"'In preparation for this, I say, God may keep these Africans here much longer. He may need more territory on which to educate still larger numbers; and we may see Him extending slavery still further in our land and on our continent. So that there may be one other way in which the purposes of God will manifest themselves with regard to the colored race here, and that is by EX-TENSION.

"'It may be that still greater portions of this land and continent are to be used, for ages to come, in the multiplication of the black race. I feel entirely calm with regard to the subject, believing that God has a plan in all this, and that it is wise and benevolent toward all who fear Him. While our relation to this people remains, the law of love, the golden rule, must preside over it. That does not require us to place the blacks on a level with us in our parlors, nor in our halls of legislation; and there may be disabilities properly attaching to them which, though they seem hard, are the inevitable consequence of a dependent, inferior condition. All this, however, has a benign effect upon us, if we will but act in a Christian manner, to make us gentle, kind, generous; and when this is the case, no state of society is happier than ours. Let Jacobinical principles, such as some of our Northern brethren inculcate, prevail here, and they at once destroy this benevolent relation. This relation will improve under the influence of the Gospel; it has wonderfully improved since Jefferson's day; and though the time may be long deferred, we shall no doubt see this colored race fulfilling some great purpose in the earth. I trust that our Northern friends will not precipitate things and destroy both whites and blacks; for a servile war would be one of extermination. Many of the Northern people I fear would acquiesce in it, provided especially, that we should be the exterminated party. This is clear, if words and actions are to be fairly interpreted.'

" 'The colored people here, as a race,' said a planter, 'are under obligations to us as partakers in our civilization. No matter, for the present, how their ancestors came here; — that does not at all affect their present obligations to us for benefits received. Now it is not a matter of course that, having been thus benefited by us, they are at liberty to go away when they please. This we assert respecting them as a whole. Are not the blacks, as a race, so indebted to us that we ought to be consulted as to the time and manner of their departure? We say that they are. They do not morally possess the right, we think, to sever the relation when they please.'

'Said an elderly, venerable man, 'A white woman in the cars, in Pennsylvania, begged me to hold her infant child for her, while she fetched something for it. She ran off, leaving the child to me. My wife and I took the child home, and have been at pains and expense with it. I question the child's right to say, whenever it pleases, Sir, I propose to leave you. I have invested a good deal in him, have increased his value by his being with me, and he has no right to run off with it.'

"'But,' said the physician, 'how long should you feel that you have a right to his services?'

"'I will answer that,' said the gentleman, 'if you will say whether my general principle be correct. Have I, or have I not acquired just what all intelligent slave-holders call "property" in that youth, that is, a right to his services, — not dominion over his soul, nor a right to abuse him, nor in any way to injure him, but to use his services^ Have I not acquired that right?'

"'I think you have,' said the physician, 'but with certain limitations.'

"'The limitations,' said Mr. W., 'certainly are not the wishes, nor caprices, nor the inclinations, of the boy; — do you think so?'

"'I agree with you,' said he.

"'That is all I contend for,' said Mr. W.

"'But,' said the physician, 'where is your title-deed from your Maker to own these fellow-creatures? Trace their history back, and they are here by fraud and violence.'

" 'Thank you, Sir,' said Mr. W., ' that is just the case with my Penn. I came into possession of him through fraud and violence! I did not sin when he was thrown upon my hands; though I confess I said, he was — what we call slavery — an incubus. My right and title to the boy I have never been able to discover in any handwriting; the mother, surely, had no right to impose the child upon me; Providence, however, placed it in my hand. I might have given it immediate emancipation through the window, or at the next stopping place; or, I might have left the child on its mother's vacant seat, declining the trust; but I felt disposed to do as I have done.'

" ' Now,' said the physician, ' will you please tell me, Sir, how long you feel at liberty to possess this boy as a satisfaction to you for your pains and expense ? '

" ' In the first place,' said Mr. W., ' I have a right to transfer my guardianship over him to another, if circumstances make it necessary. In doing so, I must be governed not by selfish motives, but by a benevolent regard to his welfare, allowing that he is not unreasonable and wicked. If when he comes of lawful age, he is judged to be still in need of guardianship, or it is expedient for the good of all concerned that he should be my ward indefinitely, the law makes me, if I choose, his guardian, with certain rights and obligations. Even if he could legally claim his freedom at his majority, circumstances might be such that all would say he was under moral obligations to remain with me. If I abuse him, he must consider before God how far it is his duty to bear affliction, and submit to oppression. There are cases in which none would condemn him, should he escape. But the rule is to "abide." He has not, under all the circumstances of our relation to each other, a right to walk off at pleasure.'

" The company agreed in this, though the physician made no remark. We conversed further on the antipathy of the Free States to a large increase among them of the colored population, ungrateful and perfidious Kansas, even, withholding civil and political equality from them; their condition in Canada; their relation to the whites in every state where they have gone to reside; and we concluded that the South was the best home for the black man, — that home to become better and better in proportion as the law of Christian benevolence prevailed. We agreed that if the South could be relieved of Northern interference, the condition of the colored people would be greatly improved, in many respects; especially, we regretted that now we did not have an enlightened public sentiment at the North to help the best part of the Southern people in effecting reformations and improving the laws and regulations. Now, the Northern influence is wholly nugatory, or positively adverse. The opinions and feelings of calm and candid neighbors and friends have great influence. This the South does not enjoy. The North is her passionate reprover; she is held to be, by many, her avowed enemy. In resistance, and in retaliation, compromises are broken, and every political advantage is grasped at in self-defence, by the South. Recrimination ensues, and civil war is threatened. The only remedy is the entire abandonment by the North of interference with this subject; but this cannot take place so long as the Northern people labor under their doctrinal error that it is a sin to hold property in man. Here is the root of the difficulty. We agreed that if reflecting people at the North would adopt Scriptural views on that point, peace would soon ensue; for all the discussions of the supposed or real evils in slavery, which would then be the sole objects of animadversion, would elicit truth, and tend to good. If the South felt that the North were truly her friend, they would both be found coöperating for the improvement and elevation of the colored race. Every form of oppression and selfishness would feel the withering rebuke of a just and enlightened universal public sentiment. But now that the quarrel runs high as to the sinfulness and wrongfulness of the relation itself, there is nothing for the South to do but to stand by their arms.

"One gentleman made some remarks which interested and instructed me more than anything that was said. He confessed that the whole subject of the relation of master and servant, — in a word, slavery, was, for a long time, a sore trouble to him, because he constantly found himself searching for his right, his warrant to hold his slaves. At last he resolved to study the Bible on the subject. He naturally turned to the last instructions of the Word of God with regard to it, and in Paul's injunctions to masters and servants, he found relief. There he perceived that God recognized the relationships of slavery, that the golden rule was enjoined, not to dissolve the relation, but to make it benevolent to all concerned. He found the Almighty establishing the relation of master and servant among his own chosen people, and decreeing that certain persons might be servants forever, being, as he himself terms them 'an inheritance forever.'

"Hereupon, he said, his troubles ceased. He gave up his speculations and casuistry, and concluded to take things as he found them and to make them better. He became more than ever the friend and patron of his servants, rendered to them, to the best of his ability that

which was just and equal, felt in buying servants and in
having them born in his household, somewhat as pastors
of churches, he supposed, feel in receiving new members
to be trained up for usefulness here, and for heaven. He
said that he had a hundred and seventy-five servants,
and that he doubted whether there was a happier, or
more virtuous, or more religious community anywhere.

"' But,' said the young Northern lady, who had recently come to be a teacher in the family where we visited,
' what will become of them when you die ? '

"' Why, Miss,' said he, ' what will become of any
household when the parents die ?   The truth is,' said he,
' I believe in a covenant-keeping God.   I make a practice of praying for my servants, by name.   I keep a list
of them, and I read it, sometimes, when I read my Bible,
and on the Sabbath, and on days set apart for religious
services.   I have asked God to be the God of my servants forever.   I shall meet them at the bar of God,
and I trust with a good conscience.   Many of them have
become Christians.'

"' Do you ever sell them ? ' said she.

"' I have parted with some of my servants to families,'
he replied, ' where I knew that they would fare as well
as with me.   This was always with their consent, except
in two or three cases of inveterate wickedness, when, instead of sending the fellows to the state-prison for life,
as you would do at the North, I sold them to go to Red
River, and was as willing to see them marched off, hand-
cuffed, as you ever were to see villains in the custody of
the officers.   But had any of your good people from the
North met them, an article would have appeared, perhaps,
in all your papers, telling of the heart-rending spectacle,—
three human beings, in a slave-coffle! going, they knew not

where, into hopeless bondage! And had they escaped and fled to Boston, the tide of philanthropy there, in many benevolent bosoms, would have received new strength in the grateful accession of these worshipful fugitives from Southern cruelty. Whereas, all which love and kindness, and every form of indulgence, instruction, and discipline, tempered with mercy, could do, had been used with them in vain. One was a thief, the pest of the county, and had earned long years in a penitentiary; but slavery, you see, kept him at liberty! Another was brutally cruel to animals; another was the impersonation of laziness. Two of them would have helped John Brown, no doubt, had he come here, and they might have gained a Bunker Hill name, at the North, in an insurrection here, as champions of liberty.'

"This led to some remarks about the great economy which there is in the Southern mode of administering discipline and correction on the spot, and at once, instead of filling jails and houses of correction with felons. But to dwell on this would lead me too far into a new branch of our subject.

"This planter asked the young lady, the school-teacher, f tare and tret were in her arithmetic? Upon her saying 'yes, in the older books,' he told her that there was, seemingly, a good deal of tare and tret in God's providence, when accomplishing his great purposes; and that to fix the mind inordinately on evils and miseries incident to a great system and forgetting the main design, was like a man of business being so absorbed by the deductions and waste in a great staple as to forego the trade. He said that he thought the Northern mind ciphered too much in that part of moral arithmetic as to slavery.

"A very excellent gentleman from the District of Columbia who had held an important office under government, gave us some valuable information. He said that the extinction of slavery in New England was not because the institution was deemed to be immoral or sinful, but from other considerations and circumstances. It was abolished in Massachusetts, without doubt, by a clause, in the bill of rights, copied from the Declaration of Independence. In Berkshire, one township, he believed, sued another for the support and maintenance of a pauper slave, and the Supreme Court decided that the bill of rights abolished slavery. The question was as incidental, he said, as was the question in the Dred Scott case which the United States Supreme Court decided. This Massachusetts case was previous to any reports of decisions, and he had some doubt as to the form in which the suit was brought, but was sure as to the decision. The question as to abolishing slavery was not submitted to the people, nor to a Convention, nor to the Legislature.

"I was specially interested in his account of the way in which the slave-trade was prohibited by our excellent sister, Connecticut. It was done by a section prohibiting the importation of slaves by sea or land, preceded by the following preamble : — 'And whereas the increase of slaves in this state is injurious to the poor, and inconvenient, Be it therefore enacted.' Another section of the same statute, he said, was preceded by the following words : — 'And whereas sound policy requires that the abolition of slavery should be effected, as soon as may be consistent with the rights of individuals, and the public safety and welfare, Be it enacted,' etc. Then follows the provision that all black and mulatto children, born in slavery, in that state, after the first of March, 1784, shall be free at twenty-five years of age. Selling

9

slaves, to be carried out of the state, was not prohibited
before May, 1792 ; thus allowing more than eight years
to the owners of slaves in Connecticut to sell their slaves
to Southern purchasers ! ' There seems to me,' he said,
' no evidence of superior humanity in this ; nor was it
repentance for slavery as a sin.'   He thought that if we
feel compelled, by our superior conscientiousness, to require any duty of the South, all that decency will allow
us to demand is, that she tread in our steps.

" ' I think,' said a planter, ' that if pity is due from
one to the other, the South owes the larger debt to the
North.   There needs to be a great reformation, namely,
The Gradual Emancipation of the Northern Mind from
" Anti-slavery " Error.'

" ' Our English friends, in their zeal against American
slavery,' said a young lawyer, ' seem to forget that the
English government, at the Peace of Utrecht, agreed to
furnish Spain with four thousand negroes annually for
thirty years.'

" ' Poor human nature ! ' said the Judge. ' What should
we all do, if we had not the sins of others to repent of
and bewail ? '

" There was a strong friend of temperance in the company from a north-western state.   Travelling in the South
for pleasure, some time ago, he was immediately struck
with the comparative absence of intemperance among the
slaves.   On learning that the laws forbid the sale of in-
toxicating drink to them, and thinking of four millions of
people in this land as delivered, in a great degree, from
the curse of drunkenness, he says that he exclaimed :
' Pretty well for the " sum of all villanies."   The class
of people in the United States best defended against
drunkenness are the slaves ! '   Some admonished him

that the slaves did get liquor, and that white men ventured to tempt them. 'I don't care for that,' said he ; 'of course, there are exceptions ; the "sum of all villanies" is a Temperance Society !'

"A Northern gentleman, travelling through the South, said, 'As to the feelings of the North respecting a possible insurrection, I am satisfied, since visiting in different parts of the South, that a very common apprehension with us, respecting your liability to trouble from this source, is exaggerated by fancy.

"'We have a theoretical idea that you must be dwelling, as we commonly hear it said, with a volcano under your feet. Very many regard your slaves as a race of noble spirits, conscious of wrong, and burning with suppressed indignation, which is ready to break out at every chance. They think of you at the North as having guns and pistols and spears all about you, ready for use at any moment. But when I spend a night at your plantations, the owner and I the only white males, the wife and seven or eight young children having us for their only defenders against the seventy or hundred blacks, who are all about us in the quarters, the idea of danger has really never occurred to me ; because my knowledge of the people has previously disarmed me of fear.'

"'Emissaries, white and black,' said a planter, 'can make us trouble ; but my belief is that we could live here to the end of time with these colored people, and be subject to fewer cases of insubordination by far than your corporations at the North suffer from in strikes. Your people, generally, have no proper idea of the black man's nature. God seems to have given him docility and gentleness, that he may be a slave till the time comes for him to be something else. So He has given the Jews

their peculiarities, fitting them for His purposes with regard to them ; and to the Irish laborer He has given his
willingness and strength to dig, making him the builder
of your railways.   If we fulfil our trust, with regard to
the blacks, according to the spirit and rules of the New
Testament, I believe God will be our defender, and that
all his attributes will be employed to maintain our authority over this people for his own great purposes.   We
have nothing to fear except from white fanatics, North
and South.'

" ' I have no idea,' said the Judge, ' of dooming every
individual of this colored race to unalterable servitude.
I am in favor of putting them in the way of developing
any talent which any of them, from time to time, may
exhibit.   More of this, I am sure, would be done by us,
if we were freed from the necessity of defending ourselves against Northern assaults upon our social system,
involving, as these assaults do, peril to life, and to things
dearer than life.   But I see tenfold greater evils in all
the plans of emancipation which have ever been proposed than in the present state of things.'

" The pastor of the place, who was present, had not
taken much part in the discussion, though he had not
purposely kept aloof from it.   He was Southern born,
inherited slaves, had given them their liberty one by one,
and had recently returned from the North, where he had
been to see two of them — the last of his household —
embark as hired servants with families who were to
travel in Europe.

" Some of us asked him about his visit to the North.
Said he, ' I went to church one day, and was enjoying
the devotional services, when all at once the minister
broke out in prayer for the abolition of slavery.   He

presented the South before God as " oppressors," and prayed that they might at once repent, and " break every yoke," and " let the oppressed go free." I took him to be an immediate emancipationist, perhaps peculiar in his views. But in the afternoon I went into another church, and in prayer the minister began to pray " for all classes and conditions of men among us." I was glad to see, as I thought, charity beginning at home. But the next sentence took in our whole land; and the next was a downright swoop upon slavery; so that I regarded his previous petitions merely as spiral movements toward the South. If the good man's petitions had been heard, woe to him and to the North, and to the slaves, to say nothing of ourselves.

" 'I stopped after service, and, without at first introducing myself, I asked him if he was in the habit of praying, as he had done to-day, for slave-holders. He said yes. I asked him if it was a general practice at the North. He thought it was. I inquired if he would have every slave liberated to-morrow, if he could effect it. " By all means," said he. — " Would they be better off?" said I. — " Undoubtedly they would," said he. " But that is not the question. Do right, if the heavens fall." — " What would become of them?" said I. — " Hire them," said he; " pay them wages; let husbands and wives live together; abolish auction-blocks, and " —— " But," said I, " some of the very best of men in the world, at the South, are decidedly of the opinion that such emancipation would be the most barbarous thing that could be devised for the slaves." — " Are you a slave-holder?" said he. — " I was," said I; " but I have liberated my slaves, and I am in your city to see the last two of my servants sail with your fellow-citizens, —— and —— " (naming them). — " You don't

say so!" said he. "What did you liberate them for?"—
"I could not take proper care of them," said I, "situated
as I am." — "But," said he, "did you do right in letting
them go to sea as you did? One of them will get no
good with that man for a master. I would rather be
your dog than his child." — "Then," said I, "you have
'oppressors' at the North, it seems." — "Well," said he,
"some of our people are not as good as they ought to be."
— "It is so with us at the South," said I. — "Preach for
me next Sabbath, Sir," said he. — "Are you going to stay
over?" — "Why," said I, "my dear Sir, would you and
your people like to hear a man preach for you whom
you, if you made the prayer, would first pray for as an
'oppressor?'" — "But you are not an oppressor," said
he. — "But I am in favor of what you call 'oppression,'"
said I. — "One thing I could pray for with you," said I. —
"What is that?" said he. — "Break every yoke," said I.
"This I pray for always. But how many 'yokes,'" said
I, "do you suppose there are at the South?" — "I forget
the exact number of the slaves," said he, in the most artless manner.'

"Hereupon the company broke out into great merri-
ment. After they had enjoyed their laughter awhile,
my Northern lady-friend said, 'Did you preach for him?'

"'Yes,' said the pastor; 'and prayed for him too.

"'Walking through the streets of that place in the
evening, I saw evidence that no minister nor citizen there
was justified in casting the first stone at the South for
immorality. I lifted up my heart in thanks to God that
my sons were not exposed to the temptations of a Northern city. Being in the United States District Court there,
several times, I had some revelations also with regard to
the treatment and the condition of seamen in some North-

ern ships, which led me to the conclusion which I have
often drawn, — that poor human nature is about the
same, North and South.

" ' So, when I conducted the services of public worship,
I prayed for that city and for the young people, and alluded to the temptations which I had witnessed ; and I
referred also to mariners, and prayed for masters and
officers of vessels who had such authority over the welfare and the lives of seamen ; and I prayed that Christians in both sections of our land might pray for each
other, considering each themselves, lest they also be
tempted, and that they might not be self-righteous and
accusatory ; and that our eye might not be so filled with
the evils of other sections of the land as not to see those
which were at home.

" ' After service the good brother said, " I suppose you
referred in your prayer to my praying against the South,
as you call it. Well," said he, confidentially, " the truth
is, some of our people make this thing their religion, and
they will not abide a man who does not pray against
slavery." Some gentlemen, with their ladies, stopped to
speak with me. One shook me by the hand most cor-
dially. " We are glad to see our good Southern brethren," said he ; " thankful to hear you preach so, and pray
so, too," said he, with an additional shake and a signifi-
cant look, while the rest were equally cordial with their
assent. One of the gentlemen took me home with him.
" This is most of it politics," said he, " and newspaper
trade, this anti-slavery feeling. The people generally
are not fanatics ; they are kind and humane, and their
sensibilities are touched by tales of distress." — " Especially Southern," said I. " Last eve I read in your papers
four outrages which happened within fifteen miles of this

city, and two in your city, which equalled, to say the least, in barbarity anything that ever comes to my knowledge among our people."

" 'The next Sabbath, as I have since learned, my good brother was very comprehensive, discriminating, and imimpartial in his supplications. He really distinguished between those at the South who "oppress" their fellowmen, and those who "remember them that are in bonds as bound with them." But,' said the pastor, 'the most of those who use that latter expression at the North really think the Apostle had slaves, as a class, in mind. I have no such belief. I suppose that he referred to persecuted Christians, suffering imprisonment for their religion, and to all afflicted persons.

" 'My landlord said to me,' he continued, ' " They tell us you are afraid of free discussion at the South, that you are afraid to have your slaves hear some things, lest it should excite them to insurrection. How is this ? "

" 'I told him that the slaves, being the lower order of society with us, were not capable of so discriminating in that which promiscuous strangers should see fit to say to them as to make it safe to have them listen to every harangue or to every one who should set himself up to teach. "Of course," said I, "there are liabilities and dangers in our state of society. We must use prudence and caution. We have some loose powder in our magazine. No one denies this. What if one who was rebuked for carrying an open lamp into the magazine of a ship, should reproach the captain with being 'an enemy to the light,' and as 'loving darkness rather than light' ? "

" 'While at the North,' said he, 'I read Mr. Buckle on civilization, and I reflected upon the subject. Being in a great assembly, once or twice, listening to abolitionist orators, lay and clerical, and hearing their vile assaults on personal character, their vulgar and reckless ridicule of fifteen States of our Union, their affected, oracular way of saying the most trite things as though they were aphorisms, but reminding me of the piles of short stuff which you see round a saw-mill, and hearing the great throng applaud and shout, I asked myself whether we have really made any decided advances in civilization since the Hebrew Commonwealth. I really doubted whether those orators could have collected an audience of Hebrews even in the wilderness. Under the "Judges," the people were, at times, low enough to enjoy such drivelling. The willingness at the North to hear these men, and to applaud them, gave me a low idea of the state of society.'

" ' But,' said I, ' confess now that you found specimens of cultivated life there such as you never saw surpassed.'

" ' I did,' said he, ' many times. And I must tell you,' he added, ' of my enjoyment in looking on your pastures in autumn, — the sun shining aslant upon them of an afternoon, — and in noticing what shades of scarlet and crimson were given to the picture by the whortleberry leaves, which, I found, contributed most to the coloring of the landscape. I also saw a peculiarity of the whortleberry's flower, which, when stung by an insect sometimes swells to twenty-five times its natural size, and becomes a fungus.'

" ' Now,' said I, ' why not apply this, — perhaps you were intending to do so, — and say that society at the North is generally like our whortleberry pastures in autumn, which pleased you so much, with here and there a fungus, made by the sting of radicalism.'

9 *

"A planter's Northern wife said, 'I should like to move the adoption of that simile.'

"'We will have it so,' said the Judge to me, 'if the lady and you tell us that we must.'

"'A fungus,' said I, 'gets more attention from one half of the people who go into the woods, than all the pure and beautiful garniture of the pastures.'

"The ladies of our company having been rallied for not having done their part in the conversation, and also, of course, having been complimented for keeping silence so long, the wife of one of the planters, a Northern lady, made this remark that considering how God, in his providence, had made such provision for the welfare of the human family through slavery in our land, and, in doing it, had shown mercy and salvation to so many hundreds of thousands of Africans, she thought it both ungrateful and narrow-minded in people anywhere to confine all their thoughts to the incidental evils of the slaves. She said that in the North she was not an abolitionist, but on coming to the South and finding things so different from that which her fancy had pictured, she had concluded to be very charitable toward the most of her Northern friends who she said were no more in the dark than she herself had been all her days, from reading newspapers and tales which had concealed one whole side of slavery from the view of Northern people. She added that she preferred life at the North without the blacks, but had found more disinterested benevolence toward them in one year at the South than she had charity to believe existed in the hearts of all the good people at the North toward them, counting in even the professional benevolence of the 'friends of the slave.'

"After refreshments, the pastor was called upon to read

the Scriptures, and to offer prayer. He read the fifteenth chapter of Revelation. Never can I forget the impression which one of the verses in that chapter made upon me, in connection with some of the thoughts awakened by our conversation about the sovereignty of God as displayed in his dark and awful dispensations towards races, nations, and men : 'And the seven angels came out of the temple, having the seven plagues, clothed in pure and white linen, and having their breasts girded with golden girdles.' 'Those who are in any way associated with the administration of God's great judgments towards their fellow-men,' said he, 'have need of special purity; and their honor should be like the untarnished gold.'

"This pastor told me, during the repast, that one day, returning suddenly from his study in the church just after breakfast, to the house of one of the gentlemen present, with whom he lived, and who was one of the wealthiest men in the South, and passing through the parlor to get a book, he found the room darkened, and the lady of the house kneeling in prayer with her servants. He of course withdrew at once, but he learned afterward from one of the 'slaves,' that it was the lady's daily custom. He often thought of that incident when reading Northern religious newspapers and noticing their lamentations over 'slave-holding professors.'"

So much for my Southern visit.

Mrs. North said that in our next conversation she would suggest that we consider the relation of Christianity to Slavery. I told her that I had some night thoughts on that subject, which I would with pleasure submit, at another time.

As the rain continued, Mr. North and I resorted to the wood-pile in the shed for exercise, till dinner-time, Mrs. North following us to the door, and charging us not to converse upon this subject till she should be present.

CHAPTER IX.

DISCUSSION IN PHILEMON'S CHURCH AT THE RETURN OF ONESIMUS.

" My equal will he be again
Down in that cold, oblivious gloom,
Where all the prostrate ranks of men
Crowd without fellowship, — the tomb."

JAMES MONTGOMERY.

" I WILL now relate to you," said I, as we resumed our conversation, " the thoughts which came to me one night as I lay awake meditating on this subject. I wrote them down the next day.

" The subject in our conversation which suggested them was, The relation of Christianity to slavery.

" About the year A. D. 64, two men, travellers from Rome, entered the city of Colosse, in Phrygia, Asia Minor, both of them the bearers of letters from the Apostle Paul, then a prisoner at Rome.

" A Christian Church had been gathered at Colosse. Its pastor was probably Archippus. Some think that Epaphras was his colleague. This church, according to Dr. Lardner and others, was most probably gathered by the Apostle Paul himself. Mount Cadmus rose behind the city, with its almost perpendicular side, and a huge chasm in the mountain was the outlet of a torrent which flowed into the river Lycus, on which the city was built, standing not far from the junction of this river with the Mœander.

" One of the two men who bore these letters was a slave. His name was Onesimus. He robbed his master, Philemon, of Colosse, fled to Rome, heard Paul preach, was converted, and now by the Apostle is sent back to his master with a letter, in charge of Tychicus, who, with this Onesimus, was the bearer of a letter to the Colossian Church.

" Let us attend the church-meeting. The pastor, Archippus, presides. Epaphras is at Rome.

" What an interesting company do we behold as we sit near the pastor's table, in full view of the audience ! The inhabitants of this place were noted for the worship of Bacchus, and Cybele, mother of the gods; hence her name, *Phrygia Mater*. Every kind of licentious language and actions was practised in the worship of these deities, accompanied with a frantic rage called orgies, from the Greek word for *rage*. This was a part of their religious worship. From among such people, converts had been made to Christianity, together with some who had been turned from Judaism.

" The letter from the Apostle Paul is brought in and is laid on the pastor's table, and some account is given of the manner in which it was received. The letter is read. It refers the Colossians, at the close, to the bearers, for further information and instructions. ' All my state shall Tychicus declare unto you, who is a beloved brother and a faithful minister and fellow-servant in the Lord. Whom I have sent unto you for the same purpose, that he might know your estate, and comfort your hearts. With Onesimus, a faithful and beloved brother, who is one of you. They shall make known unto you all things which are done here.'

"Tychicus relates his story, and, when he has finished, Philemon, a member of the Church, addresses the meeting. He was evidently a man of distinction in that community, as we infer from the large number of persons in his household, (ver. 2,) his liberality to poor Christians, (ver. 5, 7,) and from the marked respect and deference paid to him by the Apostle. He also had received a letter from the Apostle, and he asks leave to read it.

"He then tells them that Onesimus is present; that he has been sent back by the Apostle Paul, and with the full, cordial consent of Onesimus himself. He would ask permission for Onesimus to say a few words.

"'Come hither,' says the pastor, 'and tell us what the Lord hath done for thee, and how he hath had mercy on thee.'

"'Let me wash the saints' feet,' says Onesimus, 'but I am not worthy to teach in the church.'

"He proceeds to tell them, in full, of his escape from his master, after robbing him; of his meeting the Apostle at Rome; of his conversion; of his voluntary return to spend his days, if such be the will of God, as the servant of Philemon.

"The account of these proceedings reaches Laodicea, not far distant, to which place Paul had also sent a letter, and the Colossians, agreeably to the Apostle's charge, exchange letters, and no doubt the letter to Philemon is also read to the Church which is at Laodicea.

"Whereupon, we will suppose, a controversy at once springs up. There had already appeared in this region of Phrygia, as we infer from the Epistle to the Colossians, serious errors, among them a kind of angel worship and asceticism, or abstinence from things lawful, and a state of things called Gnosis, (Eng. knowledge,) or

Gnosticism, a pervading spirit of worldly wisdom, science, philosophy, which treated the simplicity which was in Christ as too rudimental and plain for the human mind, and therefore sought to furnish it with speculations and mysticism, to gratify its desires for a more extensive spiritual knowledge than it seemed to many of them was provided for by Christianity.

" Among the speculations and theories of those days, we will suppose that the idea began to prevail that Christianity was inconsistent with holding a fellow-being in bondage. A motion is made in the Laodicean Church that a committee be appointed to confer with the Colossian Church on the return of Onesimus into slavery. Such a motion would have found ready advocates in the Church at Laodicea, if, as at a later day, they were ' neither cold nor hot' in religion ; in which case any collateral subjects wholly or partly secular, would have a charm for them. These supplied that lack of warmth which they were conscious of as to religion ; their church-meeting, no doubt, seemed to them dull, unless a subject was introduced which gave opportunity for discussion, and for things which gendered debate, whereof cometh envy, strife, railings, evil surmisings.

" The result of the conference on the part of the Laodicean Committee with the Colossian Church was, that a general meeting was appointed to discuss the subject of the return of Onesimus into slavery. It was a private session of members of the two churches. They claimed the privilege as Christians of discussing any question relating to the government and the laws, taking care that no spies were present ; still, with all their precautions, false brethren made trouble for them by giving private information to the civil authorities against some of their number, whom they disliked ; and this led to some oppression and persecution.

"But the meeting was fully attended. Two members of the church who were faithful servants to slave-holding brethren were set to guard the doors. The slaves were allowed to be present and listen to the discussion. This was carried after much debate, some contending that it would expose the Christians to just reprehension from the civil authorities; and others maintaining that it would do the slaves good to hear such doctrines advanced and enforced as would be quoted from the Apostle relating to masters and servants.

"The discussion was opened by a brother from Laodicea, an office-bearer in the church, a private citizen, devoted to study, and an author of some repute. He was formerly odist at the festivals of Cybele. His pieces were collected and published under the title of ' Phrygian Canticles.' His name was Olamus.

"He took the ground that Christianity abrogated slavery. He quoted the well known words of Paul, so familiar to all who had heard him preach : ' In Christ Jesus there is neither Jew nor Greek, barbarian, Scythian, bond nor free ; but all are one in Christ.' ' The Spirit of the Lord is upon me because he hath sent me to preach deliverance to the captives, the opening of the prison doors to them that are bound.' ' Whatsoever ye would that men should do unto you, do you even so to them.'

"He maintained that to own a fellow-creature was inconsistent with this law of equal love ; that it was giving sanction to a feature of barbarism; that, practically, slavery was the sum of all villanies ; an enormous wrong ; a stupendous injustice.

" If any one should reply that the Mosaic institutions recognized slavery, he had one brief answer : — 'which things are done away in Christ.' Moses permitted this and some other things for the hardness of their hearts. Polygamy was allowed by Moses, not by Christianity ; its spirit is against it ; the bishop of a church must be 'the husband of one wife ; ' slavery is certainly none the less contrary to the spirit of the gospel.

" But inasmuch as it is inexpedient to dissolve at once, and in all cases, the relation of master and slave, he contended that while the relation continued, it should be regulated by the laws which God himself once prescribed. Every seventh year should be a year of release ; every fiftieth year should be a jubilee. And as to fugitives, he would refer his brethren to that Divine injunction : ' Thou shalt not deliver unto his master the servant which is escaped from his master unto thee ; he shall dwell with thee, even among you, in that place which he shall choose, in one of thy gates, where it liketh him best ; thou shalt not oppress him.'

" That a slave having escaped from his master could not rightfully be sent back into bondage, was evident from these considerations :

" All men are born free and equal, and have an inalienable right to life, liberty, and the pursuit of happiness. If a slave sees fit to walk off, or run off, or ride off on his master's beast, or sail off in his master's boat, he has a perfect right to do so. Slavery is violence ; every man may resist violence offered to his person, except under process of law ; the person cannot be taken except for crime, or debt, or in war ; every man owns his body and soul ; the person cannot become merchandise, except for the three causes above named, which he acknowledged were justifiable causes of involuntary servitude at present. But to forcibly seize a weaker man, or race, and hold them in bondage he declared to be in violation of the laws of nature, and contrary to the Christian religion.

"If it should be replied that Paul the Apostle countenanced slavery by sending back Onesimus, he would answer, that Paul was a Jew, and was not yet freed wholly from Jewish practices and associations of ideas. Gnosticism has supervened upon the rudimental childhood of spiritual truth. He believed in progress. It was contrary to the instinct of human nature to send back a poor fugitive into bondage, and he was glad for one that he lived in an age when the innate moral sentiments, under the lucid teachings of our more transcendental scholars were becoming more and more the all-sufficient guide in the affairs of life. He would, therefore, publicly disclaim his allegiance to the teachings of the Apostle Paul, if, upon reflection, Paul should insist that he was right in remanding Onesimus to be Philemon's property 'forever;' it was well enough that he should be sent back to restore what he had taken by theft, provided Philemon would immediately release him; otherwise, to steal from Philemon was doing no more than Philemon had done to him, in taking away that liberty which is the birthright of every human being; and Onesimus probably stole merely to assist his escape. He was justifiable in doing so.

"If one should insist that there can be no intrinsic wrong in holding a fellow-being as property because God allowed Hebrews to sell themselves, and in certain cases to be servants forever, and directed the Israelites to buy servants of the heathen round about them, who should

be an inheritance to the children of the Israelites, he
would simply say either that the whole pentateuch which
contained such a libel on the divine character, is thereby
proved to be a forgery, or, that if the pentateuch is to be
received, it only proves that in condescension to a race
of freebooters who were employed, as the Israelites were,
in bloody wars of extermination, slavery was allowed
them, to prevent, perhaps, worse evils, and in consistency
with their dark-minded, semi-barbarous condition.   In
this enlightened age when Greece and Rome had shed
superior light on human relationships and obligations, and
especially since Christ had promulgated the golden rule,
the idea that man could own a fellow-creature was so
preposterous that he would be an infidel, nay, he would
go farther, he would be an atheist, rather than believe it.
Our moral instincts are our guide.   They are the highest
source of evidence that there is a God, and they are a
perfect indication as to what God and his requirements
should be.   He was for passing a vote of disapprobation
at the act of Paul the Apostle in sending back Onesimus
into bondage.   Tell me not, said he, that the Apostle
calls him ' a brother beloved,' and ' one of you ;' these
honeyed phrases are but coatings to a deadly poison.   Slavery is evil, and only evil and that continually.   Disguise
it as you will, Philemon holds property in Onesimus.
By the laws of Phrygia, he could ' put Onesimus to
death for running away.   He deplored the act as a
heavy blow at Christianity.   It would countervail the
teachings of the Apostle.   He sincerely hoped that the
Epistle to Philemon would not be preserved ; for should
it be collected hereafter, as possibly it may, among Paul's
letters, unborn ages might make it an apology for slavery,
it would abate the hatred of the world against the sum

of all villanies. He would even be in favor of a vote requesting Philemon to give Onesimus his liberty at once, even without his consent, sending him back, with this most unwise and unblest epistle to Philemon, to Paul, who says that he ' would have retained him,' but would not without Philemon's consent. He did hope that the brethren would speak their minds, be open-mouthed, and not be like dumb dogs. For his part he wanted an anti-slavery religion. He acknowledged that the truths of the Gospel needed the stimulant of freedom to give them life and power.

" His remarks evidently produced a great sensation, for a variety of reasons, as we may well suppose.

" A man took the floor in opposition to this Laodicean brother. He was a Jewish convert, a member of the Colossian Church. His name was Theodotus. Born a Jew, he had renounced his religion and became a Greek Sophist, practised law at Scio, and heard Paul at Mars Hill, where, with Dionysius the Areopagite, with whom he was visiting, he was converted. He had established himself at Colosse, in the practice of law. He was un-usually tall for a man of his descent, had beautifully reg-ular Jewish features, and was a captivating speaker.

" He said that they had ' heard strange things to-day. If they are true, we have no foundation underneath our feet. Every man's moral sentiments, it seems, are to be his guide. Where, then, is our common appeal? For his part he believed that if God be our heavenly Father, he has given his children an authentic book, a writing, for their guide, unless he prefers to speak personally with them, or with their representatives. When he ceased to speak by the prophets, he spoke to us by his Son ; and now that his Son is ascended, I believe,' said

he, ' that inspired men are appointed to guide us, and
seeing that they cannot reach all by their living voice, I
believe that the evangelists and apostles are to furnish us
with writings which shall be inspired disclosures of God's
will and our duty.   The Old Testament is as truly God's
word as ever ; Christ declared that not one jot or tittle
should pass from it, till all be fulfilled.   Some of it is
fulfilled, in him, the end of the types ; parts of it refer
to local and temporary things ; all which is not local and
temporary is still binding upon us.   At least, the spirit
of its laws is benevolent and wise.   Damascus and its
scenes are too fresh in the memories of the brethren to
need that I should argue the inspiration of the Apostle to
the Gentiles.   His miracles are known to us.   Nay, what
miracles are we ourselves, reclaimed from the service of
the devil, once the worshippers of Bacchus and of our
Phrygian mother ; now, clothed, and in our right minds.
The Apostle claims to speak and act by divine authority.
We must question everything, if we set aside this claim.

" ' I maintain,' said he, ' that the Apostle Paul regards
the holding a fellow-creature as property to be consistent with Christianity.   To prevent all misunderstanding,
however, let me declare that he insists on the golden rule
as the law of slave-holding, as of everything else ; that
he discountenances oppression, that he warns and threat-
ens us with regard to it ; and that he considers slave-
holding as consistent with the Christian character and
happiness of master and slave.

" ' In the very Epistle just received by our Church, and
by the hands of Tychicus and Onesimus himself, from
the Apostle, we find these words : " Servants, obey in all
things your masters according to the flesh ; not with eye-
service, as men-pleasers, but in singleness of heart, fear-

ing God; and whatsoever ye do, do it heartily, as unto the Lord, and not unto men, knowing that of the Lord ye shall receive the reward of the inheritance : for ye serve the Lord Christ. But he that doeth wrong shall receive for the wrong which he hath done ; and there is no respect of persons. Masters, give unto your servants that which is just and equal ; knowing that ye also have a Master in heaven."

" ' Where, in this, is there a word that countenances the wrongfulness of being a slave, or of holding men as slaves? He directs all his exhortations to the duties which are to be performed in the relation, and he leaves the relation as he finds it. He does not enjoin slavery ; he treats it as something which belongs to society, to government, and he leaves Christianity to regulate it as circumstances shall make it proper. If any one says that the Apostle was afraid to meddle with it, I reply, that there was never anything yet that Paul was afraid to meddle with, if it was right to do so. He " meddled " with Diana of the Ephesians and her craftsmen ; he " meddled " with the " beasts " there ; he " meddled " with idolatry on Mars Hill at Athens, I being witness ; he has been beaten, stoned, imprisoned, and is now the second time before Nero for his life. Afraid to " meddle " with slavery ! I am ashamed of the man who makes the suggestion. He who thinks it, has never yet understood him.

" ' Now, where in all his teachings has he ever intimated that it is wrong to hold property in man ? Nowhere ; I repeat it, nowhere. But is he ignorant of the nature of slavery ? We all know what has lately happened at Rome, in connection with slavery. The very year that Paul arrives at Rome, the prefect of the city, Pedanius Secundus, was murdered by his slave ; and

agreeably to the laws of slavery all the slaves belonging to the prefect, a great number, women and children
among them, were put to death indiscriminately, though
innocent of the crime.* Such is slavery under the Apostle's eye ; and yet '——

"'And, therefore,' interrupted the Laodicean brother,
'the Apostle approves of murdering innocent slaves for
the sin of one. That is the conclusion to which your
reasoning will bring us.'

"'Excusing the brother for interrupting me, I ask, Is
that agreeable to the plain facts in the case?' said the
speaker. 'Are the abuses of parentage chargeable upon
the relationship of parent and child? Moreover, does
not the Apostle expressly teach us, in this Epistle, that
such things are wrong? but still, does he condemn the
relation of master and slave?

"'The tale of that horrid butchery was present to the
mind of the Apostle when he sends Onesimus back into
slavery. Moreover, he knew that by our laws Philemon
could put Onesimus to death ; yet he sends him back.

"'It is said by my brother that Paul enunciated principles which in time would kill slavery, and therefore he
did not care to denounce it, but prudently let it alone.
What else, I inquire, did Paul fail to denounce? and
why is this "enormous wrong," this "stupendous injustice," alone, left to die, without being attacked? No, Paul
treated slavery as he did all other forms of government ;
he did not denounce government, not even its despotic
forms ; for he knew that a despotism may be the best
form of government in some circumstances. But he
spoke against the abuse of power by rulers, and in the

* Tacitus, *Annals*, xiv. 42. — A thrilling tale. See Bohn's Classical
Library, 53.

same way he speaks against the abuse of power by the master.

" ' My brother tells us that slavery is " the sum of all villanies." A comprehensive term, truly. Let us admit the correctness of the phrase. " All villanies " includes all " the works of the flesh," and the Apostle enumerates the principal of them, where he says, " Now the works of the flesh are these ; " — concluding his account with the expression, " and such like." With unsparing denunciation, he portrays each and every " villany," and shows how the wrath of God is revealed from heaven against it.

" ' But while he is thus bold and faithful with regard to " all villanies " in particular, we cannot but think it strange that a thing which is said to be the " sum " of them all, is nowhere spoken against by the Apostle ! On the contrary, he recognizes the duties which grow out of slave-holding.

" ' Let us suppose him to do the same with regard to each villany which he does to that which my brother calls the " sum " of them all. Then we should hear him say ! Murderers, do so and so ; thieves, do so and so ; and ye that are mutilated, do so and so ; and ye that are pillaged, do so and so. I am curious to know how my brother will answer this. What are the religious " duties " of murderers and thieves, but to repent, to forsake their evil ways at once, and to make lawful reparation ? And what are the " duties " of those whom murderers and thieves assault, but to resist, and to seek the conviction of the evil-doer ? Oh how strange it seems for the Apostle to counsel masters and slaves to imitate their " Master which is in heaven," in their relation to each other, if holding men in bondage be " the sum of all vil-

10

lanies," and how strange for him to send Onesimus back
to the system to behave in it as Christ would act in his
place!

   " ' Onesimus escapes, we will say, from a gang of murderers, or from a company of thieves, and the Apostle's
preaching is the means of his becoming a good man.
Paul writes a letter to the chief murderer of the gang,
or to the captain of the robbers, sends Onesimus back,
and " beseeches " the brigand for " his son Onesimus,"
telling him that now he receives him " forever," and then
calls the desperado " our dearly beloved fellow-laborer " !
Why not, with equal propriety, if slavery be, necessarily,
as our brother describes it? There is some mistake in
our brother's theory.

   " ' I venture to state the distinction which I think he
overlooks, and which, if observed, will relieve his difficulty. Paul never denounces government ; " the powers
that be are ordained of God." He appeals to " Cæsar " ;
he goes before " Nero " ; he never counsels insurrection,
nor denounces government, in whatever hands or under
whatever forms it may be ; but he enjoins principles
and duties which, if observed, would make " Cæsars,"
even though they be " Neros," blessings, and their despot-
isms even would cease to be a curse. So with slave-
holding. It is incorporated into the state of society ; it
is, moreover, a relation which can exist and no sin be
committed under the relation ; hence, it is not sin in
itself, any more than the throne of Nero is sin in itself ;
and the Apostle speaks to the slave-holding Philemon as
he would to a father receiving back a wayward son.

   " ' The claim of Philemon to Onesimus rests only on
his having purchased him. Who had a right to sell
him? Trace the thing back, and you come to fraud or

violence, or some form of injustice to Onesimus in making him a slave. Paul knew that this is the case with
regard to every slave; yet he does not "break every
yoke," even when, as in this case, he had one so com-
pletely in his hands, and could have broken it in pieces.

" ' But we will suppose, with my brother, that the laws
which God ordained for slavery should prevail under
Christianity, if slavery is to exist. Let every Phrygian,
then, a fellow-countryman who has lost his liberty, go
free at the end of six years; and at every fiftieth year,
whether six years be completed or not, since the last
seventh year of release, let all such go free. This, for
argument's sake, we approve. But we must take the
whole code. Every foreigner who becomes a slave, and
the child of every such slave, was to be an "inheritance
forever." Husbands, who are Phrygians, must choose,
in certain cases, whether to go out free by themselves, or
remain in perpetual bondage with their wives and their
offspring. Paul knew the Jewish laws with regard to
slavery; he knew how favorably they compared with
our code; but he says not a word on that score, and simply sends Onesimus back to his bondage.

" ' Yet see how beautifully the spirit of Christ works
itself into the relation of master and slave, and into Paul's
views and feelings with regard to it. In his letter to our
Church, he expressly names Onesimus as one of the bearers of the epistle. He speaks of him as "one of you," a
resident with us; and he calls this slave " a faithful and
beloved brother." He speaks to Philemon about him as
"my son Onesimus whom I have begotten in my bonds;"
" thou therefore receive him, that is, mine own bowels."
" Not now as a servant, but above a servant, a brother
beloved, specially to me, but how much more unto thee,

both in the flesh and in the Lord." " If thou count me, therefore, a partner, receive him as myself."

" ' What a comment is this on the words : " In Christ Jesus there is neither bond nor free." Not that there shall be " no bond," according to the brother's interpretation ; for then it would be equally right to interpret the other part of the passage literally, — there is no Jew, no Greek, and none free ! How perfectly does the relation become absorbed by that state of heart which makes it proper for Paul to say : " Art thou called being a servant, care not for it; but if thou mayest be made free, use it rather." Notwithstanding this advice, he sends back this man-servant.

" ' Paul might have manumitted Onesimus by his authority as an apostle ; this, however, would have been rebellion against government, for our laws recognize slavery.

" ' My brother says that the Hebrew law forbade the surrender of a fugitive slave. Yes, if the slave fled into Israel from a heathen master, he must not be sent back to heathenism ; but ' ——

" ' But,' said the brother from Laodicea, ' there is no limitation of that kind. I insist that it was of universal application to slaves of all kinds.'

" ' Find the passage, if you please (in Deut. xxiii.),' said the Colossian speaker.

" The passage was found by the pastor, and was read, as already quoted : ' Thou shalt not deliver unto his master the servant that is escaped from his master unto thee. He shall dwell with thee even among you, in that place which he shall choose in one of thy gates where it liketh him best ; thou shalt not oppress him.' Deut. xxiii. 10, 15.

" ' Now,' said Theodotus, ' it is absurd to say that God proclaimed to all the servants throughout Israel, If any of you are dissatisfied, for any cause, and wish to run away, you may do so ; and wherever you wish to live, the people of that place shall provide a residence for you. After being there for ever so short a time, if you do not like it, you may flee again ; and so keep moving all your lifetime, the people everywhere being obliged to allow you a place of abode. Did the Most High mean to encourage such vagabondism ?

" ' No ; He merely provided that a fugitive from a heathen master should not be sent away from the worship of Jehovah into heathenism.'

" ' That is undoubtedly the true meaning,' said the pastor, ' if Theodotus will allow me to put in a word. " Thee," in that passage, means Israel as a nation, not each man.'

" ' I thank you, Sir,' said Theodotus ; ' and now I maintain that the injunction not to give up a fugitive to his heathen master, but to keep him in Israel, is a powerful argument in favor of retaining slaves where they will be most benefited in their spiritual concerns. God thus makes the soul of man and its eternal welfare paramount to all external relations, including slavery.'

" ' May I inquire, then,' said the Laodicean : ' Suppose that Philemon had been a cruel heathen master, and Onesimus had fled for his life, would Paul have sent him back ? '

" ' If the case were clear and beyond doubt, I am not sure that he would,' said Theodotus. ' While he would not counsel Onesimus to run away, yet I can only say, that, fleeing from certain cruelty and death, I doubt if he would have been remanded. But Paul told servants to be "subject to their masters," "not only to the good and gentle, but also to the froward." He speaks to them of "suffering wrongfully;" of "doing well, and suffering for it;" and he refers the suffering slave to Christ, "who, when he was reviled, reviled not again; when he suffered, threatened not." Moreover, he says: "For even hereunto were ye called; because Christ also *suffered for us*, leaving us an example that ye should *follow his steps*." That is certainly death.'

"'If Paul did not send Onesimus back to Philemon, however, it would not be because it was wrong, in his view, for Philemon to hold him in bondage; please observe this distinction; but, judging the case by itself, he would decide whether the slave ought not, under the circumstances, to have the right of asylum, — Paul himself having once been "let down by a basket," to escape from the Damascenes. Paul and any other man would, in certain cases, protect even a fugitive son or daughter from a father; and this consistently with his recognition of the parental and filial relation.

"'Let me remind my brother, and you, my pastor, and my brethren, of one fact which occurs to me at the moment. Manslayers, in cities of refuge, were to go free at the death of the High Priest then in office; no such release, however, was granted to the Gentile slaves, showing that slavery was not a crime in the estimation of the Most High. Otherwise, He would have legislated for the departure of slaves from their Hebrew masters, as He did for manslayers fleeing from the avenger of blood. Excuse the digression. The thought struck me at the moment.'

"'I put it to the brother,' said the Laodicean, 'whether he himself would not flee to Rome, were he a single man, if he should be made a slave to that monster in human shape, Osander of Hieropolis ? '

" ' I cannot say,' replied the Colossian, ' what my temptations might be, nor how well I should resist them ; but slavery being incorporated into the government, and I being, in the providence of God, sold into bondage to Osander, — I being either the child of a slave, or one of those who are called " lawful captives," — my race, or my capture in war, or my indebtedness, or my crimes, subjecting me to bondage according to the constitution of government, I ought to consider my slavery as the mode which God had chosen for me to glorify him, — by my spirit and temper, by my words and conduct, by my Christian example in everything, for the good of Osander's soul, and the honor of religion. I believe that I should please God more by staying to suffer, and even to die, than to run away. I doubt even the expediency of running away, as a general rule. It implies a want of faith. He is the Christian hero who stays where God has manifestly placed him.

" ' I know,' continued he, ' how easy it is to make this appear ridiculous ; and also how often cases occur in which flight, and even the taking of life, are proper, under extreme hardships. It is frequently the case that a servant sees and feels his mental superiority to the man who owns him. Now one may be so disgusted, and be so constantly vexed and chafed at this, as to make out a strong case for escaping ; another, in the same circumstances, will feel that God has placed him in charge of his master's soul, to please him well in all things though he be " froward." Whether is better, to run off or to " abide " ? There can be no doubt how the Apostle would answer the question. Exceptional cases of extreme dis-

tress do not make a rule; the rule is for each one to
"abide" in the calling in which he is called of God. See
what perfect insubordination would everywhere follow
if every one who is oppressed, or believes himself to be
oppressed, should flee: children would desert their parents; husbands and wives would flee from each other,
at any supposed or real grievance. This is not the
Christian rule. Patience and all long-suffering, obedience, endurance, committing one's self to him that judg-
eth righteously, is the temper and spirit of the Gospel.
This is the tone-note of the Sermon on the Mount. At
the same time, who blames or judges harshly a man in
peril of his life if, in self-defence, he flees? I say that
Paul would probably judge every fugitive slave case by
itself. One thing is clear: It is not his rule to help a
fugitive from slavery in his flight, as a matter of course.
His rule is evidently the reverse of this. I cannot argue
with regard to the exceptions. They generally provide
each for itself. The New Testament rule is for slaves
not to run away; and for us, and for all men, not to encourage them to do so; but to encourage them to return,
and to deal with the masters on such principles, and in
such a fraternal, affectionate way, that the appeals to their
Christian sensibilities may permanently affect their consciences and hearts.

"'I stand by the record. Let me forsake it, and I am
like Paul's ship when it was driving up and down in
Adria, and neither sun nor stars appeared. My im-
pulses were not given me as my guide. They are to
be compared with the divine will. Many questions may
be asked which I cannot answer, and many difficulties
encompass this subject of slave-holding which I cannot
solve. I abide by the example and teachings of inspired

men, and am safe in following them, even if I cannot explain everything connected with their principles and conduct to the satisfaction of others. I only know that if our masters and servants would take the Apostle Paul's Epistle to Philemon as the rule of their spirit and life, there would be no such thing as oppression, nor fugitive servants. Now, as to revolutionizing society to eradicate slavery, I would no more attempt it than I would try to dig down Cadmus to dislodge yonder snow and ice upon his top. The sun will in due time melt them and pour them into the Lycus and the Mœander. So the Gospel, when it has free course, will dissolve every chain, break every yoke, and sorrow and sighing shall flee away.'

" Philemon was now the first to rise.

" ' I am the master to whom Paul the Apostle sends back my fugitive servant. This man, Onesimus, is my brother in Christ; in heaven, it may be, I shall see him far above me as a faithful servant of our common Lord. He has given a proof of obedience to the Gospel, of submission, of patience and long suffering, of implicit compliance with the rules of Christ, which excite my Christian emulation. My endeavor shall be to imitate Onesimus as he has imitated Christ, and to surpass him in likeness to that Lord who is meek and lowly in heart. The bonds which hold Onesimus to me are no stronger than those which bind me to him. (Great sensation and much emotion.) Can I ever treat this servant in an unfeeling manner? Can I recklessly sell him? Can I deprive him of comforts? Can I fail to provide for his highest happiness? God do so to me and more also, if I prove deficient in these particulars.

10 *

" 'Let me ask, What would be the state of things among us if the benign influences of Christian love pervaded every case of slave-holding as, by the grace of God, I hope it will in my case? We must have a serving class; our customs and laws ordain the relationship of involuntary servitude, property in the services of others, by purchase of their persons. While this is so, suppose that every servant is an Onesimus and every master such as I ought to be, under the influence of the Apostle Paul's directions! It is plain that in no way can we better promote the spiritual and eternal good of certain men, as the times are, than by standing in the relation of Christian masters to them. This is the great thing with Paul. We can mitigate the sorrows of their bondage; we can compensate for the appointments of providence reducing them to slavery, by making them the freemen of Christ. While this state of things continues, it may be a blessing to both parties. God will open a way for any change which he decrees in our social relation, in his own time and manner.

" ' Now, let us suppose what would happen if, departing from the rule and example of Paul, we follow the counsels of our good brother from Laodicea. The community would be in constant excitement by the departure of servants asserting each his natural liberty; laws would become rigid; hardships would be multiplied; cruelties would be perpetuated; insurrections would become frequent; sacrifices of servants, the innocent with the guilty, would be made to deter from insubordination. Instead of the spirit of the Gospel in our dwellings, alienations, suspicion, jealousy, wrangling, strife, and every form of evil would prevail. He is no real friend of servant or master who would enforce the principles of

our Laodicean brother. I adhere to the Apostle. If
questioned as to my right to hold Onesimus in bondage,
the answer immediately suggested is that an inspired
Apostle sanctions it in my case. If right in my case,
it is right in principle ; for if slave-holding be a violation
of rights, I am guilty of that violation, however humane
a master I may be. The Apostle does not reprove me,
nor require me to manumit Onesimus, but tells me that I
now receive him "forever," and he teaches me how to treat
him. I could occupy your time by arguing the abstract
question relating to property in the services of men, —
but I rest my case for the present on the letter of Paul
the Apostle, brought to me by the hand of my fugitive
servant, returning to what the laws call his bonds.

" ' Let me add a few words, however, on the general
subject, to the argument of Theodotus.

" ' Our good brother from Laodicea tells us that slavery and polygamy are "twin barbarisms." He argues
that slavery was winked at, like polygamy; was "suffered,"
by the Most High. But I propose to refute this, and I
will throw myself on your candor to judge if I succeed.

" ' God, in Eden, appointed the marriage of one man
and one woman to be the law of matrimony. " And
wherefore one ? " says the prophet. " He had the residue
of the spirit," and could have ordained otherwise. "Wherefore one ? " The answer is, " that he might seek a godly
seed." The arrangement was for the highest elevation
of the race.

" ' Polygamy is in direct conflict with the ordinance of
God. Of course God never ordained it. On the contrary, the appointment in Eden was equivalent to a pro-
hibitory act, which Jesus Christ revived, forbidding polygamy, and the Apostles have enjoined upon us that we
observe the law of marriage as given in paradise.

" ' So much for polygamy. God never recognized it. The edict requiring the marriage of a childless widow to the brother of her husband, takes it for granted that a man would leave but one widow.

" ' But how is it with slavery? God never forbade it; he recognized it; when He framed the Jewish code it was perfectly easy to exclude slavery; but hardly are the Ten Commandments out of his lips when He ordains slave-holding, gives particular directions about it, decrees that certain persons shall be an inheritance forever. Jesus Christ never uttered one word against slavery, though he did against polygamy; the Apostles have never written nor preached to us against slavery, but on the contrary here is the Apostle to the Gentiles sending back a servant escaped from his master; and in that letter on the pastor's table he enjoins duties on masters and slaves. I have confidence that my brother will not again class slavery with polygamy, for it would be a reflection upon divine wisdom and justice.

" ' One thing more. My brother says slavery is the sum of all villanies.

" ' But did not the Most High God place his people in slavery for seventy years, in Babylon? This does not prove that slavery is a good thing, in itself; for by the same proof heathenism might be shown to be a blessing. Slavery was a curse, a punishment; but still, God would not have made use of slavery to punish his people, if, theoretically and practically, it is by necessity all which my brother alleges. It surely did not, in that case, prove a " villany " to Babylon. They were the best seventy years of their probationary state, when that people held the Jews in captivity. Now I beg not to be misunderstood nor to have my meaning perverted. I am not pleading for slavery. I simply say that God

would not have put his people, whom He had not cast
off forever, into slavery, if slavery, *per se*, were the sum
of all villanies, or, if the practical effect of it on them
would be, necessarily, destruction, or inconsistent with his
purposes of benevolence. I will add, that every people
and every man, who hold others in bondage, should be
admonished that when God puts his captives, his bondmen, into their hands, He is most jealous of the manner
in which the trust is discharged. I do think, I say it
here with all possible emphasis, it is the most delicate,
the most solemn, the most awful responsibility, to stand
in the relation of master to a bondman.

"No further discussion was had at that time, the hour
being late, and so the meeting was closed with prayer and
singing. Masters and servants joined to chant a hymn,
of which the following, written many years after by
Gregory of Nazianzum, might almost seem to be the
expansion : —

> "'Christ, my Lord, I come to bless Thee,
>   Now when day is veiled in night,
>   Thou who knowest no beginning,
>   Light of the eternal light.

> "'Thou hast set the radiant heavens,
>   With thy many lamps of brightness,
>   Filling all the vaults above;
>   Day and night in turn subjecting
>   To a brotherhood of service,
>   And a mutual law of love.

> "'Own me, then, at last, thy servant,
>   When thou com'st in majesty ;
>   Be to me a pitying Father,
>   Let me find thy grace and mercy ;
>   And to Thee all praise and glory
>   Through the endless ages be.'

" Leaning on the arm of Onesimus, Philemon returned to bless his household.

" Thus far," said I, " you have my Night Thoughts."

I asked Mr. North if he accepted the present New Testament Canon as correct?   He said that he did.   I then inquired if he regarded the Scriptures as the only and sufficient rule of faith and practice.

To this he also agreed.   I then asked him if he did not think that, in making up the canon, that is, in directing what books and epistles should go into it, God had reference to the wants of all coming times?   He signified his assent.   I then asked his attention to a few thoughts connected with that point.

" Here is the Epistle to Philemon, placed by the hand of the Holy Spirit himself in the Sacred Canon.   It is on a small piece of parchment, easily lost; the wind might have blown it from Philemon's table out of the window, beyond recovery; it was not addressed to a Church, to be kept in its archives; it is a private letter, subject to every change in the condition of a private citizen.   Yet, while the epistle to Laodicea, sent about the same time, is irrecoverably lost, this little writing, addressed to a private man, goes into the Bible, by direction of God !

" Do you not suppose," said I, " that God had a meaning in this beyond merely informing us how a master received a servant back to bondage ? "

" What further purpose do you think there was in it ? " said he.

" I only know," said I, " that slave-holding was to be a subject, as has proved to be the case, which would involve the interests of at least two of the continents of the earth, one of them being then unknown. Here the Church of God was to have large increase. Here, too, slavery was to exist, and to thrill the hearts of millions of citizens from generation to generation. It is very remarkable that one book of the Bible, which was to be made known to all nations by the commandment of the everlasting God, for the obedience of faith, should be exclusively on the subject of slavery, and that the whole burden of the Epistle should be, The Rendition of a Fugitive Slave!"

"This never occurred to me before," said Mr. North.

"Suppose," said I, "that instead of sending back Onesimus, the epistle had been a private letter from Archippus at Colosse to Paul at Rome, clandestinely aiding Onesimus to escape from Philemon, and that Paul had received Onesimus, and had harbored him, and had sent him forth as a missionary, and that not one word of comment had appeared in the Bible discountenancing the act. What would have happened then?"

"Then," said Mrs. North, "one thing is certain; the business of running off slaves to Canada would now have been more brisk even than it is at present."

"Why?" said I.

"Simply because," said she, "the New Testament would have sanctioned the practice of running off slaves."

"Why, then," said I, "does it not now equally countenance the 'running' of slaves back to their masters?"

"Please answer that for me, husband," said Mrs. North.

He smiled, and rose to put some coal on the fire. We waited for his words.

"Well," said he, "I do not know but it is all right, provided the master be in each case a Philemon."

"That is a good word," said I. "You show that the Bible has an ascendency in your mind. You will be safe in following the Bible wherever it leads you, even into slave-holding, if it goes so far. But I must now question you a little. You may answer me or not, as you please.

"One day a black man appears at your door, and says, 'I have just escaped from the South. I was owned by Rev. Professor A. B. of New Orleans. I preferred liberty to slavery, and here I am.' Would you shelter him, and encourage his remaining here, and, if necessary, send him to Canada?"

"What would you have me do?" said he.

"Take him in," said I, "if you please, and give him some breakfast. You would not object to this. After breakfast you have family prayers. 'Can you read, Nesimus?' you inquire. 'O yes, master; missis and the young missises taught us all to read.' Your little boy hands him, with the rest, a Testament, and names the place of reading. Strange to say, yesterday you finished 'Titus,' and the portion to be read in course is 'Philemon!'"

"Almost a providence," said Mrs. North.

"How would you feel, Mr. North?" said I.

"Why, feel? How should I feel?" said he. "You will answer for me, perhaps, and say, 'Read Philemon; pray; and then say, Come, Nesimus, I am going to send you back to Professor A. B. I will write a letter to him, and pay your passage.'"

"What objection would you make to this?" said I.

He thought a moment, and in the meanwhile his shrewd wife said, —

"Why, husband, do you hesitate? Say this: 'What!

I? and Bunker Hill within a day's march of my house, and grandfather's old sword over my library door?' "

"I am sick of hearing about Bunker Hill in this connection," said he. "Any one would think that it is one of the 'sacred mountains' in Holy Writ."

"But," said his wife, "If some of Paul's ancestors had had Bunker Hill privileges and influences, do you think Paul would have written the Epistle to Philemon? Unfortunate Apostle! Say," said his wife again, before he spoke, "that you believe in progress, that that epistle might have been right enough in its day, but that now 'we need an anti-slavery Bible and an anti-slavery God.' "

She made up a very expressive smile as she said it and stretched her work across her knee.

"Yes," said I, "the Bible is antiquated! God never gave a written revelation to be a perpetual guide to the end of time! I can supersede the Epistle to Philemon: Mrs. North, Hebrews; you, James; and another the whole of the Old Testament."

"Now," said Mr. North, "I will tell you what I have been thinking of all this time.

"I will put you into bondage in Algiers or Tunis. Somebody has bought you or captured you. But by some means you escape to me at Gibraltar. Now I will read 'Philemon' to you, and send you back to your Algerine master. What objection can you make to this, as a believer in inspiration?"

I answered, "If I were a slave in my own country, and slavery existed in Algiers, you would need to consider the relation which existed between this country and Algiers. If the governments had treaties with each other, the surrender of persons held to service in either of the countries would probably be provided for, and then you would have to consider whether you would obey what is called the 'higher law,' or yield me to the requisition of the proper authorities. This brings up the question of the rendition of fugitive slaves, which we have just considered.

"But being free in my own country, and having been, therefore, unlawfully sold into Algerine Slavery, or having been captured, or stolen, you would, I trust, make proper resistance in my behalf."

"But," said Mr. North, "The ancestors of my fugitive friend Nesimus, were taken from freedom in their own land and were reduced to slavery. Must he and his descendants be slaves forever for the sin of the original captors, or for the misfortune of his ancestors?"

"Birth in slavery long established makes all the difference in the world, Mr. North," said I. "If I am born in slavery, under a government ordaining slavery, that is a different case from that of one taken out of a passenger ship and sold as a slave."

"Then if you and your wife," said he, "were taken out of a passenger ship, and you should happen to have a child born in slavery, that child must remain a slave, even if you go free?"

"No, Sir," said I; "the child born under such circumstances is as rightfully free as its parents. But take this case: I, being captured and held as a slave, my master gives me a wife, lawfully a slave. Then, the child born of her is lawfully a slave. You see the distinction. God recognized it. The condition of both is a limitation and qualification of natural rights. So the lapse of time qualifies the right to collect debts, bring suits for libel, or slander, and for the right of way, or for the possession of land. Will we live under law? or shall each man or any set of men set up laws for their own conscience?"

"Then," said he, "If a slave-trader lands a cargo of slaves from Africa, at Florida, I have no right to buy them; they are not lawfully slaves. Is that your belief?"

"Assuredly," said I; "and if the fugitive whom I have supposed you to be sending back to the gentleman at New Orleans, were a fugitive from the cargo just imported from Africa, you would be sustained by the law of the land in delivering him from bondage; he was piratically taken; the laws would make him free, and punish his captors, if the laws were faithfully executed."

"But a poor fellow born in slavery must remain a slave!" he replied.

"He is not lawfully a slave," I said, "if his parents were both of that cargo. But if his father had received a wife from his master, then the child is lawfully a slave."

"How do you establish that distinction?" said he.

"The child is born of one known to be, herself, lawfully a slave. It is born under a constitution of government which recognizes slavery; while that government provides for slavery, the child must submit or violate an ordinance of God, unless freedom can be had by law, or by justifiable revolution."

"I feel constrained," said Mr. North, "to hold that liberty is the inalienable right of every human being, except in cases of crime."

"You mean," said I, "that every human being is entitled to all the civil rights and immunities which others enjoy."

"Yes," said he, "in proportion to his age, and his capacity. Minors, and the imbecile, are entitled to protection, but may not be oppressed."

" Ah," said I, " how soon you find your general rules intercepted and qualified by circumstances. Minors, and the imbecile, then, may not be admitted to equal privileges with us. But are not all men born free and equal?"

" Now let me add to 'minors' and 'the imbecile' one more class. There are two races existing together in a certain country. One has always been, there, a servile race. The other are the lords of the soil; the institutions of the country are by their creation; they have acquired a perfect right and title to the government.

" You know, from all history, that two races never could, and never did live together on the same soil, unless they intermarried, or one was subject to the other. You admit this historical fact.

" It is proposed, now, by some, to give the subject race a right to vote and to hold office, so that their equality in all things shall be acknowledged."

" Pray," said Mr. North, " will you object to this? Has not God 'made of one blood all nations of men'?"

" Yes," I replied, "but read on, in that same verse: — 'and hath determined the bounds of their habitation.' There is a law of races; races must have antipathies, unless they intermarry; he who seeks to confound them may as well labor for the conjugation of all the tribes of animals. He and his results would prove to be monsters.

" The Anglo Saxon race on this continent properly say to the Negro, ' If by conquest you get possession of the land, we must, of course, succumb to you. We are now in possession, and mean so to continue. Hard, therefore, as it seems not to let you vote in parts of the country where your numbers are such as to endanger our majority, or afford temptation to demagogues to inflame your prejudices and passions by historical appeals to them, and severe as it may seem not to let you form military companies, (which would also be mischievous in the same way) we nevertheless propose to exclude you from this right of suffrage, and from separate organizations, for our own defence, and that we may preserve our institutions for our proper descendants. We are very sorry that our English ancestors began to impose you upon us, and that Newport and Salem vessels brought so many of you here into slavery; but we cannot think of requiting you for this by jeoparding our own peace; nor would it be kind to you, as things are, to be made prominent in any way as a class. When the Northern people are, generally, your true friends, and cease to use you in an offensive manner, to excite civil war, we shall join to elevate you in every way consistent with your true interests.'

"There will be cases of extreme hardship," said I, "if a slave, fleeing from the South, however unjustifiably, nevertheless becomes surrounded here with a family, and the owner comes and claims him. There are principles of natural humanity which come into force at such a time to modify or set aside a claim. I know, indeed, that to build a valuable house on land not mine, does not vacate the land-owner's title; and, moreover, I know what may be alleged on the principle illustrated by Paley, who speaks of a man finding a stick and bestowing labor on it which is more in value than the stick itself. These cases of slaves who have gained a settlement here, call for the utmost kindness and forbearance between the sectional parties in controversy; clamor will never settle them, nor the sword; but the reign of good feeling will cause

justice to flow down our streets like a river, and righteousness like an overflowing stream."

" As we have conversed a good deal upon this subject,"
said Mr. North, " perhaps we may bring our conversation
to a close as profitably as in any other way by your telling
us, summarily, what you think of this whole perplexing
subject; what would you have me believe ; how ought a
Christian man, who desires to know and do the will of
God, to feel and to act with regard to it ?   Good men, I
see, are divided about it ; I respect your motives, I approve many of your principles, I cannot object to your
conclusions, in the main.   Let us know what you consider to be, probably, the ultimate issue of the whole
subject."

" I will do so with pleasure," said I.

" But," said Mrs. North, " let us wait till after dinner."

" As the storm is over," I said to her, " I must go
home, but we will have one more council fire, if you
please, and end the subject."

So in the afternoon, my kind friends gave me their attention while I made my summing up in the next and
concluding chapter.

CHAPTER X.

THE FUTURE.

"It is heaven upon earth to have a man's mind rest in providence, move in charity, and turn upon the poles of truth."

LORD BACON.

"SLAVERY, as human nature now is, cannot be otherwise than one of the Almighty's curses upon any race which is subject to bondage.

"True, it may nevertheless, be an amelioration of their original state; they may fall into the hands of a Christian people, and hundreds of thousands of them be civilized, and be converted to Christianity; redeemed from a barbarous condition they may contribute immensely to the general good of the race both as producers and consumers. Wherever commerce needs them, unquestionably they will do more good to the world by being compelled to work than by wearing out their miserable and useless existence in Africa.

"All this may be true; still, is it not a curse to be hewers of wood and drawers of water? Does not God say to Israel that if they sin, they 'shall be the tail and not the head?' National degradation, exposing a people to be the prey and the captives of a superior race, is, of course, a curse, though, like death itself, and even sin, it may, by the grace of God, turn to good. Still, it is a curse.

" But in governing a fallen world like ours, God now and then ordains the subjection of one race to another; and he makes bondage one of his ordinances as truly as war. The extermination of the Canaanites by the sword, was an ordinance of Heaven. War is a part of God's method in governing the world; as well as sickness and death.

"I never had any sympathy for that amiable but weak concern for the character of God which represents him as finding slavery in existence and merely legislating about it, and doing the best he can with an inevitable evil. This view belongs to a system which makes God, as it seems to me, the most unhappy Being, continually striving to destroy that which sprung up contrary to his plan. To dwell on this, however, would lead us too far into theological questions.

" I tremble to think of our responsibility as a nation in being put in charge of a people with whom God has some terrible controversy for their own sins and those of their ancestors.

"Through our abuse of power, God may say to us, ' I was a little angry, and ye helped on the affliction.' God's purposes in having the chastised nation afflicted, will be accomplished, but He will punish every one who inflicts the chastisement with a selfish, unchristian spirit.

" Our people generally take it for granted that slavery is like one of the self-limiting diseases of childhood, to be outgrown, and to cease forever, in process of time, and before many years have passed away.

" The ground of this conclusion is a doctrinal error, namely, that slave-holding, the relation of master and servant, ownership, property in man, or by whatever name slavery may be designated, is in itself wrong, and

that as soon as practicable it will be abjured and no man
will stand to another in the relation of master, or owner.
But whether for good or for ill, slavery will be in existence at the last day.   We read that ' every bondman
and every freeman' will see the sign of the Son of Man.

" But should slavery be at any time, or in any country,
or part of a country, utterly extinguished, it will ever
remain true that ownership, or property in man is not in
itself wrong, and that it may be benevolent to all concerned.   It is interesting to recollect that in proportion
as human relations are cardinal, or vital, they approach
most nearly to ownership, as in the case of parent and
child.   The highest relation of all, that between man
and God, finds its most perfect expression in terms con-
veying the idea of ownership on the part of God.   'For
ye are not your own; — therefore glorify God in your
body and spirit which are God's.' If God should send
one of us to a distant part of the universe, under the
charge of an angel, where superior intelligence and wisdom were needful for our safety in temptation and amid
the bewildering excitements of new scenes, ownership for
the time being, absolute dominion over us, on the part of
the angel, would be in the highest measure benevolent.
In those days when universal love reigns, it is just as
likely as not that there will be more 'ownership' in
man than ever before.   By ownership I mean such
relationships as we see in the households of those who
are represented in the letter of the Southern lady to
her father.   There we see the weak, the unfortunate,
the dependent nature clinging to the stronger, and
receiving support and comfort, and even honor, from
those who in rendering kindness and in receiving service have their whole being refined and cultivated to the

11

highest degree. There are no rigors in those relationships; everything which contributes to the welfare and
happiness of a serving class is enjoyed, and all its liabilities to care and sorrow are removed, to as great a degree
as ever happens in this world.

"Allowing that there are always to be inequalities of
mind and condition, and that what we call menial services
will need to be performed; that there must be those who
will have a disposition and taste to work over a fire all
day and prepare food; and that men of business or study
will not all be able to groom their own horses and wash
their vehicles; and that possibly the Coleridges and
Southeys, and their friends the Joseph Cottles, may,
from being absorbed in their ideal pursuits, still be ignorant of the way to get off a collar from a horse's neck,
and must call upon a servant-girl to help them, we shall
need those who will be glad to be servants forever, and
who will require for their own security that their employ-
ers shall 'own' them, and thus be made responsible for
their support and protection. This may always be necessary for the highest welfare of all concerned. But the
history of this relationship in connection with our human
nature has been such, to a great extent, that we associate
with it only the idea of pillage, oppression, cruelty. Already there are cases without number in which no such
idea would ever be suggested to a spectator, and they
will increase in proportion as Christianity prevails.
There is more real 'freedom' in thousands of these
cases of nominal slavery than in thousands who are
nominally free. How did it happen that the Hebrew
servant, who chose to stay with his master rather than
leave his wife and children, was not made nominally free,
and apprenticed or hired? Why was his ear bored, and

perpetual relations secured between him and his master?"

"For the master's security, I presume," said Mr. North.

"I should say," said I, "for the mutual benefit of both. The master then became responsible for him; his support was a lien on his estate, the children must always be responsible for his maintenance. The awl made its record in the master's door-post, as well as in the servant's ear.

"Now, suppose," said I, "that God chooses to supply this nation with menial servants to the end of time. Suppose that he has designed that one race, the African, shall be the source from which he will draw this supply, and that down through long generations he proposes to make this black race our servants, seeking at the same time, by means of this, their elevation, by connecting them with us, and keeping up the relation; and that for the permanence of the relation, and for the security of all concerned, there should be 'ownership,' such as he himself ordained when he prescribed the boring of the ear? For my part, I cannot see in this 'the sum of all villanies,' 'an enormous wrong,' 'a stupendous injustice.' Yet this would be slavery. I am not arguing for such a constitution of things. As was before observed, the whole black race may, in a few years, be swept off from the country; but who will undertake to say that, as the people of other nations have been employed by Providence to make our railroads and canals, the black race may not be employed for a much longer term to be our servants, both North and South, both East and West? And who will say that the tenure of 'ownership' may not be the wisest and most benevolent arrangement for all concerned? I repeat it, I am not arguing for this; I am only trying to show you that the present abuses in slavery are no valid argument against the relation itself; that this may remain when the abuses cease, and therefore that at the present time we ought to discriminate in our arguments against slavery, and direct our assaults, if we continue to be assailers, against its abuses."

"On one disagreeable subject," I said to him aside, "I will make this general remark: The Southern slaves are, as a whole, a religious people; their religion, indeed, is of a type corresponding to their condition. But still, if the South were one festering pool of iniquity, as many at the North fancy, would the colored people show such evidences as they do of moral and spiritual improvement? Look at Hayti. A very large majority of the children are not born in wedlock. Slavery is a moral restraint upon the Southern colored people. Evil as slavery is, it is, in many things, taking the slaves as they are, a comparative blessing."

"But," said Mr. North, "our people generally insist that abuses, oppression, cruelty, are so inherent in slavery that they cannot be removed without destroying the relation itself."

"Here," said I, "is the mistake under which Southerners perceive that we labor, and which prevents us from having the least influence with them.

"This, however, is unquestionably true: as human nature is, we would not choose to give men unlimited power over their fellow-men who are slaves. If, in the course of events, it is found by good men that the abuses flowing from such power are inevitable, that legislative enactments and public opinion cannot control the relation, their consciences will not be quiet till it is abolished.

I am willing to confide this to men as good as we, acting as they will on their responsibility to God. It may be, that the system, stripped of everything which can be taken away, will be perpetuated, for the best good of the slave and his master.

"But," said I, " while this perpetual relation of the black race to us is possible, and may be the design of a benevolent God for our happiness and that of the Africans, and while I love to use it in replying to those who, with short-sighted and somewhat passionate reasoning, as I think, contend that slavery must utterly be rooted out of the land, I confess that my own thoughts turn to the Continent of Africa as the great object for which an all-wise God has permitted slavery to exist on our shores.

" I love to look at American slavery in connection with the future history of that great African continent, containing one hundred and fifty millions of people. History and discovered relics make the Ethiopian race to be older even than Egypt. The once powerful nations of Northern Africa, Numidia, Mauratania, as well as the Egyptian builders of pyramids, have disappeared, or they exist only in a few Coptic tribes; and even they are of doubtful origin. But the Ethiopian people, notwithstanding the slave-trade which has extended its degrading influence far and wide among them, and though civilization long since departed from their tribes, have continued to increase till now they are the most numerous of the human families except the Chinese. The slave-holding nations which have pillaged them for ages, have not been able to destroy them. Ethiopia may well say, stretching out her hands to God, ' Thy wrath lieth hard upon me, and thou hast afflicted me with all thy waves.' It is sublime to think what triumphs of redemption there are yet to be

on that African continent.   But how little, apparently,
from all that they ever say, do some of our abolitionist
friends seem to think about Africa as a future jewel in
Immanuel's diadem!   Utterly foreign from all their
thoughts appears to be the great plan of Providence
which by means even of slavery in this land, has done
so much to extend the work of human salvation among
the African race.   And there are some ministers of the
Gospel and professed Christians, I regret to observe, who
reply to all that you say about the vast proportion, to
white converts, of converts among the colored people, in
a manner which would awaken great fears in the most
charitable breast with regard to their own personal interest in the salvation by Christ, did we not all know
how far we may be blinded by passion. If you visit in
the South, you will find that African missions take the
deepest hold on the hearts of Southern Christians.   The
time will come, God hasten it! when they and we will be
united in plans and efforts for the good of the African
race.

"But I am not in favor of stealing Africans from their
native land to bring them here, even though it were certain that the majority of them would be converted to God.
We are not to do evil that good may come. If Providence makes it plain that tribes of them shall be removed
to new districts of our country, suitable measures can and
will be devised for that purpose.   That they are better
off here, even in slavery, than in their own land, under
present circumstances, I do not see how any one can
question; but that does not justify man-stealing. I remember to have seen a letter from a Missionary in Africa, in which he says, speaking of the slaves and of the
South, 'Would that all Africa were there; would that

tribes of this unhappy people could be transferred to the privileges which the slaves at the South enjoy. I would rather take my chance of a good or bad master, and be a slave at the South, than be as one of these heathen people. In saying this, I refer both to this world and the next.' I need not say, he is an enemy to the slave-trade.

"A missionary who had spent much time among the Zulu people, was appealed to by a zealous anti-slavery person to commiserate our slaves as being so much worse off than the Zulus. 'Madam,' said he, 'if our Zulus were in the condition of your slaves, eternity would not be long enough to give thanks.'

"Mrs. North," said I, "you will not impute it to mere gallantry when I appeal to you if we may not generally measure the refinement and elevation of society by the position of woman, and by the sentiments and manners of the other sex with regard to yours. The deference, the delicate attentions, the gentleness, the refinement of behavior, in word and act, which you inspire, are both the means and the evidence of the highest cultivation. In public and in private life, in assemblies, public con-veyances, at table, around the evening lamp, in all the intercourse of the family, the susceptibility of impression, the restraints and the chastised utterances, in word and action, of husbands, fathers, brothers and friends, which are due to the presence of woman, are a correct gauge of civilization and refinement."

"All right," said Mr. North, bowing very politely to his wife.

"Nowhere," said I, " do we see this more conspicuously than in Southern society. Chivalry there seems to blend with the genial influences of Christianity, and together they give a tone and manner to Southern life which is peculiar.

"I am often struck with a Southern gentleman's reverence, here at the North, for the female sex. He is displeased at seeing daughters serving at table in boarding-houses kept by their worthy parents or widowed mothers. We, indeed, respect a young woman who serves us in this manner, (if we reflect at all,) and we resent rudeness or an unfeeling mode of addressing those who are in such situations. But the Southern gentleman goes further. He has, perhaps, not been accustomed to see the daughter of a white family serve. When a respectable young woman, therefore, at a boarding-house, brings him his tea, he feels impelled to rise and ask her to be seated, and to wait upon her. I have been an eye-witness to scenes of this kind, and have been much pleased and not a little amused at some exhibitions of the feeling. If our sentiments toward the sex, and their position in social life, mark the degree of civilization and cultivation in a community, I am compelled to accord a high degree of it to Southern society, in its best estate.

"This is one effect of slavery. It takes mothers, wives, daughters, away from occupations which, though honorable, do not always elevate them in the eyes of the other sex. Perhaps there is no value (and some will say it) in all this; that every labor and service is right and good for woman; and that we are to prefer a state of society where woman does these things with her own hands, instead of having them done for her, and that this is our only safeguard against luxury and degeneracy. I will not debate it. I am only showing that, tried by an ordinary test, — the position of woman, — Southerners are really not barbarians."

" I verily believe," said Mrs. North, " that if you take the Southern constitution and give it a Northern training, the result is as perfect a specimen of man or woman as is to be found on earth."

"People at the North," said I, "may, in their zeal against slavery, make light of the abounding sustenance which the slaves enjoy, and call it a low and gross thing in comparison with ' freedom ; ' but, in the view of all political economists and publicists, how to feed the lower classes is a great problem. It is solved in slavery.

" There is another topic," I added, " which is interesting and important.

" Here," said I, taking a newspaper-slip from my wallet, " is something which fairly made me weep. It is a picture of one of our poor, virtuous, honest New England homes, in which I would rather dwell and suffer, than be an ' oppressor ' with my hundreds of slaves, and wealth counted by hundreds of thousands. A slaveholder, blessed be God, is not a synonyme of ' oppressor ; ' nor are the slaves as a matter of course ' oppressed.' Our people to a great extent think otherwise, and it is useful to see how we appear to others when this error leads us into folly. This little picture in the newspaper-slip gives us a transient look into an abode whose honest poverty and want are made more painful by evil-doing under the influence of fanaticism."

I then read to my friends the following from a Southern paper ; — I here omit the names which are given in full : —

" The touching letter which was found on the body of —— ——, one of the insurgents, from his sister in ——, ——, has been published. The following paragraph in that letter is a suggestive one :

" ' Would you come home if you had the money to
11 *

come with ? Tell me what it would cost. Oh! I would
be unspeakably happy if it were in my power to send
you money, but we have been very poor this winter. I
have not earned a half-dollar this winter. Mattie has
had a very good place, where she has had seventy-five
cents a week ; she has not spent any of it in the family,
only a very little for mother. Father has had very small
pay, but I think he has more now ; he is a watchman on
the —— ——, that runs from here to ——.'

"Here, says the Southern editor, is a family, one of
thousands of families in New England in similar circumstances, where one daughter thinks it a ' very good place'
where she can get seventy-five cents a week ; another
has not earned a half-dollar during the winter, and all are
' very poor ; ' yet the son and brother goes off and deserts
a mother and sisters thus situated, — a mother and sisters
who, though poor, have evidently the most affectionate
feelings and tender sensibilities, — for the purpose of lib-
erating a class of people, not one of whom knows anything of the want or privation from which his own family
is suffering, or who would not look without contempt upon
such remuneration as seemed the height of good fortune
to the destitute sisters and mother of this abolitionist.
When we bear in mind the intelligence and sensibilities
which characterize the wives and daughters of the poorest
classes equally with the richest in New England, it is
most amazing that men should overlook such misery at
their own doors — nay, should forsake their own kith
and kin who are suffering under it — the mother who
bore them, the sisters who love them with all a sister's
tender and solicitous love, and run off to emancipate the
fattest, sleekest, most contented and unambitious race
under heaven."

"This shows," said I, "how God has set one thing over against another, in this world. You and Mrs. North and myself would rather be the poor honest 'watchman,' or earn our 'seventy-five cents a week,' with 'Mattie,' or even, with the loving sister who writes this letter, 'not' have 'earned a half-dollar this winter,' than be the 'sleekest' of well-fed slaves.

"Yet, when we are summing up the evils of slavery in the form of indictments, we must honestly confess that it is no small thing to feed a whole laboring class in one half of a great country with bread enough and to spare."

Mrs. North asked if I had ever seen a slave-mart, or if I knew much by observation of the domestic slave-trade.

"Yes," said I, " and it is in connection with this feature of slavery that we at the North are most easily and most painfully affected. Some of the most agonizing scenes are enacted at these auctions. They are a part of slavery; so is the domestic slave-trade, which is the necessary removal of the slaves from places where they cannot have employment, to regions where their labor is in demand. In no other way can they be disposed of, unless they are at once freed; and with many the evils of the domestic slave-trade are the most powerful argument in favor of emancipation. That there are grievous trials and sorrows, as well as wrongs and violence, in the disposal of slaves, is known to all. As to those who are to remain within the State, we are told to go, if we will, and inquire into the history of slaves who are to be publicly sold, and take the number of cases in which a wanton disregard of a slave's feelings can be detected. An owner is compelled to part with his property in his slave; or, the slave is taken for debt; estates are to be divided; an owner dies intestate ; titles are to be settled, mortgages foreclosed, the number of the household is to be reduced ; and for these and numerous other reasons new owners are to be sought for the slaves. Here is a man and his wife and children to be sold. There is a general interest felt in arranging the sale so that the family may be in the same neighborhood. This is for the interest of the owners; it promotes contentment and cheerfulness in the servants. Cases of hardship are the exceptions to the general rule in disposing of servants. Admitting all that can properly be said of such cases, and of the various other evils connected with it, the question recurs, What is to be done but increasingly to mitigate the sorrows of the bondmen, to cultivate a kind and generous disposition toward them, and to prepare them, as far and as fast as the good of all concerned will warrant, for any other condition which Providence may in time point out? My belief is, that if you take four millions of laboring people anywhere under the sun, and put down in separate columns the good and the evil in their conditions, the balance of welfare and happiness, from the supply of their wants, will be found to be greater among our Southern slaves than elsewhere. But, still, this leaves them slaves. My reply to myself, when I say this, is, They were so in their own land ; or, they were in a condition of fearful degradation and misery. Their God is their judge; we have not increased their degradation; woe to us if we add needless sorrows to their lot. But as for thrusting them up to an ideal state of elevation, before their time and ours has come, I am not disposed to aid in it. Moreover, Southern Christians are doing all that we would do if in their place ; I will not affect to be more humane or just than they ; this is our great error.

"Here," said I, "is another view of the subject":

"In the sale of slaves (in America) nothing but labor is transferred. It passes from master to master, as it passes, in countries of hired labor, from employer to employer. The mode in which the transfer is made differs in the two systems of labor. The slave-laborer is never compelled to hunt for work and starve till he finds it. Is this an evil to the laborer? Would it be thought an evil, by the hired man in Europe, that his employer should be obliged, by law, to find him another employer before dismissing him from service?

"But, it is said, the slave is too much exposed to the master's abuse of power; he is liable to wrongs without a remedy; and, so far, his condition is below that of the hired laborer.

"If this be true at all, it is true as regards the able-bodied hired man only. But take into the account children and women, those, for example, that work naked in coal-mines, or wives whose sufferings from the brutal treatment of husbands daily fill the reports of police courts; take these into the reckoning, and the difference in the consequences of abused power will be very small. The negro-slave is as thoroughly protected as any laborer in Europe. He is protected from every other man's wrong-doing by the ready interference of his master; he is guarded from the master's abuse by the laws of the land, and a vigilant, earnest public opinion. Let all cruelty be punished; let all abuse of power be restrained; but to abolish the relation of master and slave, because there are bad masters and ill-treated slaves, would not be a whit wiser than to abolish marriage, because there are brutal husbands and murdered wives.

"Yet, surely, it will be said, it must be admitted, after all, that slavery is an evil. Yes, certainly, it is an evil; but in the same sense only in which servitude or hired labor is an evil. To gain one's bread by the sweat of one's brow, is a curse. But it is a curse attended with a blessing. It is an evil that shuts out a greater evil. Labor for wages, labor for subsistence, and subjection to the authority of employer or master, are the conditions on which alone the laboring masses, white or black, can live with advantage to themselves and to society." — *De Bow's Review*, Jan. 1860, pp. 56, 57.

Mr. North asked if I did not think that the colored people should be assisted in their efforts to get an education.

"There are collegiate institutions," I told him, "for colored people, in Oxford, Pa., and in Xenia, O. With great sorrow have I observed, that applications to aid these institutions and to endow others for similar purposes have been received with coldness and distrust by many who could have made liberal contributions, for no other reason than the suspicion that they were designed by Abolitionists to thrust forward the colored man in an offensive manner. I have known the name of a leading Abolitionist to be the death of a subscription-paper for such an institution. This was a bitter prejudice. When philanthropy with regard to the colored race among us falls into its natural channel, we shall see the South and the North opening wide the doors of ·usefulness in every department for which the colored people shall, any of them, manifest an aptitude. The idea that this race is to be debarred from any and every development of which it is capable, is not entertained by any respectable people at the South. The negro at the South is not doomed, by the Christian people, to an inexorable fate. They will help him rise as fast and as far as God, in his providence, shows it to be his will to employ any or all of that race in other ways than those of servitude.

"'If American slavery,' says one, 'be the horrid system of cruelty, ignorance, and wickedness represented by some writers of fiction and paid defamers of our institutions, how happens it that those who have been reared in the midst of it, when freed and planted in Africa at once exhibit such capacity for self-government and self-education, and set such examples of good morals?

" ' Have the negroes under British care at Sierra Leone made similar progress in improvement? Do the free colored subjects of Britain in the West Indies show the capacity, industry, and intelligence manifested by the Liberians, whose training was in the school of American servitude? Nor have the best specimens of this tutelage been sent out. Thousands and tens of thousands of colored servants in the Southern States are church-members, instructed in their duties by faithful Christian teachers, and the children are trained in the fear and love of God.' — I then observed,

" I have come to this conclusion: if Southern Christians say to us, as they do, Auction-blocks, separation of families, and similar features of slavery, in the limited and decreasing extent to which they prevail, are as odious to us as to you; — we tolerate these things as parts of a system which we all feel to be an evil, and which we are constantly striving to ameliorate; — I will leave the whole subject in their hands; I will trust them in this as I would in anything and everything; I feel absolved from all responsibility to God or to them with regard to the matter."

" Pray tell me," said Mrs. North, " what is all this discussion about ' the territories,' and keeping slavery out of them?"

" I told her that slavery, which fifteen States of the Union maintain as a part of their domestic life, is, by many of the people in the Free States, regarded as they regard the plague and death; they prescribe certain degrees of latitude as barriers to it, as though they enacted thus : 'North of 36° 30′ whooping-cough is prohibited, measles are forbidden, cholera-morbus is forever interdicted.' They regard slave-holders as living in a moral pestilence, and seeking to carry it with them into new districts.

" But, practically," I said, " the thing will now regulate itself, and both sides are contending very much for an abstract right. It is a war of feeling, and no one knows where it will end. If the North would say, ' Free labor, which cannot thrive where slavery exists, requires an amicable division and allotment of the territorial regions ; let us agree where our respective systems shall prevail,' — there would be no difficulty. But the effort has been to shut out slavery, as men use sanitary legislation and quarantine to keep out a pestilence. This is treating fifteen States of the Union as polluted and polluting. Hence they say, We cannot live together as one people, and we will not."

" What do you honestly think," said Mr. North, " is the true cause of our present national calamities ? "

" They are owing," said I, " originally, to the peculiar state of feeling on the part of the North toward the South. This was not in consequence of injury experienced ; for slavery had not inflicted injury upon the North ; but, right or wrong, Northern disapprobation of slavery, and the ways of manifesting it, are the fountain-head of our present national trouble. Let great numbers in one section of such a nation as this conscientiously disapprove of their brethren in another section, and not only so, but hold them guilty of an immoral and an inhuman system, and deal with them in such ways as Conscience, that most merciless of inquisitors and persecutors, alone employs, and if the indicted section be not exasperated, it will be because the accusation is true, — that their system has destroyed their manhood."

"But my hope and belief," said he, "are, that all these changes are to result in the overthrow of slavery."

"I can only say," said I, in answer to such a remark, "that he who expects relief from our trouble through the eradication of slavery, and urges on secession and division as the means to effect it, is in danger of having his enthusiasm counted as fanaticism, if not madness."

"How I wish," said he, "that we could join and buy up these slaves and set them free."

"Kind and well meant as this proposal is," said I, "nothing is really more offensive to the South. It implies that her conscience is debauched by self-interest, and that by offering to remunerate her if she will part with what we call her ill-gotten booty we shall assist her to become virtuous. Such a proposal makes her feel that fanaticism has assumed the calmness which is its most hopeless symptom."

"Then," said he, "is the North to change all its opinions?"

I said, "If this implies the abandonment of moral or religious principle in the least degree, Never. Our only hope lies in our possibly being in the wrong, and in magnanimously changing our views and feelings, and our behavior. This, upon conviction, it will be most noble to do for its own sake, leaving the effect of it to Him by whom actions are weighed, and to those who, we shall have concluded, are naturally as magnanimous and just as we, and who, if guilty of oppression, were

liable to the very same accusation when we first con-
federated with them, and when Northern slave-import-
ers put their hands with Southern slave-holders to the
Declaration of Independence, both averring that all
men are created free and equal.

"We seem now to have concluded that we have
put ourselves entirely right, and that our Southern
brethren are entirely wrong."

"I cannot feel," said Mr. North, "that we are to
blame for having our opinions, and for expressing them
honestly and fearlessly. What more have we done?"

I replied, "They say that we have held them up to
universal execration; that we have quoted, with readi-
ness, the testimony of foreign nations against them, —
of nations who know nothing of domestic slavery like
ours, mixed up with the qualifying influences of our
own civilization; that our imaginative literature has
made them odious, associating cruelty and vulgarity
with the relation of slave-holding; that we have labored
to cripple their Institution, hoping to destroy it; that we
have striven to save the District of Columbia from their
system as from corruption; that a thousand millions of
dollars of their property we have treated as contra-
band, and have made it perilous for them to recov-
er it; that we have lain in wait and molested them
in their transit through our borders, with their servants, to embark for sea. We dispute their right to
go with their servants into territories jointly acquired,
and belonging by constitutional right equally to them
as to ourselves. This, they say, has not been a just
and sincere demand for an equitable division of territory in view of the naturally conflicting interests of
slave labor and free, but rather a vindictive determina-

tion to hem in the slave-holder, to force the scorpion
into fires where he shall die of his own sting, or, —
to borrow the metaphor, with the language, of a present Senator from Massachusetts, — where the ' poisoned rat shall die in his own hole.'

" Two confederacies or one, our prospect is fearful
if we continue to feel and act toward each other after
this temper, and to cherish our respective grievances."

" There is another side to all this," said Mr. North.
" I ascribe the excitement at the South to the loss on
their part of political power, or to a grasping spirit
which breaks compromises, and which requires that the
national legislation be always shaped in its favor."

" But," said I, " if we can trust the convictions of
just men, in private life, at the South, — men removed
from all suspicion as to the purity of their motives, — it is certain that our Northern feelings toward
slave-holders, and the expressions of those feelings in
ways which have been applauded among us for many
years, are the real causes of the irritation and exas-
peration which have brought us to the present brink.

" Now, as these two sections must continue to exist,
side by side, they will go on to repel each other until
either slavery ceases, or a change of feeling takes
place in the non-slaveholding section. Secession and
permanent division will not cure the trouble, but will
increase it. Moreover, the contrariety of feeling between people in the non-slaveholding States, made
intense by the departure of the Southern section,
may inaugurate hostilities among ourselves more fearful than those which drive away the Southern people.

" Perhaps we are to be two nations. I cannot but
regard this as the greatest calamity which will have

happened to the cause of human improvement. Nor do I see how it will help Northern philanthropy, nor the negro; but it may be greatly for his injury. The truth is, we must live together for self-defence against each other, if from no other consideration. Israel began its downfall in secession, which was compelled by Rehoboam.

"But," said I, "let us contemplate a different issue. Let us think what a result it will be if such a government as ours, whose speedy ruin has been so often predicted and is still confidently looked for, shall pass through these trials and dangers without bloodshed, and we become again a united people. Self-government will then have vindicated itself; constitutional liberty will have triumphed; arms and coercion will lose their old authority and power; for there will be an example of a republican people recovering from convulsions which would have demolished any throne or power which trusted in the sword. The serf-boats in ports of the Bay of Bengal, which ride the swift, enormous surges, are not nailed, but their parts are lashed one to another, and thus the boats yield easily to the force of the water. Our government has been likened to them; and now, by yielding, one part to another, where a theoretically stronger government would have used coercion, we shall, if it please God, pass safely through these fearful hazards, furnishing a demonstration, which God may have been preparing by us for the instruction of mankind, that fraternal blood is not the best nourishment of the tree of liberty, and that 'wisdom,' resulting in the victories of peace, 'is better than weapons of war.'

" I look, therefore, toward some change in Northern feelings with regard to the South. A change in this respect will end our troubles. Opinions may not be wholly reversed; people born and bred under totally different institutions may not, for they cannot wholly, yield their convictions on controverted sectional topics, even when they cherish mutual respect and deference; but, the belief that the North will change its feelings toward the South and its institutions, under a modification of views entirely consistent with independence of judgment and self-respect, and that the South will not be wanting in a corresponding temper, rests on the same conviction as that God does not intend to destroy us by each other's hands, nor to make the life of the two sections weary with perpetual hatred and strife."

" Our form of government, Mr. North," said I, " is the very best on earth if it goes well, and the worst if it goes ill. We have no standing army to fight for an administration as for a throne or dynasty; so that if a State secedes, the question is how to coerce that people, if it be best to attempt it. Citizens do not like to march against their brethren. Think of our taking up arms against our correspondents; against people that have gone from our churches and settled in that State; against cousins, and brothers-in-law, and people who lived or did business under the same roofs with us."

" It is awkward, indeed," said Mr. North, " especially if they simply withdraw and hold the fortifications of the general government, in their own territory, to keep the government from destroying their lives."

" Why, yes," said Mrs. North, " it would be simple in

them, after seceding, to suffer themselves to be bombarded. But have they any right to secede?"

"As to that," said Mr. North, "my mind has been much exercised of late with this thought: I have always advocated the right of the negroes to make insurrection, or to flee from oppression. But now their masters complain of being oppressed by the North. Why have not the masters the same right to secede from their government as the negro from his?"

"Well, husband," said his wife, "I think that you are getting on fast."

"Why," said I, "Mr. North, is not slavery 'the sum of all villanies?' Did the negro ever consent to his form of government?"

"Well," said he, "I never consented to be born; I find myself in existence; I have no more consented to the government of the United States than I suppose the negroes, generally, have submitted to their civil condition. My question is, Who shall decide when the Southern masters say, We are intolerably oppressed; we are under a yoke; 'break every yoke!' 'let the oppressed go free!' If I interpose and say, 'You are not oppressed; you are better off as you now are,' is not this the reply of the masters when we seek to free their slaves? Do we not say that the oppressed must be the judges of their necessity? And why may I coerce the master, if it be wrong for him to coerce the negro?"

"I must let you work out that question at your leisure, and on your own principles," said I.— "We were speaking of seizing and holding the forts and arsenals. The French proverb says, 'It is the first step that costs.' Seceding involves the necessity of seizing the forts. If they who do this embarrass other persons in their lawful rights, they must risk the consequences; but if they secede from the government, the question is, Do circumstances justify a revolution? for secession is revolution. Is revolution justifiable in the present case?

"But not to discuss that question," said I, "all that I wished to say was this, that our government seems admirably suited for a people who will behave well under it. We can take care of isolated cases of rebellion. But if any important part of the country rises up and departs, it is exceedingly difficult to know what to do. Prevention is excellent; but cure is next to impossible. So long as there is a general acquiescence in the exercise of executive power against insurrectionists, one or more, we have a general government; but when States depart, we are a house divided against itself. We find that we have been living, as it were, not so much under paternal authority, as under fraternal rule. If broken irretrievably, the alternative is to be divided, or for one part of the country to coerce its neighbors and brethren. This we find to be extremely inconvenient and really impracticable without civil war; and after the war, — whose horrors, in our case, can never be pictured, — we would either find ourselves in the same divided state as before, or if politically united, it will have been effected at a cost which it is fearful to contemplate.

"So that we are illustrating the question, whether such a government as ours is really practicable, — whether a people can govern themselves. Already we hear it said, 'We have no government.' The explanation is, We are not disposed to destroy each other's lives to preserve the confederation. We can have a monarchy, with its 'divine right,' and with its standing army, if we choose; or, if we remain as a republic, we must be liable to just our present exigency. Our only defence, then, consists in mutual conciliation and agreement.

" What a land this is," said I, " with its diversified interests and its unparalleled variety of products, — its agriculture, mechanic arts, science, and literature. Separation will embarrass every form of intercourse, and make us hostile."

" Jews and Samaritans," said Mrs. North. " And all for an idea ! "

" Yes," said I, " and for an idea which to one whole section, and to a very large part of the people in the other section, is false. — Four millions of negroes are destroying us. As a foreign writer said, ' In trying to give liberty to the negro, we are losing our own.' "

Said Mrs. North. " Can nothing be done to save us ? "

" Bishop Butler tells us, Mrs. North," said I, " that a nation may be insane as well as an individual. But reason seems to be returning in some quarters. Secession and its consequences are having a wonderful effect to open the eyes of people. John Brown's foray and its end were a providential demonstration of certain errors, which we may conclude will not soon be revived. Secession is now leading the world to look more narrowly into the subject of negro slavery. Let me read to you these extracts from a recent number of ' Le Pays,' Paris. The writer is arguing that Europe must recognize the Southern confederacy :

' But in awaiting these results which would flow from the cordial welcome given by Europe to the new confederation, let true philanthropists be assured that they are wonderfully mistaken in regard to the real condition of the blacks of the South. We willingly admit that their error is pardonable, for they have learned the relations of master and slave only from "Uncle Tom's Cabin." Shall we look for that condition in the lucubrations of that romance, raised to the importance of a philosophic dissertation, but leading public opinion astray, provoking revolution, and necessitating incendiarism and revolution? A romance is a work of fancy, which one cannot refute, and which cannot serve as a basis to any argument. In our discussion, we must seek elsewhere for authorities and material. Facts are eloquent, and statistics teach us that, under the superintendence of those masters, — so cruel and so terrible, if we are to believe "Uncle Tom," — the black population of the South increases regularly in a greater proportion than the white; while in the Antilles, in Africa, and especially in the so very philanthropic States of the North, the black race decreases in a deplorable proportion.

' The condition of those blacks is assuredly better than that of the agricultural laborers in many parts of Europe. Their morality is far superior to that of the free negroes of the North; the planters encourage marriage, and thus endeavor to develop among them a sense of the family relation, with a view of attaching them to the domestic hearth, consequently to the family of the master. It will be then observed that in such a state of things the interests of the planter, in default of any other motive, promotes the advancement and well-being of the slave. Certainly, we believe it possible still to ameliorate their condition. It is with that view, even, that the South has labored for so long a time to prepare them for a higher civilization.

' In no part, perhaps, of the continent, regard being had to the population, do there exist men more eminent and gifted, with nobler or more generous sentiments, than in the Southern States. No country possesses lovelier, kinder hearted, and more distinguished women. To commence with the immortal Washington, the list of statesmen who have taken part in the government of the United States shows that all those who have shed a lustre on the country, and won the admiration of Europe, owed their being to that much abused South.

12

' Is it true that so much distinction, talent, and grandeur of soul could have sprung from all the vices, from the cruelty and corruption which one would fain attribute now to the Southern people ? The laws of inflexible logic refute these false imputations. And — strange coincidence — while Southern men presided over the destinies of the Union, its gigantic prosperity was the astonishment of the world. In the hands of Northern men, that edifice, raised with so much care and labor by their predecessors, comes crashing down, threatening to carry with it in its fall the industrial future of every other nation. For long years the constant efforts of the North, and a certain foreign country, to spread among the blacks incendiary pamphlets and tracts have powerfully contributed to suspend every Southern movement towards emancipation. Its people have been compelled to close their ears to ideas which threatened their very existence.' "

"But," said Mr. North, "here we have been, for thirty years or more, living on an anti-slavery excitement. Grant that it is all wrong; will you ask or expect that we shall change all at once ? in a week? or in a month? or in a year? We will not kneel to anybody; if we change, it must be upon conviction."

"I strike hands with you there," said I, "most heartily. Our Southern friends must understand this; they must now approach us once more with reason and persuasion. The people at large are in a frame to be reasoned with and persuaded; for if we can do anything within the bounds of reason to retain the South in the Union, it will be done. We will say of concession as the antithesis of secession, as was said of two other things : 'Millions for defence, but not a cent for tribute.' I think that both sections need forgiveness of God, and of each other."

"Well," said Mr. North, "after all we shall get along and get through, even if there should be a separation."

" Mr. North," said I, " when you were studying Cicero, could you understand — for I could not — how he and other patriots could feel so strongly about the fortunes of their country as to declare — which they frequently do — that they would rather die than survive their country's honor? It has come to me vividly of late. I see it and feel it. The sunshine will seem to have gone out of our life when we become two unfriendly nations.

" It is easy," said I, " for it gratifies some of the lower passions, to ridicule a whole section of the country for their act of secession or a disposition towards it ; to boast that the South cannot do without us ; to prophesy that they will get sick of it, and wish to return ; to express wonder that they should feel so much hurt ; to remind them that, if they will do as we have always counselled them, there would be no trouble ; and there is a temptation to say, as friends in a quarrel will hastily say, Let them go. But when they are irrecoverably gone, justifiably or not, I tell you, Mr. North, there will be mourning in our streets. I know, indeed, that there are some among us to whom it will be a carnival ; but — "

" They will have a long Lent after it," said Mrs. North ; " pray excuse me."

" Ties of kindred," said I, " patriotism, Christian friendships, will not go down to hopeless graves without leaving behind them sorrows ending only with life.

" It appears to me," said I, " that our ship is where nothing but an immediate calm and then a change of the wind, can save us. If we become two nations, it may be for judgment and destruction ; and it may be for some great, ultimate good. But it will be hard parting. To think of having no South ! and of their having no North ! We shall each become provincial. We are wonderfully fitted to qualify and improve each the other. How strange it would be to have these two sections love each other! No one among us under twenty-five years of age, has probably ever thought of us but as in controversy."

"Speaking of Southern life," said Mrs. North, "I have not seen our friend Grant since he came back from the South."

"I have seen him," said I, "and have heard his story. He made his home with an old friend, a clergyman. It was known that he was a stranger, and at once he was made to feel at home by many of the citizens. The morning after he arrived, Jack, a servant of a neighboring family, came into the breakfast-room, with a waiter filled with dishes, which he deposited on the side-board. 'Master and Missis send their compliments, and want to know how the family is, and how Mr. Grant is this morning.' Now they had never seen Mr. Grant; but they knew that he had arrived the night before. 'Well, Jack,' says Mrs. ——, 'I see you have got some good things for us.' 'O, not much, Missis; but they thought you and Mr. Grant would excuse 'em for sending it.' So there were deposited on the breakfast-table, 'big hominy' in one or two shapes, rare fish, puff-muffins, and several dishes which called for Jack's interpretations. 'And Master says, shall he send the carriage round for you this forenoon? and he will call himself.' The evening talk was interrupted by a black woman, all smiles, bearing a waiter of ice-cream and other refreshments, from another house; and so the visit was a succession of surprises from families who, at the South, count each other's guests their own. Mr. Grant was a strong anti-secessionist, and he spent much breath in arguing with the people in private.

On his return to his room, one day, he found a glass dish on the table, filled with japonicas, camellias, roses, and other early flowers, with the card of a married lady, — with whom he had had a debate, — inscribed, ' From the hottest of the Secessionists.' He seems modified in his views a little about 'the sum of all villanies,' since his return."

" Yes," said Mrs. North, " and the people here explain it by saying, ' O, he was fêted, and flattered.'

" Yes," she continued, " some of our people will sacrifice their confidence in man or angel, rather than believe anything good about slavery."

I said to her, " Add the Bible to those witnesses, Mrs. North."

" Husband," said she, " please reach me that long, thin, brown-covered book on the what-not." She then read an extract from the sixty-third page; it was a book by one now deceased, called, " Experience as a Minister " :

" I had not been long a minister, before I found this worship of the Bible as a fetish hindering me at every step. If I declared the Constancy of Nature's Laws, and sought therein great argument for the Constancy of God, all the miracles came and held their mythologic finger up. Even Slavery was ' of God,' for the divine statutes in the Old Testament admitted the principle that man might own a man, as well as a garden or an ox, and provided for the measure. Moses and the Prophets were on its side ; and neither Paul of Tarsus, nor Jesus of Nazareth, uttered a direct word against it."

" But here is the sun ! " said I.

" We are all more cheerful," said Mrs. North, " than we were when he left us ; for we have been able to converse on a trying and perplexing subject with good feelings."

"Now," said I, "here is the Southern lady's letter, which has given occasion to all our conversation."

"It has also introduced us," said Mr. North, "to that goose, Gustavus, and to his good aunt."

"What shall I say to the Southern lady," said I, "if I write to her father?"

"Tell her," said Mrs. North, "that if she comes to the North she must come directly to our house and make it her home. If you will allow me, I will put a note into your envelope to that effect. I shall beg her to bring Kate with her. Wouldn't I love to see Kate!"

"My dear," said Mr. North, "do you know what a time there would be if the lady should bring Kate with her?"

"The good time coming! I think it would be," said his wife, "to see the Southern lady and her Kate under our roof."

"Why," said he, "we should all have to go to court?"

"Well, that would be interesting," said she; "but for what?"

"Why," said he, "you know that this is free soil: Kate is a slave; she can have her freedom for nothing if she comes here. Some of our Massachusetts gentlemen are as chivalrous and attentive to Southern colored people, as our good friend tells us Southern gentlemen are to a white woman: a committee would wait on Kate, with an officer of the peace, and invite her to visit the court-house with them, to be presented with 'freedom'; and Kate's mistress must go with her, to show that she is not restraining Kate of her liberty."

"Why," said Mrs. North, "if I could not be allowed, in visiting Sharon Springs, to take Judith with me to give me my baths, because she is free, I should call it barbarism. Who was that gentleman that broke his collar-bone and sent to you, husband, to get him a nurse?"

Mr. North said it was a student in a medical school, from the South.

"Did you find him a nurse?" said she.

"Yes," he replied; "but he groaned and said, 'Mother wanted to send on my mammy that nursed me, but your laws will not allow her to come. Now,' said he, 'mammy will not tamper with your servants here, and entice them away, as free colored men might do to our slaves if they landed at the South from your vessels. O, mammy,' said he, 'if I had your 'arbs and your nursing, what a pleasure it would be to be sick.'"

"Poor fellow!" said Mrs. North. "What did you say to him?"

"O," said he, "I told him that we lived under different institutions; and that when we are among the Romans we must do as the Romans do."

"Well," said Mrs. North, "if all such prohibitions are not downright impertinence, then I will give up."

"It's the law of the land, here," said her husband.

"Is there no 'Higher Law' in such a case?" said she.

"'Higher Law,' I believe, is sometimes the rule in Massachusetts."

"Some of our most estimable colored fellow-citizens would attend her," said I, "and tempt her by their own prosperity and happiness in freedom, at the North, to cast in her lot with them and abandon her Southern home, her mistress, and her little charge, Susan; and her own little Cygnet's grave. They would send her, if she wished, free of charge, to Canada, and leave her there. She could be perfectly free."

"Now, what is all this for?" said Mrs. North. "Do the people here really believe that Kate is ' oppressed?' that her mistress is a tyrant? that Kate is a victim to the ' sum of all villanies?' that she suffers an ' enormous wrong?' that her mistress does her a ' stupendous injustice?' If they wish for objects of charity, and will go with me, I will engage to supply them with ' the oppressed' in any quantity, with some of ' the down-trodden' also."

" But, my dear Mrs. North," said I, " ' 'tis distance lends enchantment to the view.' Besides, to get a slave away from a Southerner is worth unspeakably more to the cause of human happiness than to help scores of Northern people."

" But to be serious," said Mr. North, " we are afraid that slave-holding may get a foothold in Massachusetts; so we have to challenge every one who comes here with a slave, to show proof that he or she is not holding the servant to involuntary servitude among us."

" But," said Mrs. North, " are the people so conscientiously fearful lest bondage should get established here in Massachusetts? Is that the true reason for hurrying every colored servant, who travels here with his or her invalid master or mistress, before a court to know if he or she would not prefer to quit the family and the South? It seems to me we are sadly wanting in good manners."

" Now, please do not smile at your good wife for her simplicity, Mr. North," said I, " for I suppose that you are thinking, What have ' good manners' to do with the 'cause of freedom'? She is right in her impressions; a lady's sense of propriety against all the world."

" Do publish the Southern lady's letter by all means," said Mrs. North.

" How surprised she would be," said I, " to see it in print, or to know that it had wandered here, and was taking part in the discussions about slavery."

" The letter," said Mrs. North, " would, just now, seem like Noah's poor little dove, wandering over wrecks and desolations."

"True," said I, " and to finish the illusion, it might come back to her after many days, and lo! in its mouth an olive-leaf plucked off! "

" Give my love to her," said Mrs. North; " her letter has made me a better and happier woman. Now I love my whole country. I do justice in my feelings to hundreds of thousands whom I have hitherto regarded as perverse. I now see God's wonder-working providence in connection with the slave. It seems plain to me in what way the Union can be saved, and that is, by the general prevalence at the North of such views about slavery as the very best people at the South declare to be just and right."

" You would be deemed simple for saying that, Mrs. North," said I. " But you are right."

" Three things," she continued, after a moment's pause, " are more strongly impressed on my mind; please see if I am right: — That the relation of master and slave is not in itself sinful; That good people at the South feel toward injustice and cruelty precisely like us; and, That Southern Christians can correct all the evils in slavery, or abolish it, if necessary, better without our aid than with it."

"Mrs. North," said I, "unless we accept those propositions, the North and South never can live together in peace; and if we separate, the Northern conscience will be in a worse condition than ever, and we shall have long wars."

"It is a marvellous thing to me," said she, "as I now view it, that our good Christian people here are not willing to confide in that which good Southern Christian people say about slavery. We should trust their judgments, their moral sentiments, their consciences, on any other subject. How is it that when men and women, who are the excellent of the earth, tell us the results of their observation, experience, and reflections, with regard to slavery, we treat them as we do? When ill-mannered people, who must be vituperative and saucy to every body and in every thing, behave thus, it is not surprising; but I cannot explain why truly good men should not either adopt the deliberate sentiments of good people at the South, or at least consent to leave the subject, if beyond their faith or discernment, to the responsibility of Southern Christians. I condemn myself in saying this. But having myself been converted, I have hope for everybody."

During this talk, Mr. North was affected somewhat as he said his wife was when he first read the Southern lady's letter to her. He was a little incoherent by reason of his emotions; but he made out to say something about the sweetness and the strength of reconciled affections, and of the happiness which there would be when it should be proclaimed that the North and the South are once more friends.

"What is your whole name, Mrs. North?" said I; "for I shall wish to speak of you to the Southern lady, if I write to her father."

" My Christian name," said she, " is Patience."

" Patience North ! " I said to myself, once or twice, as I stood at the parlor door. I was musing upon the name perhaps ten or fifteen seconds, and when I looked up, they were each both smiling at me and crying.

We shook hands, and I went my way.

THE END.

F Ada

Adams, Nehemiah, 1806-1878.

The sable cloud